Some Historical
Stories of Chicago

Contents

Foreword 9

Chicago History Museum—A Reverie 23
Chicago: Geology, Town And City—A Reverie 30
Chicago, Early Discovery, 1673—A Reverie 36
The Immigrants—A Reverie 41
Growth of Immigrant Cities—A Reverie 54
Wild Chicago—A Reverie 62
Two Declarations—A Reverie 71
Potter and Bertha Palmer—A Reverie 83
The Chicago Fire and Haymarket Affair—A Reverie 92
Reverie—Year Of St. Paul 109
Canal and Railroad (1848),
    Union Stock Yards—A Reverie 133
Chicago Buildings—A Reverie 142
Abraham Lincoln—A Reverie 153
World's ColumBian Exposition—A Reverie 172
Valentine's Day Massacre—A Reverie 184
Century of Progress—A Reverie 194

The Apostle of Freedom—A Reverie 208
University of St. Mary of the
    Lake Mundelein Seminary—A Reverie 213
A Mid-Lenten Reverie 221
A Year For Priests—A Reverie 225
A Religious Reverie 232

Tom Zbierski, Rita Goodman and Bert Hoffman
sharing a meal and art at Monesteros Restaurant in Chicago.

FOREWORD

I was a volunteer interpreter for ten years of the many exhibits at the Chicago History Museum. In our training the Museum's Research Department gave us fact sheets and background information on the exhibits. This forward is written based on the hand outs distributed by the research department.

DISCOVERY, 1673

In the spring of 1673 seven white men set out from the mission of St. Ignace, on the mainland near Mackinac Island, to find and explore the Mississippi River. They hoped that the great stream, which they knew only by rumor, would offer a highway to the fabulous riches of the Orient. Father Jacques Marquette, French-born missionary of the Jesuit order, and Louis Jolliet, Canadian explorer and mapmaker, led the expedition; the other five were voyageurs or canoe men. The Voyageurs were French Canadians who were very strong and rugged and could not be taller than five feet six inches tall in order to control the canoes in the water. They had to be able to carry 100 pounds on their back, 100 pounds on their chest and 100 pounds on their head in order to make any portage from water to water to continue their travel by water. The explorers followed the Fox and Wisconsin rivers to the Mississippi, and then floated with the current as far as the mouth of the Arkansas. There, satisfied that the river emptied into the Gulf of Mexico, and fearing to encounter enemies if they traveled farther, they turned back.

On their return trip Marquette and Jolliet, instead of retracing their previous route, paddled up the Illinois River. Near the present city of Ottawa they found a great Indian village. There Marquette preached the gospel and promised the friendly savages that he would return. Led by Indian guides, the explorers ascended the Des Plaines and crossed the low-lying ground between that river and the South Branch of the Chicago River. As the leaves were beginning to turn they floated into the waters of Lake Michigan and pointed their canoes toward Green Bay. They were the first white men to lay eyes on the site of the future city.

THE MISSION OF THE GUARDIAN ANGEL, 1696-1700

For a quarter of a century after 1673 Frenchmen frequented the site of Chicago. Marquette, keeping his promise to the Indians of the Illinois valley, spent the winter there in 1674-75. La Salle, Tonty, Joutel, and other traders and explorers used the portage repeatedly on their journeys to the Illinois and Mississippi rivers. Near the end of the century a large band of Miami Indians, seeking refuge from the implacable Iroquois, established two villages at Chicago, one on the south side of the main river between the forks and the lake, the other two miles away on the South Branch. There, in 1696, Father Francois Pinet, a Jesuit missionary, founded the Mission of the Guardian Angel. For four years, with one interruption, Father Pinet sought to save the souls of his savage wards. The task, however, was a hopeless one, and in 1700 the French abandoned the mission. From that date until the early 1780's, when Jean Baptiste Point Sable established a trading post on the north bank of the Chicago River near the lake, the history of Chicago is a void. For eighty years hostile Indians blocked the natural passage between the Great Lakes and the Mississippi. Traders must have slipped through from time to time, but no traces of their activities are to be found in the surviving records.

THE TREATY OF GREENVILLE, 1795

The scene shifts from the swampy shore of Lake Michigan to Fort Greenville in western Ohio. There, in the summer of 1795, the tribes gather to make their peace with General Anthony Wayne-"Mad Anthony" of the Revolution, who had routed them at the Battle of Fallen Timbers on August 20, 1794. The treaty, concluded August 10, 1795, opens most of the present State of Ohio to white settlement, but stipulates that certain tracts in the Indian country to the westward may be used by the United States for forts and portages. One of these is described as follows: "one piece of land six miles square, at the mouth of Chicago river, emptying into the southwest end of Lake Michigan." Thus title to the site of the future city passes to the United States. The comment of Milo M. Quaife in Checagou: From Indian Wigwam to Modern City is pertinent: "From every point of view, this is the most momentous real estate transaction in the history of Chicago. It embraced an area which today the fabled wealth of the Indies would scarcely suffice to purchase, and it directly prepared the way for the subsequent founding of Fort Dearborn. Although the tract was never formally surveyed, its approximate boundaries are easily indicated. From Fullerton Avenue on the north to Thirty-first Street on the south, and from the lake westward to Forty-eighth Avenue (Cicero Avenue); such were the dimensions of Mad, Anthony's purchase."

THE FIRST FORT DEARBORN, 1803-1812

Eight years passed before the United States moved to erect a fort at the mouth of the Chicago River. Early in 1803 the War Department made the decision. With the summer Lt. James Strode Swearingen led a detachment of the First Infantry overland from Detroit while Capt. John Whistler, who would command the new post, traveled by water. The troops reached their destination on the afternoon of August 17 and set to work at once building shelters and a stockade. A year later Fort Dearborn, named in honor of the Secretary of War, stood complete.

At this time the Chicago River made a sharp bend to the south just east of the present Michigan Avenue Bridge and emptied into the lake at the approximate location of Madison Street. On elevated ground in the bend of the river stood the stockade, with blockhouses at the northwestern and southeastern corners. The main gateway, in the middle of the south side, looked down the future Michigan Avenue. Inside the enclosure were barracks for officers and men, a storehouse, and a stone powder magazine. A visitor in 1809 characterized the fort as "the neatest and best wooden garrison in the country." Year after year, little happened at Fort Dearborn. A ship with trade goods called annually, and mail came at long intervals. Hunting, fishing, and games gave some occupation to the troops, but for the most part, life was almost intolerably monotonous. But with the spring of 1812, the situation changed. Word reached the outpost on the Chicago River that war with Great Britain was imminent. Indians, sullen and aggressive, collected at the fort. In mid-July a runner arrived with official notice that war had been declared. On August 9 a messenger brought Capt. Nathan Heald, who had replaced Captain Whistler in 1810, an order directing him to evacuate Fort Dearborn and withdraw with the garrison to Fort Wayne. Preparations began at once. On the 13th Capt. William Wells, with thirty friendly Miami warriors, arrived at Chicago to accompany the troops on their long and dangerous journey. The next day Heald distributed the goods of the government store to the Indians; the garrison liquor and the surplus arms and ammunition he destroyed.

At 9:00 o'clock on the morning of August 15 the stockade gate swung open. Captain Wells and some of his Miami headed the procession that emerged. The garrison followed, and after them, the women and children and a dozen militiamen. The remainder of the Miami brought up the rear. The Potawatomi surrounding the fort had promised an escort, but the few who appeared soon deserted. The column moved south, taking a route between the lake and a row of low sand hills a hundred yards from the water. After covering a mile and a half, Captain Wells discovered that the Indians were lying in ambush behind the sand hills. Heald ordered his men to charge. They gained the ridge, but they were hopelessly outnumbered, and doomed to defeat in the confused fighting that followed. In thirty minutes more than half of the whites lost their lives. When promised that the survivors would be spared, Heald surrendered. In spite of the promise, some of the wounded were put to death, and several of the prisoners were tortured. On the day after the massacre the Indians set fire to the fort and left for their villages, taking their captives with them. Only smoldering ruins, with mutilated bodies in the distance, marked the site of the first Fort Dearborn (the second Fort Dearborn was reestablished in 1816).

Albert A. Hoffman, Jr.

RECOLLECTIONS OF FORT DEARBORN
By Julia Fearson Whistler, Army Wife

COMING TO CHICAGO, AUGUST 1803

(From Detroit) the U.S. Schooner "Tracy" was dispatched with supplies, and having also on board Captain John Whistler, (his wife, several of their children, and an older son), Lieut. Wm. Whistler and (his wife Julia, aged 16). The schooner, on arriving at Chicago, anchored half a mile from the shore, discharging her freight by boats. Some 200 Indians visited the locality while the vessel was here, being attracted by so unusual an occurrence, as the appearance in these waters of "a big canoe with wings." There were then here, says Mrs. W., but four rude huts or traders' cabins, occupied by white men, Canadian French, with Indian wives; of these were Le Mai, Ouilmette, and Pettell. Capt. Whistler, upon his arrival, at once set about erecting a stockade and shelter for their protection, followed by getting out the sticks for the heavier work. There was not at that time, within hundreds of miles, a team of horses or oxen, and, as a consequence, the soldiers had to don the harness, and with the aid of ropes drag home the needed timbers.

>From 29 October 1875 personal interview
>By Henry Hurlbut, who used it in his
>Chicago Antiquities (1881), 23-28.

A GRANDDAUGHTER PASSES ON FAMILY LEGENDS

Our grandmothers (Julia Whistler and her mother-in-law Anne Whistler) were the only women in the fort all the winter of 1803-1804. They lived in tents up to some time in December, and grandmother (Julia) says the soldiers on one occasion had to dig her out of her tent after a heavy snow storm. Their provisions gave out six weeks before navigation opened in the spring, and all she or any of them had to eat in that time was pork (salt) and hard tack or sea biscuit. They were once attacked by the Indians and they had only 57 men all told in garrison. A friendly Indian came and told Grandfather (John Whistler) that they were to be attacked by 500 Indians, so he had the men drive sticks in the ground and tie guns to them and wrap coats about them and put caps on; they he put the men in front which gave the appearance of being quite a lot of soldiers. A dreadful thunder storm came up that night and with every flash of lightening grandmother said she could see the heads of the Indians above the hazle bushes. Grandfather had taken a cannon with him from Detroit and he had it loaded with a lot of old chain which made a dreadful report which frightened the Indians so that they thought it was a warning for the "Great Spirit," and dispersed.

> Caroline Clench Bixby (granddaughter of
> Julia Whistler) to "Lizzie" (great-grand-
> Daughter of Julia Whistler), St. Catherines,
> Ontario, September 20, 1903. Typed letter
> Copy with handwritten annotations,
> Missouri Historical Society, St. Louis.

THE SECRETARY OF WAR'S PLAN FOR FRONTIER FORTS 1804

War Dept., 28th June, 1804 SIR-Being of the opinion that, for general defense (sic) of our country, we ought not to rely on fortifications, but on men and steel; and that works calculated for resisting batteries of cannon are necessary only for our principal seaports, I cannot conceive it to be useful or expedient to construct expensive works for our interior military posts, especially such as are intended merely to hold the Indian in check. I have, therefore, directed stockade-works, aided by block-houses, to be erected at Vincennes, at Chikago (sic), near the mouth of the Miami of the Lakes (the Maumee River), and at Kaskaskias, in conformity to the sketch herewith enclosed, each calculated for a full company; the block-houses to be constructed of timber, slightly hewed, and of the most durable kind to be obtained at the respective places; the magazine for powder to be of brick of conic figure, each capable of receiving from fifty to one hundred barrels of powder. Establishments of the kind here proposed will, I presume, be necessary for each of the military posts in Upper and Lower Louisiana, New Orleans and its immediate dependencies excepted. I will thank you to examine the enclosed sketch, and to give me your opinion on the dimensions and other proposed arrangements. You will observe the block-houses are intended to be so placed as to scour from the upper and lower stories the whole of the lines. The back part of the barracks are to have portholes which can be opened when necessary for the purpose of musketry for annoying an enemy. It will, I presume, be proper, ultimately, to extend the palisades around the block-houses.

>Secretary of War Henry Dearborn to
President Jefferson, 28 June 1804, as
quoted in Allan Eckert,
THE TWILIGHT OF EMPIRE (1988), 36-37.

JOHN WHISTLER'S ACCOUNT OF HIS WIFE'S ILLNESS AT FT. DEARBORN, 1805

... Mrs. Whistler is in a very low state with a Reumatism or____in the left side of her head, she scarce get a moment of ease frequent bleeding is the only remedy that gives her any kind of relief, we are at this moment preparing a warm bath for her while there is life there is hope that is all I have to comfort me at present, as my case must be very unhappy should I be so unfortunate as to loose so good a companion at this state with so large a family of small children, these circumstances I write you as knowing you my friend and a man of family yourself ...

> John Whistler to Jacob Kingsbury,
> 12 July 1805, Kingsbury Letter Book,
> Chicago Historical Society.

NOTE by WGC: Later letters say she recovered fast, then had a relapse within the month; letter of 27 May 1810 says she has been ill for a "length of time, but this (JW's removal as commander of Ft. Dearborn) adds greatly to her ill health ..." She lived until 1814.

REMOTENESS OF FORT DEARBORN, 1810-1811

Captain Nathan Heald was single while he commanded Fort Wayne 1807-1810. However, he found his next command at Fort Dearborn so isolated that, shortly after his arrival, he asked for a winter's leave under threat of resigning. In recommending a friend to be his replacement Heald conceded, "(Fort Dearborn) is a good place for a man who has a family & can content himself to live so remote from the civilized part of the world." Heald returned to his post in the summer of 1811, and enroute was able to reassure his district commander, "To prevent my being troublesome (sic) in my applications for furloughs in future I am taking on a Wife with me . . ."

> Nathan Heald to Jacob Kingsbury,
> 8 June 1810, 17 June 1811, Jacob
> Kingsbury Papers, Chicago Historical
> Society, as summarized in Willa G. Cramton,
> WOMEN BEYOND THE FRONTIER:
> A Distaff View of Life at Fort Wayne (1977), 6.

Fact Sheet
Jean-Baptiste Point DuSable (1745-1818)

Du Sable was the first non-native settler in Chicago. He opened a successful trading post at the mouth of the Chicago River. Du Sable was born to African and French parents in what is now known as Haiti, and may have come to Chicago in 1772 to trade furs and other goods with both Europeans and Native Americans. His wife Katherine was a cousin to the Potawatomi Indian chief Pokogon, friend of the famous chief Pontiac. We know of Du Sable only through a few documents in which he is referenced, but it appears he was an independent and influential force at this strategic location during the Revolutionary War. In 1778, Du Sable was held by the British for presumed sympathies with the American revolutionaries and eventually released to ease tensions with the Potawatomis. Du Sable continued his business at the mouth of the Chicago River until 1800, when discouraged by declining French influence and the increase in Anglo-American competition, he sold his land and business and moved to Peoria, Illinois. Later, he moved to the French town of St. Charles, Missouri, where he died in 1818.

Note: When Du Sable left Chicago in 1800, he sold his properties and supplies. This list gives us an idea of the kind of settlement he had built in Chicago.

- A furnished mansion house including eleven copper kettles and a French cabinet of walnut wood with four glass doors.
- A trading post, with a piazza along the front, 24' by 40' feet, ranging in depth to four or five rooms.
- Two barns 24' by 30' feet and 28' by 40' feet.
- A bakehouse 18' by 20' feet.
- Several outhouses, a poultry house, a smoke house, blacksmith shop, and cut lumber for a new barn.
- Eight axes, seven saws, seven scythes, eight sickles, three carts, one ploy, a ring saw, and a cross cut saw.
- Two mules, two calves, two oxen, thirty head of cattle, thirty-eight hogs, and forty-four hens.

Source: The real bill of sale, one of the few documents through which we know of Du Sable is written in French and can be found at the Wayne County Document Building in Detroit, Michigan.

TOWN AND CITY, 1833-1837

A region inhabited only by Indians and a few hunters and trappers needs no government. But if a sizable number of permanent settlers are to live together in harmony, some agency must perform certain services for the general welfare-locate and maintain roads, settle disputes, arrest and punish law-breakers, and levy taxes to cover costs. As population increases and people become more dependent upon each other, government assumes more and more duties, at the same time that individual communities-towns and villages-demand a greater share in the control of their own affairs. In Illinois, as in most of the United States, this development has taken shape in successive forms of government. In 1800 a region occupied by only a few hundred settlers was made a part of Indiana Territory; in 1809 it had grown populous enough to be set apart as Illinois Territory; in 1818 it became a state. Concurrently, counties were being formed to provide local government, while within the counties, towns and cities came into existence. The southern half of Illinois was well settled while Indians still occupied the northern part of the state. Cook County was not organized until January 15, 1831. Even though its extent was five times as large as it is today, its population consisted of the two companies of infantry stationed at Fort Dearborn, rebuilt in 1816, and a few scattered pioneers. But after the Black Hawk War (1832) removed the Indian menace, settlers poured in. In the summer of 1833 those who lived in the vicinity of Chicago decided that they needed their own government. Of the thirteen voters, twelve favored incorporating as a town. On August 10, 1833, five trustees were elected. Two days later they chose T.J.V. Owen, one of their number, president. The settlement was still so small that they waited until November 7 to adopt a municipal code. The first ordinance established the town limits-Ohio Street on the north, Jackson Street on the south, Jefferson and Cook streets on the west, and on the east, the lake as far as the river, and south of that, State Street. Within three years a fast-growing population demanded the larger powers offered by incorporation as a city. Delegates from each of Chicago's three districts met on November 24, 1836, and decided to petition the state legislature for a city charter. At the same time, they appointed a committee to prepare a draft. This, substantially, was the charter adopted by the legislature on March 4, 1837. At the first election under the new form of organization the voters chose six aldermen, one for each ward, and elected William B. Ogden mayor. The mayor received a salary of $500 a year; the aldermen served without pay. A census, taken July 1, 1837, gave the young city a population of 4,170.

CHICAGO HISTORY MUSEUM—A REVERIE

For ten years I was a volunteer with the Chicago History Museum leading one hour tours while interpreting the many artifacts used in the exhibits. The tours were for two groups (1.) Private tours for students from High Schools and Grammar Schools, and (2.) Public tours for CHM visitors. Our research department gave us evening lectures on each exhibit along with information sheets. What follows are five such information sheets:

1. THE HAYMARKET RIOT, 1886. In the spring of 1886 many Chicagoans were uneasy. Labor unions were campaigning for the eight-hour day (with ten hours' pay), and so many social revolutionaries of European origin had attached themselves to the movement that it had become a class struggle. Employers and conservatives feared bloodshed, and looked for it to come on May 1, when many unions planned to strike for shorter hours.

   May 1, however, passed in peace, though thousands struck as they had threatened. The first real violence took place two days later, when a fight between strikers and strike-breakers took place at the McCormick Harvester plant. The police, hastily summoned, attacked the rioting strikers, killing one and wounding several others.

The following day, May 4, handbills calling workingmen to a mass meeting at the Haymarket, Randolph Street between Desplaines and Halsted, were circulated. The meeting was called "to denounce the latest atrocious act of the police, the shooting of our fellow-workmen yesterday afternoon," and some of the notices urged workers to come armed. Contrary to expectations, only a small crowd appeared, and those present gathered around a wagon on Desplaines Street rather than in the Haymarket itself. Speakers harangued them for an hour and a half. As the meeting neared its end, a police column of 180 men suddenly appeared, marched to the wagon, and halted. The commanding officer ordered the meeting to break up. As the dwindling crowd hesitated, a sputtering bomb dropped near the first rank of police, and an instant later exploded. Nearly half of the officers fell with wounds, some fatal. Those hurt closed ranks and opened fire on the crowd, causing casualties that were never accurately determined.

The city-in fact, the entire country-saw in the bomb the beginning of a campaign of terror on the part of wild eyed socialists and anarchists, and demanded that the agitators be punished to the limit of the law. The police arrested as many as they could find, and a grand jury indicted thirty-one for murder or conspiracy to murder. Of these, eight stood trial. All were found guilty. For seven, the jury fixed the penalty at death; the eighth was to be imprisoned for fifteen years. Appeals to the State Supreme Court and the United States Supreme Court were unsuccessful.

On November 10, 1887, twenty-four hours before the executions were to be carried out, Louis Lingg, one of the condemned men, committed suicide in his cell.

That evening the Governor of Illinois commuted the sentences of Samuel Fielden and Michael Schwab to life imprisonment. The next day the hangman sent Albert R. Parsons, Adolph Fisher, George Engel, and August Spies to their deaths.

From the beginning many believed that the Haymarket rioters were being tried for holding unpopular opinions rather than for the crimes with which they were charged. The men who shared this conviction-and their number included some of Chicago's most respected citizens-organized the defense of the rioters and, after the verdict, appealed to the Governor for clemency. After the executions, they continued their efforts in behalf of the three men still in prison. John P. Altgeld, elected Governor in 1892, pardoned them six months after he took office.

2. THE IROQUOIS THEATER FIRE, 1903. The Iroquois Theater-new, beautifully decorated, and believed to be completely fireproof-had a capacity crowd for the matinee on December 30, 1903. children were out of school for the Christmas holidays, and many parents had planned parties so that the youngsters might see Eddie Foy in "Mr. Bluebeard." It was a joyous occasion.

Then, without warning, disaster struck. Midway in the play a wisp of smoke curled from the flies. A few seconds later a flimsy piece of scenery burst into flames. Eddie Foy stepped to the footlights, asked the audience to be calm, urged the orchestra to play. Behind him a skylight crashed to the floor and a sudden draft blew flame and smoke from the stage. The crowd rushed for the exits, many of which were locked. In the darkness-the lights went out soon after the fire started-men, women, and children knocked each other down, tried to climb over prostrate bodies, and smothered to death. Firemen and police smashed down doors, rushed in with torches, and found piles of dead bodies. Hardened reporters sickened at the sight. In fifteen minutes 596 people-twice as many as died during the Chicago Fire-lost their lives.

The victims of the Iroquois Theater fire died needlessly but not in vain. In Europe as well as the United States the tragedy led to the adoption of safety measures that have effectively prevented similar disasters.

3. THE CHICAGO PLAN, 1909. In the years following the World's Columbian Exposition a number of leading Chicagoans began to see visions of a more orderly, more beautiful city. At first they thought only of connecting Grant Park and Jackson Park with a boulevard, although even that was an undertaking of the first magnitude. Under the leadership of Daniel H. Burnham, however, the improvements contemplated expanded in number and scope and became parts of a general plan. Early in the twentieth century the Merchants' Club and the Commercial Club made the plan their primary activity, and after the two clubs merged as the Commercial Club in 1907, offered substantial civic and financial backing.

The Chicago Plan, published by the Commercial Club in 1909, was the first comprehensive outline of development ever offered to an American city. Instead of limiting themselves to the municipality, large as that was, the planners dealt with the entire area lying within a sixty-mile radius. They foresaw a network of highways around the city, great forest preserves within easy access, and an expansion of existing parks. Within Chicago they looked forward to a wide thoroughfare and a continuous parkway from Jackson Park to Winnetka, a monumental bridge across the Chicago River, broader traffic arteries, numerous diagonal streets, an imposing civic center, and many other improvements each related to the other.

Four months after the publication of the plan Mayor Fred A. Busse appointed the Chicago City Plan Commission and designated Charles H. Wacker, a dynamic civic leader, as chairman. Backed by the Commercial Club, Wacker undertook a campaign of public education. A plan manual was distributed to school children, releases flooded the newspapers, speakers expounded the subject at every opportunity. Chicagoans caught the conception of a better city, and when the time came for voting the bond issues that were indispensable, responded favorably.

Some of the features of the original Chicago Plan have been discarded as undesirable; others have not yet been realized. Yet the gains have been notable. To the plan the city owes the magnificent stretch of park land from Jackson Park to the river and the northern extension of Lincoln park, the Outer Drive, the Michigan Avenue and Outer Drive bridges, Wacker Drive, the northern reach of Ogden Avenue, the forest preserves, and many of the smaller parks. Moreover, the Chicago Plan Commission, a continuing body, constantly sets new objectives in the light of changing conditions, and proves every year that with intelligent foresight the city can be made a better home for its millions of residents.

4. THE EASTLAND DISASTER, 1915. On the early morning of July 24, 1915, the passenger steamer Eastland lay at the Chicago River dock adjacent to the Clark Street Bridge. The ship was one of four which the Western Electric Company had chartered to take its employees and their families to Michigan City, Indiana, for the company's annual outing. Since the Eastland would depart first, crowds swarmed aboard as soon as

the gates opened. By 7:00 there were 2500 people on her decks, and the Eastland cast off. For no apparent reason the ship listed away from the dock, then righted itself. An instant later it listed again but this time, instead of recovering, slowly rolled over on its side and settled on the mud of the river bottom.

The happy, holiday crowd had paid little attention to the first list, but the second resulted in a mad panic. Some passengers, foreseeing disaster, scrambled up the sloping deck and jumped to the dock; hundreds spilled from the hurricane deck into the river and swam ashore. But those between decks had little chance. The fire and police departments sprang into action and hundreds of volunteers worked heroically, but many of the excursionists died before rescuers reached them. Altogether, 812 lost their lives, making the Eastland disaster by far the worst in the city's history.

5. REACHING SKYWARD, 1920-30. The "booming 'twenties'" are already legendary. Industry, released from war production and stimulated by vast markets for such new products as the radio and electric refrigerator, produced as never before. Automobiles broke out of the luxury class and became necessities. Wages jumped, profits rose, and the country entered an era of free-spending and speculation that finally escaped the limits of reason and ended with the shattering collapse of the stock market in October, 1929.

The 'twenties were the decade of "flaming youth," of 'coonskin coats and hip flasks, of "flappers" and rolled stockings and skirts above the knees. They were the decade of "Big Bill" Thompson and flamboyant city politics. They were the decade of prohibition and the speakeasy, with gangsters like John Torrio and Al

Capone giving Chicago a reputation for crime and vice that it has not yet lived down.

But the 'twenties were also a decade of progress. In ten years Chicago changed its face. Over many square miles buildings rose in almost every block. The thud of the pile driver and the machine-gun rattle of the riveter became the normal noises of daily living. Soldier Field, the Shedd Aquarium, and the Adler Planetarium rose to adorn the lake front. The Wrigley Building, the Tribune Tower, 333 North Michigan, the Straus Building (now the Continental), the Stevens Hotel (renamed the Conrad Hilton), and many others transformed the skyline of Michigan Avenue. In the Loop the Burnham Building, the Continental-Illinois Bank Building, and the Board of Trade-to name only a few-towered above the older structures. Nearby the Union Station and the Merchandise mart spread their masses over city blocks, while in residential districts luxurious apartments reached skyward. The great boom in building, like the great boom itself, came to an end with the crash of 1929, but the city today uses its solid heritage-the structures it produced-in its daily living.

CHICAGO: GEOLOGY, TOWN AND CITY—A REVERIE

To better understand the land forms and water systems surrounding the Chicago-land-midwest area let us go back in time about 10,000 years ago, the end of the ICE AGE, and introduce briefly the history of its geology. Once again, my friend Donald L. Miller, author of City of the Century, will supply us with this brief history.

The Wisconsin glacier gave the future city of Chicago another natural advantage over other future city sites farther south, such as St. Louis. When the final ice sheet gradually retreated up the St. Lawrence River valley, beyond Lake Ontario, a rushing river took the drainage of the Great Lakes, by way of the Mohawk Pass, to the Hudson River estuary, boring a gap through the Appalachian Mountains. This gap became the route of both the Erie Canal and the New York Central Railroad, nineteenth-century Chicago's two chief ways of reaching New York City. Because of the Mohawk Pass there is no mountain barrier between Chicago and New York, as there is between Chicago and other eastern ports, such as Boston and Philadelphia. New York, the busiest ocean harbor in the world, and Chicago, the busiest inland harbor in the world, became linked by nature and man, their economic destinies intertwined. Throughout the nineteenth century, as Chicago prospered, so did New York; and vice versa.

Lake Chicago created more than future Chicago's corridors of commerce. It created Chicago itself. As this glacial lake contracted over thousands of years to the present dimensions of Lake Michigan, its wave action and undertow smoothed the pliant surface of the site of Chicago to its tabletop flatness. This lake plain-present day Chicago—is only slightly higher than the lake itself, and its level surface, and the layers of poorly porous clay that the glacial deposited, made it extremely difficult to drain. Once a prairie swamp, the early town would be a mudhole for good parts of the year, and as it grew into a city, it would be afflicted by a succession of drainage-related public health epidemics. But the level surface of the ancient glacial lake bottom had it advantages. It made it easy to lay out streets and rail and trolley tracks and placed no physical barriers in the way of Chicago's outward expansion to the north, the south, and the west.

To the east, of course, is the lake. Until the development of a sprawling industrial district along the tiny Calumet River, the Chicago River was the city's only access to the largest inland waterway in the world, highway to ports to the north and east, such as Duluth and Buffalo, to the Atlantic, through the St. Lawrence River, and to the northern forests and ore beds that would supply Chicago with timber and iron to fuel its growth. This small prairie stream is the principal reason why Chicago grew up here, on its banks. For it is a well-protected harbor, as snug and sheltered as New York's, on a long and mostly uninterrupted shoreline. Of equal significance, it led, as we know, to the protage; and this is what made Chicagoua, an

Indian crossroads and summer trading spot, a truly exceptional site for a city.

When the waters of Lake Chicago withdrew from the Chicago plain, they left exposed a thin line of land that secured Chicago's destiny. It was a low, almost imperceptible morainic ridge—not over *10 feet high*—that Joliet, in crossing over its muddy summit, had the geographer's sense to realize was part of *a great continental divide*. This drainage barrier, or watershed, separated by only a few miles the two principal water systems of the west: the Great Lakes-St. Lawrence system, Joliet's familiar trading grounds, and the Mississippi system he had just explored. On the one side of the divide, rainfall drained into the Atlantic Ocean; on the other, into the Gulf of Mexico. Together these systems comprised over thirty-five hundred miles of navigable water roads traversing the continent, interrupted, as Joliet's map indicated, only at the Niagara and Chicago portages. By cutting a canal through the narrow place in the *continental divide* at the "river of the portage" and positioning a fort and a town to protect it and reap its largesse, New France could begin to command the continent, Joliet suggested to his governor.

His recent voyage, he reported to the powers in Quebec, had produced "a very great and important advantage, which perhaps will hardly be believed. It is that we could go with facility to Florida in a bark, and by very easy navigation. It would only be necessary to make a canal by cutting through but half a league of prairie, to pass from the foot of the Lake of the Illinois (Lake Michigan) to the river Saint Louis (the Illinois River)." Joliet asked Frontenac to send him back across the portage to build a colony "in countries so beautiful and upon lands so fertile." In his would-be role of colonizer, he almost certainly would have taken an active part in the establishment of a garrison town on the "river of the portage," where there "is a harbor," he pointed out, "very convenient for receiving vessels and sheltering them from the wind." With this "excavation of which I have spoken," the harbor could become, he dreamed, a gateway to the fertile prairies, to what even he could not imagine would become the most productive agricultural region of its size in the world. With this prophetic plan Joliet gave the design not of Canada's but of Chicago's future economic empire. And the two great water highways he drew on his map became the main axes of settlement of the trans-Appalachian West, with Chicago situated at their juncture. It is there because Joliet's dream became the dream of others centuries later.

Let us now return to Chicago and see how it grew into a town and city, 1833-1837. A region inhabited only by Indians and a few hunters and trappers needs no government. But if a sizable number of permanent settlers are to live together in harmony, some agency must perform certain services for the general welfare: locate and maintain roads, settle disputes, arrest and punish law-breakers, and levy taxes to cover costs. As population increases and people become more dependent upon each other, government assumes more and more duties, at the same time that individual communities (towns and villages) demand a greater share in the control of their own affairs.

In Illinois, as in most of the United States, this development has taken shape in successive forms of government. In 1800 a region occupied by only a few hundred settlers was made a part of Indiana Territory; in 1809 it had grown populous enough to be set apart as Illinois Territory; in 1818 it became a state. Concurrently, counties were being formed to provide local government, while within the counties, towns and cities came into existence.

The southern half of Illinois was well settled while Indians still occupied the northern part of the state. Cook County was not organized until January 15, 1831. Even though its extent was five times as large as it is today, its population consisted of the two companies of infantry stationed at Fort Dearborn, rebuilt in 1816, and a few scattered pioneers.

But after the Black Hawk War (1832) removed the Indian menace, settlers poured in. In the summer of 1833 those who lived in the vicinity of Chicago decided that they needed their own government. Of the thirteen voters, twelve needed their own government. Of the thirteen voters, twelve favored incorporating as a town.

On August 10, 1833, five trustees were elected. Two days later they chose T.J.V. Owen, one of their number, president. The settlement was still so small that they waited until November 7 to adopt a municipal code. The first ordinance established the town limits: Ohio Street on the north, Jackson Street on the south, Jefferson and Cook streets on the west, and on the east, the lake as far as the river, and south of that, State Street.

Within three years a fast-growing population demanded the larger powers offered by incorporation as a city. Delegates from each of Chicago's three districts met on November 24, 1836, and decided to petition the state legislature for a city charter. At the same time, they appointed a committee to prepare a draft. This, substantially, was the charter adopted by the legislature on March 4, 1837.

At the first election under the new form of organization the voters chose six aldermen, one for each ward, and elected William B. Ogden mayor. The mayor received a salary of $500 a year; the aldermen served without pay. A census, taken July 1, 1837, gave the young city a population of 4,170.

Let us end this Reverie in amazement at the unbelievable population growth of Chicago! This growth was the foundation for its spectacular prosperity and the city's many innovations.

1833	350
1846	4,470
1850	29,963
1860	109,260
1870	298,977
1880	503,185
1890	1,099,850
1900	1,698,575

CHICAGO, EARLY DISCOVERY, 1673—A REVERIE

In the spring of 1673 seven white men set out from the mission of St. Ignace, on the mainland near Mackinac Island, to find and explore the Mississippi River. They hoped that the great stream, which they knew only by rumor, would offer a highway to the fabulous riches of the Orient. Father Jacques Marquette, French-born missionary of the Jesuit order, and Louis Joliet, Canadian explorer and mapmaker, led the expedition; the other five were voyageurs, or canoe men. The voyageurs were French Canadians who were very strong and rugged and could not be taller than five feet six inches tall in order to control the canoes in the water. They had to be able to carry 100 pounds on their back, 100 pounds on their chest and 100 pounds on their head in order to make any portage water to water to continue their travel by water. The explorers followed the Fox and Wisconsin rivers to the Mississippi, and then floated with the current as far as the mouth of the Arkansas. There, satisfied that the river emptied into the Gulf of Mexico, and fearing to encounter enemies if they traveled farther, they turned back.

On their return trip Marquette and Joliet, instead of retracing their previous route, paddled up the Illinois River. Near the present city of Ottawa they found a great Indian village. There Marquette preached the gospel and promised the friendly savages that he would return. Led by Indian guides, the explorers ascended the Des Plaines and crossed the low-lying ground between that river and the South Branch of the Chicago River. As the leaves were beginning to turn they floated into the waters of Lake Michigan and pointed their canoes toward Green Bay. They were the first white men to lay eyes on the site of the future city.

THE MISSION OF THE GUARDIAN ANGEL, 1696-1700

For a quarter of a century after 1673 Frenchmen frequented the site of Chicago. Marquette, keeping his promise to the Indians of the Illinois valley, spent the winter there in 1674-75. La Salle, Tonty, Joutel, and other traders and explorers used the portage repeatedly on their journeys to the Illinois and Mississippi rivers. Near the end of the century a large band of Miami Indians, seeking refuge from the implacable Iroquois, established two villages at Chicago, one on the Southside of the main river between the forks and the lake, the other two miles away on the South Branch. There, in 1696, Father Francois Pinet, a Jesuit missionary, founded the Mission of the Guardian Angel.

For four years, with one interruption, Father Pinet sought to save the souls of his savage wards. The task, however, was a hopeless one, and in 1700 the French abandoned the mission. From that date until the early 1780's when Jean Baptiste Point Sable established a trading post on the north bank of the Chicago River near the lake, the history of Chicago is a void. For eighty years hostile Indians blocked the natural passage between the Great Lakes and the Mississippi. Traders must have slipped through from time to time, but no traces of their activities are to be found in the surviving records.

THE TREATY OF GREENVILLE, 1795

The scene shifts from the swampy shore of Lake Michigan to Fort Greenville in western Ohio. There, in the summer of 1795, the tribes gather to make their peace with General Anthony Wayne–"Mad Anthony" of the Revolution–who had routed them at the Battle of Fallen Timbers on August 20, 1794. The treaty, concluded August 10, 1795, opens most of the present State of Ohio to white settlement, but stipulates that certain tracts in the Indian country to the westward may be used by the United States for forts and portages. One of these is described as follows: "one piece of land six miles square, at the mouth of Chicago river, emptying into the southwest end of Lake Michigan." Thus title to the site of the future city passes to the United States.

The comment of Milo M. Quaife in Checagou: From Indian Wigwam to Modern City is pertinent: "From every point of view, this is the most momentous real estate transaction in the history of Chicago. It embraced an area which today the fabled wealth of the Indies would scarcely suffice to purchase, and it directly prepared the way for the subsequent founding of Fort Dearborn. Although the tract was never formally surveyed, its approximate boundaries are easily indicated. From Fullerton Avenue on the north to Thirty-first Street on the south, and from the lake westward to Forty-eighth Avenue (Cicero Avenue); such were the dimensions of Mad Anthony's purchase."

THE FIRST FORT DEARBORN, 1803-1812

Eight years passed before the United States moved to erect a fort at the mouth of the Chicago River. Early in 1803 the War Department made the decision. With the summer Lt. James Strode Swearingen led a detachment of the First Infantry overland from Detroit while Capt. John Whistler, who would command the new post, traveled by water. The troops reached their destination on the afternoon of August 17 and set to work at once building shelters and a stockade. A year later Fort Dearborn, named in honor of the Secretary of War, stood complete.

At this time the Chicago River made a sharp bend to the south just east of the present Michigan Avenue Bridge and emptied into the lake at the approximate location of Madison Street. On elevated ground in the bend of the river stood the stockade, with blockhouses at the northwestern and southeastern corners. The main gateway, in the middle of the south side, looked down the future Michigan Avenue. Inside the enclosure were barracks for officers and men, a storehouse, and a stone powder magazine. A visitor in 1809 characterized the fort as "the neatest and best wooden garrison in the country."

Year after year, little happened at Fort Dearborn. A ship with trade goods called annually, and mail came at long intervals. Hunting, fishing, and games gave some occupation to the troops, but for the most part, life was almost intolerable monotonous.

But with the spring of 1812, the situation changed. Word reached the outpost on the Chicago River that war with Great Britain was imminent. Indians, sullen and aggressive, collected at the fort. In mid-July a runner arrived with official notice that war had been declared.

On August 9 a messenger brought Capt. Nathan Heald, who had replaced Captain Whistler in 1810, an order directing him to evacuate Fort Dearborn and withdraw with the garrison to Fort Wayne. Preparations began at once. On the 13th Capt. William Wells, with thirty friendly Miami warriors, arrived at Chicago to accompany the troops on their long and dangerous journey. The next day Heald distributed the goods of the government store to the Indians; the garrison liquor and the surplus arms and ammunition he destroyed.

At 9:00 o'clock on the morning of August 15 the stockade gate swung open. Captain Wells and some of his Miami headed the procession that emerged. The garrison followed, and after them, the women and children and a dozen militiamen. The remainder of the Miami brought up the rear. The Potawatomi surrounding the fort had promised an escort, but the few who appeared soon deserted.

The column moved south, taking a route between the lake and a row of low sand hills a hundred yards from water. After covering a mile and a half, Captain Wells, discovered that the Indians were lying in ambush behind the sand hills. Heald ordered his men to charge. They gained the ridge, but they were hopelessly outnumbered, and doomed to defeat in the confused fighting that followed. In thirty minutes more than half of the whites lost their lives. When promised that the survivors would be spared, Heald surrendered. In spite of the promise, some of the wounded were put to death, and several of the prisoners were tortured.

On the day after the massacre the Indians set fire to the fort and left for their villages, taking their captives with them. Only smoldering ruins, with mutilated bodies in the distance, marked the site of the first Fort Dearborn.

THE IMMIGRANTS—
A REVERIE

There are many books on the immigrants and immigration of the American people. The review text of American History (1991 Edition) by Irving L. Gordon is a favorite of mine, so it is his text that I selected to introduce this reverie.

"Except for the Indians, all American are immigrants or the descendants of immigrants. During the colonial period, settlers came by the thousands. From the end of the American Revolution to today, some 52 million people have migrated to our shores.

Why they chose to immigrate:

1. Economic. European farmers were discouraged as they tried to reap an adequate crop from small and worn-out lands. Farmers were driven from the soil as the Agricultural Revolution brought about a change from subsistence to large-scale commercial farming. European city workers were disheartened by low wages, and many workers faced unemployment as the Industrial Revolution hastened the use of machines. Immigrants looked to America a a land of opportunity, where fertile lands could be acquired at little or no cost and where the expanding economy provided steady employment at decent wages.

2. Political. Most European governments were controlled by the upper classes, and the common people had little or no say in political matters. Immigrants looked to democratic America, where the ordinary citizen had a strong voice in the government.
3. Social. European society was characterized by rigid class distinctions, few educational opportunities for the lower classes, and discrimination against religious minorities. As World War I approached, most governments required young men to serve terms of compulsory military service. Immigrants looked to America as a land of equality, where they could rise in social status, provide an education for their children, practice their religion without fear, and be free of compulsory military service."

"Historians have traditionally referred to the Europeans coming before 1890 as the "old immigrants". They originated chiefly from northern and western Europe: Great Britain, Ireland, Germany, Holland, France, and the Scandinavian countries of Denmark, Norway, and Sweden. They arrived while the frontier was still open, and many settled on farms in the West. It has been claimed that, since these "old immigrants" possessed customs and traditions similar to those of Americans, they adjusted easily to American ways of life.

Historians have traditionally referred to the Europeans coming after 1890 as the "new immigrants." They came in greater numbers than immigrants had ever come before. From 1901 to 1910 some 8,800,000 persons entered the United States. Unlike the "old immigrants," the "new immigrants" originated chiefly in southern and eastern Europe: Italy, Greece, Austria-Hungary, Serbia, Rumania, Russian Poland, and Russia. They arrived when the frontier was closed and therefore settled chiefly in the cities as factory workers. It has been claimed that, since the "new immigrants" possessed customs and traditions different from those of Americans, they experienced difficulty in adjusting to American ways of Life."

I was a docent at the Chicago History Museum for 10 years (1992-2002). One of my permanent one-hour tours was the history of Chicago given to grammar school and high school students. What follows is one page of my notes used in preparation for the Chicago tour that is relevant to this reverie:

> In 1850 20% Chicagoans were Irish, 6,093 out of 29,963.
> Chicago's unprecedented growth from a marshy wilderness to a city of over 3 million in less than 150 years.
> Almost a constant flow of settlers
>
> 1.) At first: settlers from eastern United States
> 2.) Then from northwestern Europe
> 3.) Later from eastern and southern Europe
> 4.) Most recently from southern United States, Caribbean area, Mexico and parts of Asia.
>
> Chicago was mainly a city of immigrants.
> European immigration started on a large scale in the 1840's
>
> 1st large group-Irish-potato famines 1845-1860 and burden of absentee landlords
> 2nd large group-Germans-after the suppression of the democratic revolutions of the 1840s.
> 3rd large group-Scandinavians-and smaller numbers of English, Welsh and Scots-by 1860-over half of population of 112,172 was foreign born.

The movement of immigrants spurred by the first rail connection between New York and Chicago in 1853 and organized solicitation of settlers-glowing reports of Chicago opportunities. By 1890 over 79% of Chicago's 1 million people were immigrants or children of immigrants.

About 1880-immigrant shift-from eastern and southern Europe: Poles, Italians, eastern European Jews, Czechs, Slovaks, Lithuanians, Greeks, Croatians, Serbian and Hungarian immigration quotas went into effect in 1927.

Causes for Irish immigration:

    a. Potato famine 1845-60 period
    b. Over population
    c. Political dissatisfaction
    d. An oppressive land system
    e. In 1850 20% Chicagoans were Irish 6,093 out of 29,963.

Let us now turn our attention directly to Chicago especially to the Irish and the Germans. And to do this, I used the excellent writing of John D. Hicks in his book, The Federal Union."

"It is not surprising that the United States, as "the land of opportunity," attracted during these prosperous years a great host of European immigrants. The impact of the Industrial Revolution upon Europe had not been without its unfortunate aspects. Those left unemployed by the introduction of labor-saving devices found great difficulty in obtaining re-employment. Also, profound political disturbances, such as the Chartist movement in England and the Revolutions of 1848 on the Continent, accompanied the changing economic order. For those who wished to flee this turmoil, Europe had not adequate outlet of its own, but this defect the United States was fortunately in good position to remedy. Its industries were new, and could profitably absorb both skilled and unskilled European workmen. Its frontier, capable seemingly of an almost indefinite expansion, could give homes not only to its own needy millions, but to millions of Europeans as well. Before 1840 the number of immigrants who came to the United States each year was an almost negligible figure, twenty-three thousand in 1830, and eighty-four thousand in 1840; but between 1845 and 1855 the average number of newcomers admitted annually had risen to not less than three hundred thousand. They came from many lands, but, owing to special circumstances, from Ireland and Germany far more than from all other countries combined.

Unlike the Scotch-Irish who came to the United States from the north of Ireland during the eighteenth century, the new Irish immigrants came from the southern counties of Ireland; they were Celtic in origin rather than Teutonic, and Roman Catholic in religion rather than Presbyterian. Their incentives for leaving Ireland were numerous: political oppression, whether real or fancied, absentee landlordism, overpopulation, and above all a series of devastating famines that began with the failure of the potato crop in 1845. Deaths by starvation during these hard seasons were pitifully frequent, and those who were able to leave for a land of plenty such as America availed themselves of the first opportunity. Shipping companies cut the cost of transportation to a figure lower than had ever been known before, herded the immigrants together in stifling holds, and made a rich harvest from their enterprise. The Irish landed virtually destitute at Boston, New York, and other eastern ports, and went to work at small wages in the factories, on the railroads, or wherever their help was needed. Thousands of Irish girls found employment as domestics. Soon nearly every city had its "Shantytown" where the newly arrived Irish lived in quarters even more squalid than those they had known in

Ireland, and rejoiced on incomes that to the Native Americans seemed ridiculous.

The reasons for the German migration were somewhat analogous. In the vanguard were the political refugees, liberals who had taken a part in the revolutions of 1848 only to lose out in the end before the forces of reaction. Some men of this type, Carl Schurz and Franz Sigel, for example, soon achieved a greater prominence in their adopted land than they had ever known in Germany. Still others left to avoid the compulsory military service required by most German princes, and others to get away from distressing economic conditions for which no remedy seemed available. The success of the English manufacturers with factory-made textiles brought ruin to the numerous German household producers of linen, while crop failures in the Rhine Valley and a losing struggle to hold the English grain market meant critical times for agriculture.

The average German immigrant was a little higher in the social scale than his Irish contemporary, and had often saved enough money to get a start in the new land. Sometimes he went into business, and whole cities, such as Cincinnati, St. Louis, and Milwaukee, soon exhibited many of the characteristic qualities of the Germans. More frequently he bought himself a farm and unaccustomed to the thriftless methods into which an abundance of rich soil had betrayed the Native Americans, he farmed carefully, and prospered inordinately. Unlike the Irish, the Germans rarely settled in the East, but went instead to the Middle West, where lands were cheaper and opportunity more abundant. For a generation or more they continued to speak the German language, and they clung tenaciously to the manners and customs of their European homes. Great lovers of music and of good-fellowship, each German community was apt to have it Liederkranz, its Turnverein, and its Biergarten. In Wisconsin the German influence was so pronounced that there was talk of making the state over into an ideal German commonwealth."

Well, gentle readers, here are some paragraphs that relate to the Chicago immigrants.

Since the establishment of the first school fund in 1833, Chicagoans have viewed schools as vital community institutions. Compulsory school attendance laws passed by the state, combined with a widespread belief in the value of education, encouraged the expansion of educational opportunities. The acceleration of immigration into Chicago after the fire of 1871 placed new responsibilities on the schools which extended their mission far beyond the teaching of the "3 R's." Adult evening classes in English and civics helped prepare new arrivals, young and old, for U.S. citizenship. Thus the schools became the center of a large network of relationships which embraced children, adults, teachers, and other public institutions. For many Chicagoans, the acquisition of a diploma represented the first major step toward worldly success. Besides publicly supported schools, numerous privately run institutions were scattered throughout the city, reflecting the religious and ethnic variations characteristic of Chicago's people. Roman Catholic schools had the greatest number of students. By 1893 their total enrollment reached approximately 38,000 and by 1900 Chicago had the largest Catholic school system in the country. School desks were built for utility, not comfort. Often there were not enough desks to go around. In 1898 the Chicago board of Education congratulated itself on reducing the ratio of elementary students to each teacher from sixty-three to fifty-four. Overcrowding was common in parochial schools as well. The monthly tuition was only $1.00 in the parochial schools in 1935.

The diversity of the city's growing population was reflected in the variety of its religious denominations and practices. Although some houses of worship were established to serve specific locations, others were organized according to nationality, race, and common interest. Chicagoans looked to these institutions not only for spiritual guidance but also as the center of their communal life. By 1885 Chicago had more than two hundred congregations. In many denominations, disputes arose between those who wanted to preserve Old World languages and traditions and those who wanted to modernize.

A city with as many foreign-born residents as Chicago needed institutions that would help bridge the gap between Old World traditions and the ways of the new World. To counteract the immigrants' tendencies to crowd into ethnic enclaves which isolated them from the rest of society, social reformers established settlement houses in the ethnic neighborhoods. Hull-House, Chicago Commons, and similar centers offered a variety of programs ranging from language classes to recreational activities that helped integrate immigrants into the mainstream of American life. Many settlement houses sponsored classes to teach immigrants hygiene and marketable skills such as sewing, cooking, and art. They also encouraged continued use of national crafts to help immigrants retain their ethnic pride. The success of the settlement houses was due in large part to the sensitivity of the staff who lived in the neighborhood and knew the real needs of the neighborhood. By 1920 there were sixty-eight settlement houses in Chicago. Democratic in character, they were open to all and people were treated equally.

Chicagoans have long organized and used clubs and societies to serve a variety of aims and purposes. Sometimes, clubs were founded as benevolent societies to help newcomers: others sought to preserve the language and customs of former homelands. Some have been primarily athletic or recreational; others have brought together people with common intellectual, professional, or political; interests. A group of clubs has served purely social purposes. Frequently these social organizations were patterned after ones that flourished in the old country. A club's address might have been a neighborhood storefront, a posh downtown building, or a members' mailbox. But what the club offered was much the same for everybody; an opportunity to be part of a larger community with common interests. Virtually every ethnic group established mutual aid societies and "self-advancement clubs" to help members learn English and adjust to life in Chicago. Since the life span of a club was determined by its ability to attract and keep members, much effort was devoted to the development of a group image. Badges, special dress, initiation rites, and specially printed invitations to club events underscored the significance of the organization and the desirability of membership.

Newspapers were second to none in importance in the medium of the printed word. From 1870 to 1892 the number of dailies alone nearly tripled to a total of twenty-nine by 1892. Editorial columns depicted the wide range of Chicagoan's interests-urban attitudes and habits intertwined with persisting rural concepts and customs. Since Chicago was made up of a diverse public seeking different kinds of information, there was a need for a variety of newspapers. Some of them addressed particular racial and ethnic groups; others addressed the residents of a specific geographical neighborhood; and still others served as clearing houses for the news of the entire city. In addition to keeping people attuned to the events that shaped their lives, Chicago's numerous dailies and weeklies encouraged lively and sometimes heated exchanges of opinions and ideas. A survey conducted in the 1930s identified 149 foreign language papers. This figure did not include the English language dailies, the numerous black newspapers, or the many local gazettes which emanated from private homes and storefronts. The city's newspapers competed for readers in a variety of ways, from running special features series to advertising via colorful posters, radio, and later television. The Chicago Daily news cost one cent per paper or $3.00 per year in 1881. "All those who speak English read the Daily News."

In the nineteenth century, Chicago saloons were an important center of neighborhood life. In many ways, saloons were like neighborhood clubs. They provided a place where people could gather to exchange neighborhood gossip or news of their homeland, read available newspapers while having a drink, or even board for a few nights-a real help to newcomers. Neighborhood saloons reflected the interests and character of the ethnic groups living in the area. The owners were often the aldermen for the surrounding community, and their saloons were the centers of local political discussion. By the 1880s there was one saloon for every 150 people in Chicago. In the book Old Time Saloon, 1931, newspaperman George Ade writes about saloons: "The saloon gave boisterous welcome to every male adult regardless of his private conduct, his clothes, his manners, his previous record or his ultimate destination. The saloon was the rooster-crow of the spirit of democracy. It may have been the home of sudden indulgence and a training school for criminality, but it had a lot of enthusiastic comrades." The beer growler was a significant object in the working man's life. He would carry his lunch to the factory in it each morning and on the way home have it filled with beer at a nearby saloon. The cost of a growler of beer was about ten cents. Neighborhood children often made good tips by "rushing the can" back and forth for the thirsty. Many saloons competed for business by offering a free lunch. A stop at the corner saloon was part of many a Chicagoan's daily routine. Saloons, often the neighborhood center for information, also doubled as offices for ward aldermen. In 1884, the cost for a saloon license was $500, a steep price imposed by the state legislature in 1883 as part of the temperance movement. Many saloon owners could not afford to pay for a license, and by 1900 three-quarters of the saloons in Chicago were purchased by brewing companies.

Ah, friends, let us end this reverie as we have done so often in the past, by asking our friend, Donald L. Miller, to talk to us about Saloons: "The working-class saloon was a neighborhood institution second in importance only to the family and the parish church. In Jane Addam's Nineteenth Ward, where E.C. Moore, a University of Chicago graduate student, conducted a survey of saloons, there was no place but the saloon, he argued, for the men "to meet their social needs." There were forty-eight thousand residents but no coffeehouses, music halls, or theaters and only a few small trade-union halls.

The saloon's daily routine was keyed to the rhythms of the neighborhoods. Sleepy workers stopped there as early as five in the morning for an "eye-opener," and at the screaming sound of noontime factory whistles, dirt—and blood-caked men rushed out of foundries and slaughtering mills to neighboring rows of saloons for five-cent drafts, ten-cent whiskey chasers, and a free lunch of cold meats, cheese, pickles, and rye bread. Workers unwilling to fight the crowds handed over their big, empty lunch pails, called growlers, to boys at the factory gates, who charged a penny a pail to race to the nearest saloon and fill them with beer. "Rushing the can," it was called. There was a lull in the saloon's business after lunch; then the place filled up from the time the factories began letting out until last call. Some saloons stayed open all night to catch the business of workers on the late shift who stopped on their way home for a "bracer" and some conversation.

In neighborhoods where up to three-quarters of the residents were illiterate, the saloon was the local newspaper, the chief source of information about the world and, more important, about employment and lodging-house openings. For those who could read, newspapers were available, including foreign-language dailies, which some customers would comb before slipping off to a union or a political meeting in the saloon's back room, the very place where many of them had celebrated the baptisms, birthdays, and weddings of their sons and daughters.

"The saloon is a very wholesome discussion center," said a Bohemian immigrant. "Here men bring their ideas and compare them. It helps to get at the truth in a situation and fight manipulation by unscrupulous men."

Immigrants arriving fresh from the home country often came first to an ethnic saloon to inquire about a room or a job, the saloonkeeper himself sometimes being a landlord or an employment agent for a local mill. It was not unusual for a Lithuanian greenhorn stepping off a train at Dearborn Station to be clutching a note with the address of a Chicago watering hole scribbled on it, the place where he was to meet a fellow villager, perhaps a brother or a cousin who had written to him with the help of a saloonkeeper.

Saloonkeepers-successful ethnic businessmen themselves-became advisers to Polish steelworkers living in boardinghouses and saving their earnings for passage money for their families or to start a small business. They were happy to cash the paychecks of their customers, part of the money going right back into their cash drawers, and it was to them that many regular customers went first for a small loan. An immigrant's bank, the saloon was also his post office, where he picked up mail and left and received messages. When saloons began installing telephones in the 1880's, regular customers and their families were welcome to use the phone to call the hospital or the doctor in case of emergency. The local bartender was also the neighborhood pharmacist, dispensing stale beer for an upset stomach or a concoction of his own creation for a hangover or a bad cold. On sweltering summer nights in the closed-in neighborhoods of the river wards, the saloon, with its fans and big windows, its polished bar and gleaming plate-glass mirrors, was the only cool and clean place to be found. Instead of returning to their clammy rooms, some immigrant boarders would pay the saloonkeeper a nickel to sleep on his wooden floor. By 1915, Chicago had one licensed saloon for every 335 residents, and many working-class neighborhoods had up to one for every fifty males sixteen years of age or older, the age at which a boy was usually welcome to join the men at the bar. On any given day in the 1890s, more than half a million customers might find their way into Chicago's saloons."

Remember this song about a saloon which was so respected and protected by the cop on the beat?

>Saloon, Saloon, Saloon,
>Runs through my brain like a tune.
>You can have your café
>And fancy cabarets
>But I'll take saloon
>For the rest of my days.
>For it brings back a fond recollection
>Of a little low-ceiling room,
>With a bar and a rail
>A dame and a pail
>Saloon, Saloon, Saloon,

GROWTH OF IMMIGRANT CITIES—A REVERIE

Here are some reasons for the growth of cities, which of course, apply to Chicago which is the prototype of all the "big cities" of the United States.

1. INDUSTRIAL REVOLUTION. As industries arose, workers congregated about the factories. These workers added to existing city populations or created new cities. Because urban dwellers needed food, clothing, entertainment, and professional services, still more people came to the cities.
2. SOCIAL AND CULTURAL ATTRACTIONS. Many people were attracted to cities by social and cultural facilities: colleges and universities, theaters and movies, symphonies, libraries, and lecture forums.
3. IMPROVED TRANSPORTATION AND COMMUNICATION. The railroads, telegraph lines, and telephones that served the cities enabled the city dwellers to a. obtain foodstuffs and other essentials, b. distribute the products of city factories throughout the land, and c. conduct business transactions quickly and efficiently from a central office.
4. DECREASING FARM POPULATION. Farmers and farm laborers were driven from the countryside by the a.

drabness and hardships of farm life, b. low agricultural prices and difficult times, especially following World War I, and c. increased mechanization and growth of commercial farming.
5. IMMIGRATION FROM EUROPE. During the 19th century, some "old immigrants" settled in cities. After the close of the frontier in 1890, the "new immigrants" settled chiefly in cities.
6. These urban settlers found jobs in city factories and other businesses. As newcomers unfamiliar with American culture, they preferred to live among fellow immigrants who spoke their native tongue. Ethnic groups congregated in special city sections, thereby forming ghettos.
7. MIGRATION OF BLACKS. In the 20th century, blacks left the rural South for urban centers. Some blacks moved to cities in the South, but more moved to cities in the West and North. By 1980, blacks in large numbers inhabited America's most populous cities.

A major railroad center that was still a frontier town, Chicago was always filled with people passing through: tourists, farmers, immigrants, and businessmen-and hustlers who went there to prey on them. A city of strangers, it was a paradise for pickpockets, confidence men, and streetwalkers. Police occasionally hassled these small-time operators, but usually only when they threatened to scare out-of-town spenders away from the city's big, western-style gambling halls, concert saloons, and sporting houses.

There were Sunday closing laws, but they went unenforced, except on one occasion in 1855, when nativist politicians tried to shut down German beer gardens and taverns on the North Side, provoking "Lager Beer Riots" that resulted in one death, hundreds of arrests, and days later, a return to the status quo antebellum. The Illinois prohibition law was defeated by the voters that year, and Chicago had no further problem with the restriction of alcohol consumption until the 1820's.

Nor did anyone in city government try seriously to restrict gambling operations. Professional gamblers who had operated on Mississippi River boats before the Civil war gravitated to Chicago during the war, riding about town in victories, their strumpets beside them in furs and feathered hats. Gunfighters were so common on Randolph Street that it became known for decades as the "Hairtrigger Block." "We are beset on every side by gang of desperate villains!" cried the Chicago Journal. But vice paid. It drew people to the city and emptied their pockets. So it stayed, like everything else that made money in the city.

Since the Lager Beer Riot was Chicago's first civil disturbance, on April 21, 1855, which resulted in one death, 60 arrests, and the beginning of political partisanship in city elections, it may be well to read a little more of its history. On March 6, "Law and Order" coalition swept city elections. The coalition was formed by anti-immigrant, anti-Catholic nativists (Know-Nothings) and temperance advocates who were interested in moral reform and public order. With most municipal services either privatized or organized at the neighborhood level, city elections in the 1840s and early 1850s had been nonpartisan contests of little interest to anyone except real-estate owners. The extremely low voter turnout permitted this quietly mobilized coalition to win control of city hall with a thin base of popular support. Once elected, Mayor Levi Boone and the new council majority hiked liquor license fees while also shortening license terms from one year to three months. Expecting resistance, Mayor Boone "reformed" the city's police force: tripling its size, refusing to hire immigrants, requiring police to wear uniforms for the first time, and directing them to enforce an old, previously ignored ordinance requiring the Sunday closing of taverns and saloons.

These were intentionally provocative acts aimed at Germans and Irish accustomed to spending their leisure hours in drinking establishments. Germans organized to resist the $300 license ordinance, raising defense funds for tavern owners arrested for noncompliance. Prosecutions clogged the city courts and attorneys scheduled a test case for April 21. This, in effect, scheduled the riot. A huge crowd assembled to support the defendants. Mayor Boone ordered police to clear the courthouse area, which resulted in nine arrests. An armed group from the North Side German community decided to rescue the prisoners, but Boone held them off by keeping the Clark Street drawbridge raised until he was able to assemble more than two hundred policemen. When the bridge was lowered and North Siders surged across, shooting began. Boone called in the militia, and the riot ended in minutes. The riot mobilized Chicago's immigrant voters. In March 1856, a heavy German and Irish turnout defeated the nativists, causing the $50 liquor license to be restored. More important was the renewed attention to city elections on the part of political party leaders, ending the era of municipal nonpartisanship. Never again would city elections be of such limited interest that a small group of extremists could win surreptitiously.

It is no wonder that so many saloonkeepers found their way into politics. (In 1900, half the Democratic Party's precinct captains were saloonkeepers.) They built up their businesses on the basis of neighborhood trust and became local men of respect. Running a saloon was also a way to move up in the world. In the 1880's the city's big breweries, following the British "tied-house" system, began to buy out privately owned saloons and turn them into retail outlets, where only the company's product was sold. This drove out many small entrepreneurs but opened opportunities for cash-starved immigrants who wanted to avoid the factory floor. As one Chicago barkeeper said, a saloon was "the easiest business in the world for a man to break into with small capital." With two hundred dollars, he could get a brewer to set him up in business; the brewer paid the rent and the license fee and supplied the bar fixtures and the beer.

Protestant purifiers complained that there were too many bars in the city, but Carter Harrison thought there were not enough of them. He depended on the money from the license fees to pay for the urban services the middle-class reformers who were trying to close the saloons were pressuring him to provide. The rural-dominated Illinois legislature put tight restrictions on Chicago's ability to raise taxes or float bond issues, and township tax assessors kept property assessments ridiculously low in order to stay in office or to please big interests, which kept the assessors in their pay. In 1893 the total assessed value of all Chicago property was actually less than it was in 1871, even though the city had more than quadrupled in size; and the average assessment of real estate was only a little more than 10 percent of its actual value. This left the government heavily dependent on saloon-license revenues, which in 1886 accounted for over 12 percent of all city income. "While much has been said about the evils of saloons, . . . the fact is that we are dependent on the saloons to enable us to eke out a municipal existence," remarked one observer. "The taxpayers of Chicago ought to take off their hats to them."

As mayor, Harrison used his control of the police force to protect saloonkeepers from Protestant reformers. With the advice of Democratic Party officials, he appointed all policemen but left control of the force largely to the ward bosses, who allowed saloons to stay open on Sundays and after the legal midnight closing in return for a payoff. So ethnics had to pay to protect their lifestyles but were willing to do so, even though it sometimes meant tolerating gambling and prostitution in their neighborhoods, trades also protected by the enterprising aldermen.

This was the real source of Harrison's popularity. He understood that Chicago was a city of neighborhoods, each with its own unique customs and folkways. Whereas cultural uplifters like Charles Hutchinson and Joseph Medill had a citywide orientation and a desire to see all of Chicago's people brought up to an Anglo-American standard of taste and behavior, Harrison was willing to let people in the precincts lead their own lives. As Willis J. Abbot, one of his advisers, wrote of him, he "consistently held that the masses are better judges of their own needs than are the constituted censors of the press or of 'citizen's associations.'"

But the working people of Chicago wanted more than this from their government. They wanted politicians who were willing to defend the right of labor to organize and demonstrate for better wages and benefits. Modern urban historians like Richard Oestreicher claim that in most American big cities there was "no meaningful difference" between Republicans and Democrats on "the rights of labor." Most big city mayors were not "spokesmen of workers," Oestreicher writes. But Carter Harrison was. And he aligned his party with the city's organized labor movement, giving Catholic and German Lutheran workers an additional reason to vote for him. Harrison offered his own view of the differences between the city's two main parties: "The Republican Party is made up of the rich and monopolistic classes, while the Democratic Party is the party of the people." If you want to read more on this history, go once again to Donald L. Miller's book, CITY OF THE CENTURY. By the way, the Democratic Party is no longer the party of the people. The Republican Party is Pro-Life, the Democratic Party is not.

Since June 2008 to June 2009 is the year of St. Paul as declared by Pope Benedict XVI and since November 30th is the first Sunday of Advent, the beginning of our liturgical year, let us end this reverie by quoting from a "Bible Study Guide For Catholics" authored by Father Mitch Pacwa, S.J. Father Mitch was born and raised in Chicago, who earlier in the year talked to RRC in our Chapel. He is a weekly speaker on EWTN, the Eternal Word Television Network.

St. Paul in his Letter to the Galatians directly links the Holy Spirit with interior virtues:

> "But the fruit of the Spirit is love, joy, peace, patience, kindness, goodness, faithfulness," gentleness, self-control; against such there is no law. And those who belong to Christ Jesus have crucified the flesh with its passions and desires.
>
> "If we live by the Spirit, let us also walk by the Spirit. Let us have no self-conceit, no provoking of one another, no envy of one another. (Gal 5:22-26)

In this passage, St. Paul speaks of the "fruit" of the Holy Spirit. The choice of "fruit" points to a profound difference from the spiritual gifts. A gift is bestowed upon a person, either in its entirety or in parts and sections. A fruit grows slowly and develops its sweetness over a length of time. This is an apt image for the Spirit's fruit of love, joy, peace, patience, kindness, goodness, faithfulness, gentleness, and self-control (or chastity). Like a fruit, each one of these virtues may begin as a blossom that smells sweet and appears beautiful. Many converts see an initial improvement in their personality, accompanied by great joy. However, blossoms fade and fall away, leaving a small, green, bitter nub. At some point, Christians find it difficult, even bitter, to try to live the virtues. Only with much time and growth does the fruit grow in size and eventually gain color. Yet even when color appears, the fruit may be hard and sour on the inside. Only full development allows the sweetness to come through. The Christian must remain united with the Church, the Body of Christ, like fruit on a tree. The sap of the Holy Spirit will continue to flow into the soul, increasing the size, color, and sweetness of the virtues.

So, my dear friends, what better way to start our new Liturgical year then with meditations on St. Paul. The presence of the Holy Spirit is made known in more visible ways through the gifts he bestows on Christians. St. Paul wrote three lists of these gifts 1.) 1 Corinthians 12:4-11, 2.) Ephesians 4:7-14, and 3.) Romans 12:3-8. Why not meditate on the gifts the Holy Spirit gave each of you and how their fruits are working in your life?

WILD CHICAGO—A REVERIE

There developed in the second decade of the nineteenth century in Chicago a group of men and women that later became known as the "old settlers." Two of their best known names were William Butler Ogden (1805-1877) and Gurdon Saltonstall Hubbard (1802-1886).

William B. Ogden, Chicago's first mayor, had a philosophy of "get on with it." His friend, Isaac Arnold, said that if a thousand picked men were cast upon a desolate island, Ogden "would, by common, universal, and instinctive selection, have been made their leader." Arnold also said Ogden was the man you would want along on a long stage ride because he made ... the longest day short by his inimitable narration of incidents and anecdotes, his graphic descriptions, and his sanguine anticipation of the future.

Ogden had a lot of reasons not to be sanguine about the future. He was, nevertheless, the incurable optimist the young town needed to jumpstart it and keep it pushing along. The 4,000 residents (or rather, the 706 voters) of Chicago who selected him as mayor in 1837 thought so. He defeated the son of furtrader John Kinzie, John H. Kinzie, who had grown up outside of Fort Dearborn and who had escaped the massacre in 1812.

When Ogden first arrived two years earlier, he was unbelievably disappointed. He was born in Delaware County, upstate New York, in 1805, and loved the mountains, streams and rivers of his native place. By contrast, Chicago was frantic and mired in mud. He came to Chicago on a business trip to look after some property that his brother-in-law, Charles Butler, and several others had earlier purchased for $100,000. Ogden wrote back to the men whom he represented and told them that they had been taken in a land auction, however, he recouped the $100,000 by selling off one-third of what they had bought. He expressed his new attitude to a friend: When you are dealing with Chicago property the proper way is to go in for all you can get and then go on with your business and forget all about it. It will take care of itself.

The land speculation bubble burst during Ogden's term as mayor. The situation became exactly what it was called, "a panic." He pushed hard for the city not to go bankrupt and renounce its debt. Comparing the situation to a city besieged, he argued passionately: . . . many a fortress has saved itself by the courage of its inmates and their determination to conceal their weakened condition. His optimism and fight carried the day.

Ogden stayed enthusiastic. He designed the city's first swing bridge, donated the land for its first medical school (Rush Medical College), dealt in real estate, twice served on the City Council, built a fine home and established a literary and cultural tone for the community.

Chicago's first railroad had been started in 1836, and abandoned the next year, when hard times hit the city. It faded for almost everyone; not, however, for William Ogden. When Ogden wanted to resume building the railroad, William F Weld, a Boston financier, told him to do so, but that it would go broke and then he and other Eastern financiers would finish it. Ogden climbed on a horse, rode out to the farmers along the proposed route and got the money from them, a few dollars at a time. His Galena & Chicago Union Railroad in 1848 purchased a third-hand engine, The Pioneer, and started operation from Chicago to a point 10 miles west. It never reached Galena, but it became the first spoke in the great railroad system that within a decade made Chicago the railroad hub of North America. He later formed another line, the Chicago & Northwestern which eventually became the Chicago Union.

His vision was broader than his Midwestern lines, however, in 1850 Ogden became chairman of the National Pacific Railway Convention. He would serve in 1862 as president of the Union Pacific Railroad, a position he held until 1866. He would later help drive in the golden spike at a place named after him, Ogden Flats, Utah, when the country was finally spanned by a railroad line in 1869. As a man who steeled himself to handle adversity, William Ogden would need all that strength to face what was ahead. As his railroads spread throughout Wisconsin, he invested in the lumber trade that dominated sections of the state. The focus of his interests was the town of Peshtigo, where large numbers of the residents worked for Ogden companies.

On Oct. 8, 1871, major fires burned both Chicago and Peshtigo, devastating the cities and killing 1,000 people in Peshtigo and 300 in Chicago. The former mayor lost his home in Chicago as well as his investments. In the Wisconsin fire, he lost close to $1,000,000 plus the lives of friends and workers. He stayed in Chicago only four days to handle business and personal matters. He then spent two months in Peshtigo, helping to save the city with the same optimism for its future that he had for Chicago in 1837. In 1875, at the age of 70, the busy and determined Ogden finally married.

Now gentle reader, rather than include more biographies, I think you'd enjoy much more the lives and activities of the "old settlers." Their individual biographies are really beyond the scope of this Reverie but they can be found in any library if you are so inclined to read them. So, I once again turn to my friend, Donald L. Miller, author of the "City of the Century."

The canoe that carried sixteen-year-old Gurdon Saltonstall Hubbard to Chicago in the fall of 1818 was not one of the light and fleet birchbarks used by Marquette and Joliet. It was a bateau, or freight canoe, fifty feet long, with a crew of five voyageurs, four of them rowing while the fifth steered from the stern. Although made of bark, it carried, in addition to its crew, several traders and clerks and over three tons of merchandise and provisions. Owned and outfitted by John Jacob Astor's American Fur Company, which had recently gained a monopoly on the Indian trade in the regions Joliet opened up for New France, it was one of twelve boats—a "brigade"—headed for the Illinois wilderness by the route Marquette had taken back from there on his final voyage.

Descendant of Reverend Gurdon Saltonstall, a colonial governor of Connecticut, he was also the adopted son of Waba, chief of the Kikapoo, and for a time was married to a Kankakee woman and wore his hair long, like an Indian. The Potawatomi called him Pa-pa-ma-ta-be, "the Swift Walker," for he could cover fifty miles between daylight and darkness without great effort. Fellow traders at Fort Dearborn called him "Yankee Hubbard." Both names fit the man, for his life linked two cultures and two epochs of Chicago's earliest recorded history.

Chicago's transition from fur-trading outpost to capitalist town, a cultural revolution Gurdon Hubbard lived through and helped bring forward, shows that in the city-building process in the West there were clear winners and losers. The western town did not evolve organically out of the nucleus of the trading village, as Frederick Jackson Turner suggested in his famous essay "The Significance of the Frontier in American History." In

Chicago's case, town and hamlet were wholly different types of human settlements, and the explosive emergence of one meant the complete disappearance of the other. To appreciate what was gained and lost in this transformation is to achieve a fuller understanding of the urban process on the American frontier and the larger historical importance of Chicago's beginning. The history of early Chicago is a history, in small measure, of the American frontier. To know Gurdon Hubbard is to know that story.

Early Chicago had two focal points: the fort and Wolf Point. They were only a half mile apart, but the only convenient means of communication between them was by canoe or rowboat. "I passed over the ground from the fort to the Point on horseback," a visitor to Chicago in the 1820's reported. "I was up to my stirrups in water the whole distance. I would not have given sixpence an acre for the whole of it." The wet, shallow soil and the raw winds that blew off the lake for most of the year made it impossible to grow crops, and "the village . . ." wrote another traveler, William H. Keating, "consists of but few huts, inhabited by a miserable race of men, scarcely equal to the Indians from whom they are descended. Their log or bark houses are low, filthy and disgusting."

Keating might have made a single exception had he paid a visit to the Kinzie house, with its fenced-in orchard and wide, poplar-shaded piazza. John Kinzie had acquired the property in 1803 from a man who had bought it from Jean Baptiste Point du Sable, a cultivated mulatto fur trader from Santo Domingo.

The Canadian-born Kinzie had a reputation as a sharp-dealing Indian trader when he first arrived in Chicago in 1804 at the age of forty to establish a trading post near newly constructed Fort Dearborn. Until fighting broke out along the northwestern frontier during the War of 1812, Kinzie had been the head man at Chicago, fashioning a trading fiefdom. His ties with the local

Potawatomi tribe had allowed his family to be spared in the slaughter on the dunes south of the fort, and they later escaped to Michigan.

In the summer of 1816, when troops and mechanics arrived to begin rebuilding the second Fort Dearborn, the only signs they saw that this had been a place of habitation were the abandoned Kinzie house, a shabby trader's cabin on the southern shore of the lake, the blackened brick magazine of the plundered and burned fort, and the scalped bodies of the massacred victims, which had been left unburied in the shifting sands, an eerie reminder of the fragility of life on the Indian frontier, where Chicago was the only white settlement between Fort Wayne and Green Bay. The soldiers buried the victims on the steep banks of the lakeshore, where the windblown waters would uncover parts of the pine coffins. It was to this desolate place that a much-aged and financially strained John Kinzie returned in 1816 to try to regain his stature in the fur trade.

John Kinzie might have been Chicago's first white resident, but Point du Sable has the strongest claim to being its first permanent non-Indian settler. His house at the mouth of the river is commonly referred to in early histories of Chicago as a primitive cabin, but a document listing the property he sold to Jean Lalime in 1800, before leaving Chicago for Missouri Territory, gives a picture of a man of some substance. Had he not been black, Jean Baptiste Point du Sable would not have been an embarrassment to old settlers; indeed, one historian speculates that his father was a descendant of a famous French family. That is pure conjecture, but the fact remains that "the First Chicagoan" was a proud and prosperous black man who lived at the head of the river for almost twenty years in a house that his white-skinned pretender was too impoverished in his old age to hold on to.

The center of early Chicago was not the place where John Kinzie's homestead faced the lime-slaked walls of the fort. It was just upriver at Wolf Point, the rollicking gathering place of a racially mixed settlement of Indians, half-breeds, French Canadians, and Anglo-Americans. There was a lot of bickering and petty crime and even an occasional murder in this wilderness settlement that hugged the river to the north and south of the Point, but its inhabitants were bound together into a community by three things: isolation from civilized society, trade in furs, and drinking and reveling at the river taverns on Wolf Point. The most popular of these makeshift hotels was managed by a devil-may-care Creole from the Detroit area named Mark Beaubien, the spirit of the long-forgotten Chicago that lived for a brief but turbulent moment in the years just after Gurdon Hubbard arrived in 1818.

Mark Beaubien was the younger brother of one of Chicago's earliest fur traders, Jean Baptiste Beaubien, who lived with his large, part-Indian brood on a government field just south of the fort and helped his brother get started in the tavern business in a building Mark Beaubien named after his half-breed friend Billy Caldwell, who was called "the Sauganash," or Englishman.

By 1830, there were three taverns in the area of Wolf Point, and the next year they were connected by a log-raft ferry run by Mark Beaubien. These taverns, and frontier Chicago itself, attracted every manner of humanity. At various times there were Frenchmen in the village who had fought with Napoleon at Jena and Waterloo, Yankees who had been with Andrew Jackson at New Orleans, and Indians, like Billy Caldwell, who had fought alongside the legendary Tecumseh. Occasionally, a gambler or a criminal on the run showed up and stayed for a bit, for there were few better spots in the Old Northwest to find a card game or a place to disappear.

At the Sauganash and its neighboring hotels, men and women of every color and class were welcome; and whiskey, song, and dance were the great democratizers. Visitors from more civilized parts were shocked to see Indian braves spinning the white wives of fort officers around the dance floor of the Sauganash to the frenzied fiddling and toe tapping of Mark Beaubien, or Indian and white women drinking home-distilled liquor straight from the bottle. To add an edge to the evenings, local white traders, usually led by the raucous Kinzie clan, would put on feathered headdresses and spring into the crowded tavern with war whoops and raised tomahawks, scaring the wits out of tight-buttoned easterners.

Years later, when the traders were long gone, old settlers, who arrived in Chicago just as Mark Beaubien's world was disappearing, would remember him as "a jolly good fellow . . . full of fun and frolic," who would play his fiddle and call out the figures for the dancers in his mangled English. "I plays de fiddle like de debble," he once told a group of eastern spectators who asked him what he did for a living, "an I keeps hotel like hell." To old settlers, he was "our Beaubien," part civilized, part savage in spirit, a reckless but lovable man who managed to spend whatever he made. But Mark Beaubien, father of twenty-three children, was not the one-of-a-kind village character of old-settler memory. He was a representative figure in a precapitalist community that flaunted progress and prided itself on its disdain for proper public conduct, a wild town with three taverns but no churches, school buildings, or meetinghouse. "Oh them was fine times," he declared toward the end of his life, "never come any more."

Mark Beaubien and his riverside neighbors ran a barter economy on the rim of civilization. Until the town was officially surveyed and platted in 1830, they were squatters on their land. They traded parcels of real estate, in what became the center of the world's first skyscraper city, for saddles and bridles, or won or lost them in noisy games of stud poker. Convivial Mark Beaubien often gave away land to people he took a liking to in an effort to get them to settle in the village that was "a mighty lonesome, wet place" when the first Beaubiens arrived from the other side of the lake. No one thought things would change as they did. After lots he gave away became fantastically valuable only a few years later, Mark Beaubien could only remark, with a shrug: "Didn't expect no town."

Well, gentle reader, do you agree with me that Wild Chicago was quite a city?

Let's end this reverie with three statements worthy of quiet reflection:

1.) "Wolf Point" in 1832 was the center of frontier Chicago.
2.) Gurdon Saltonstall Hubbard, fur trader, merchant, and town founder; his biography is the history of Chicago from 1818 to the mid-1880's.
3.) William Butler Ogden was Chicago's first mayor. A land dealer and railroad builder, he more than anyone else, turned Chicago from a mudhole into a metropolis.

TWO DECLARATIONS— A REVERIE

We celebrate our Declaration of Independence every fourth of July. But in the second paragraph we state our declaration of dependence:

> "We hold these truths to be self-evident, that all men are created equal; that they are endowed by their Creator with certain unalienable rights; that among these are life, liberty, and the pursuit of happiness."

Our Founding Fathers knew that the federal government could not give the people these rights, for if they could, they could also take them away. They understood and acknowledged their dependence on their Creator.

"The fundamental principle of our Constitution enjoins that the will of the majority shall prevail." Since the 1960's, the Supreme Court has issued judgments that undermine our liberties enumerated in the Constitution. Many books are now available that urge a return to the limited government originally set forth in the Constitution and Bill of Rights. One such books is Original Intent written by David Barton.

Here are some selected quotes from his book concerning their concern with the courts, the Constitution, and religion:

* George Washington's Farewell Address:

"Of all the dispositions and habits which lead to political prosperity, religion and morality are indispensable supports. In vain would that man claim the tribute of patriotism who should labor to subvert these great pillars of human happiness?"

* John Adams:

"We have no government armed with power capable of contending with human passions unbridled by morality and religion . . . Our Constitution was made only for a moral and religious people. It is wholly inadequate to the government of any other."

* John Quincy Adams:

"Three points of doctrine, the belief of which, forms the foundation of all morality. The first is the existence of a God; the second is the immortality of the human soul; and the third is a future state of rewards and punishments. Suppose it possible for a man to disbelieve either of these articles of faith and that man will have no conscience, he will have no other law than that of the tiger or the shark; the laws of man may bind him in chains or may put him to death, but they never can make him wise, virtuous, or happy."

* Abraham Baldwin, signer of the Constitituon:

 "A free government . . . can only be happy when the public principles and opinions are properly directed . . . by religion and education. It should therefore be among the first objects of those who wish well to the national prosperity to encourage and support the principles of religion and morality."

* Nathaniel Greene:

 "Truth, honor, and religion are the only foundation to build human happiness upon. They never fail to yield a mind solid satisfaction, for conscious virtue gives pleasure to the soul."

* George Mason, Father of the Bill of Rights:

 "We are now to rank among the nations of the world; but whether our Independence shall prove a blessing or a curse must depend upon our own wisdom or folly, virtue or wickedness . . . Justice and virtue are the vital principles of republican government."

* Thomas Jefferson:

 "The practice of morality being necessary for the well-being of society, He (God) has taken care to impress its precepts so indelibly on our hearts that they shall not be effaced by the subtleties of our brain. We all agree in the obligation of the moral precepts of Jesus and nowhere will they be found delivered in greater purity than in His discourses."

* Alexander Hamilton:

 "The law . . . dictated by God Himself is, of course, superior in obligation to any other. It is binding over all the globe, in all countries, and at all times. No human laws are of any validity if contrary to this."

* George Washington:

 "Reason and experience both forbid us to expect that national morality can prevail in exclusion of religious principle . . . Promote, then, as an object of primary importance, institutions for the general diffusion of knowledge."

* Benjamin Rush, signer of the Declaration of Independence:

 "The only foundation for a useful education in a republic is to be laid in religion. Without this there can be no virtue, and without virtue there can be no liberty, and liberty is the object and life of all republican governments. Without religion, I believe that learning does real mischief to the morals and principles of mankind."

* Oliver Ellsworth, Delegate to the Constitutional Convention; US Senator; Chief Justice of the US Supreme Court:

 "The primary objects of government are the peace, order and prosperity of society . . . To the promotion of these objects, particularly in a republican government good morals are essential. Institutions for the promotion of good morals are therefore objects of legislative provision and support; and among these . . . religious institutions are eminently useful and important."

Frenchman Alexis de Tocqueville, (1805-1850), a French Statesman and author, visited the United States to discover what made us so great. He traveled throughout the nation in the early 1830's and published his findings in 1835 in The Republic of the States of America, and Its Political Institutions, Reviewed and Examined-now called simply, Democracy in America. Notice some of his observations:

Upon my arrival in the United States, the religious aspect of the country was the first thing that struck my attention; and the longer I stayed there, the more did I perceive the great political consequences resulting from this state of things, to which I was unaccustomed. In France I had almost always seen the spirit of religion and the spirit of freedom pursuing courses diametrically opposed to each other; but in America I found that they were intimately united, and that they reigned in common over the same country.

He traveled the country investigating our people, our work, our cities and lands. Upon seeing the many church steeples throughout the country and the religious practices of the people, he concluded it was our public acknowledgment of our dependence on the Creator that made us great. He ended his report with these words: "America will continue to be great as long as America continues to be good, but America will cease to be great, if America ceases to be good."

Any article on the Declaration of Independence, the Constitution and/or the Bill of Rights, must always cite Abraham Lincoln for validity (excerpts from Original Intent)

In the Declaration, the Founders established the foundation and the core values on which the Constitution was to operate; it was never to be interpreted apart from those values. This was made clear by John Quincy Adams in his famous oration, "The Jubilee of the Constitution." Adams explained:

> The virtue which had been infused into the Constitution of the United States ... was no other than the concretion of those abstract principles which had been first proclaimed in the Declaration of Independence ... This was the platform upon which the Constitution of the United States had been erected. Its virtues, its republican character consisted in it conformity to the principles proclaimed in the Declaration of Independence and as its administration ... was to depend upon the ... virtue, or in other words, of those principles proclaimed in the Declaration of Independence and as its administration ... was to depend upon the ... virtue, or in other words, of those principles proclaimed in the Declaration of Independence and embodied in the Constitution of the United States.

Generations later, President Abraham Lincoln reminded the nation of that same truth:

> These communities, by their representatives in old Independence Hall, said to the whole world of men: "We hold these truths to be self-evident: that all men are created equal; that they are endowed

by their Creator with certain inalienable rights; that among these are life, liberty, and the pursuit of happiness." . . . They erected a beacon to guide their children, and their children's children, and the countless myriads who should inhabit the earth in other ages . . . . They established these great self-evident truths that . . . their posterity might look up again to the Declaration of Independence and take courage to renew that battle which their fathers began, so that truth and justice and mercy and all the humane and Christian virtues might not be extinguished from the land . . . Now, my countrymen, if you have been taught doctrines conflicting with the great landmarks of the Declaration of Independence . . . let me entreat you to come back . . . Come back to the truths that are in the Declaration of Independence.

The interdependent relationship between these two documents was clear, and even the U.S. Supreme Court openly affirmed it. At the turn of the century (1897), the Court declared:

> The latter (Constitution) is but the body and the letter of which the former (Declaration of Independence) is the thought and the spirit, and it is always safe to read the letter of the Constitution in the spirit of the Declaration of Independence.

The Constitution cannot be properly interpreted nor correctly applied apart from the principles set forth in the Declaration; the two documents must be used together. Furthermore, under America's government as originally established, a violation of the principles of the Declaration was just as serious as a violation of the provisions of the Constitution.

Nonetheless, Courts over the past half-century have steadily divorced the Constitution from the transcendent values of the Declaration, replacing them instead with their own contrivances. The results have been reprehensible-a series of vacillating and unpredictable standards incapable of providing national stability.

Jefferson declared:

> You seem . . . to consider the judges as the ultimate arbiters of all constitutional questions; a very dangerous doctrine indeed, and one which would place us under the despotism of an oligarchy. Our judges are as honest as other men and not more so. They have, with others, the same passions for party, for power, and the privilege of their corps . . . . And their power the more dangerous as they are in office for life and not responsible, as the other functionaries are, to the elective control. The Constitution has erected no such single tribunal.

Jefferson did not oppose the courts expounding the Constitution, but he stressed that the Judiciary was not the "final arbiter." It was merely one of three branches in a system where each was capable of reading the Constitution and determining constitutionality.

Generations later, President Lincoln, in his "Inaugural Address," affirmed that this was still the belief when he declared:

> I do not forget the position assumed by some that constitutional questions are to be decided by the

> Supreme Court ... At the same time, the candid citizen must confess that if the policy of the government upon vital questions affecting the whole people is to be irrevocably fixed by decisions of the Supreme Court, the instant they are made ... the people will have ceased to be their own rulers, having ... resigned their government into the hands of that eminent tribunal.

Lincoln's statement had been prompted by the Dred Scott decision in which the Supreme Court had declared that Congress could not prohibit slavery-that slaves were only property and not persons eligible to receive any rights of a citizen. Fortunately, the other two branches ignored the Court's ruing. On June 9, 1862, Congress did prohibit the extension of slavery into the free territories; and the following year, President Lincoln did issue the "Emancipation Proclamation"-both were acts that were a direct affront to the Court's decision. Because Congress and President Lincoln were guided by their own understanding of the Constitution rather than by the Judiciary's opinion, both declared freedom for slaves.

Abraham Lincoln was a politician. To many, this word, "politician," has a pejorative overtone; but to the people who knew Mr. Lincoln, they would all sing, "Honest Abe!" Abraham Lincoln was an honest politician. His words always reflected what he believed and his actions always reflected his words. To all men and women, he would give their just due. However, his justice was always tempered with compassion. Listen to the words of President Lincoln: "With malice towards none and charity for all, let us strive to bind up our nations wounds ..." yes, indeed, the kind words of "Honest Abe" Lincoln.

On October 12, 2007, I heard a homily at a mass on EWTN given by Father Thomas Eutenier who heads up Human Life

International (Pro-Life). The Gospel for that day was Luke 11:15-26: "Jesus was driving out a demon that was mute, and when the demon had gone out, the mute person spoke and the crowds were amazed." Father Eutenier's Bishop gave him the power to drive out demons, in other words, he was appointed an exorcist. And what follows now are his thoughts expressed by him in his homily. Possessions really happen today. One demon comes first and will be joined by other demons but one at a time, that is, the person will eventually be possessed by multiple demons. A demon can enter into a body either by invitation of that person or as a victim. Examples of both (l) voluntarily, in the new age many people who dabble in the occult voluntarily let a demon enter into them and, (2) as a victim. Father related a case where an uncle said to a demon "if you give me money, I'll give you my nephew", the nephew was victimized by his uncle. It took Father Eutenier one year to exorcise the 16 demons, one at a time, even though the nephew went to daily mass. You see how powerful the demons are and how long it takes to drive them out. But the power the bishop gives to a designated priest has this infallible power that the demons (also the devil) cannot resist or stop, it is Christ's power. A demon can never possess a soul, that soul belongs to God. The exorcism could take years but it will be done if the person perseveres. It is a mystery of God's will that allows the devil and his demons to take possessions. Now, Fr. Eutenier then spoke about larger scale possessions, such as nations and the whole problem of evil. Demons are powerful beings spiritually but so are exorcists. It is possible that a whole society can be possessed; example, Nazi Germany, Communist Russia, Communist China.

Now to our country: 1965-the demon of contraception entered into the U.S.A. through the Supreme Court's decision in the Connecticut Case, and on January 22, 1973, the demon of abortion was invited into the U.S.A. by our Supreme Court in the Roe vs Wade decision. Both demons brought other demons into our nation one at a time and this possession is growing and spreading, their political power is also growing. No popular election nor any legislation will ever chase out these demons. You cannot cast them out by human efforts, only the Catholic Church can do this. Bishops, priests, and all the laity (all Christians of all denominations) must stand as a group before legislatures and capital Buildings (Federal, State, Municipal, City) and pray to God to drive out these demons from our country and demand these evils to leave our country. Laity are doing their job now through pro life activities but many Bishops and Priests are not doing their job, not giving the leadership we need, giving us a very bad example. *All Bishops, all Priests, all citizens who want to free our country from these evils should surround these aforementioned buildings and pray for exorcisms of these demons. It might not happen in our lifetime but eventually all these stored-up prayers will be successful and God will defeat and drive out these evil demons. We are promised victory so never give up hope, we are the church militant, we can and will do it but we must continually pray for it and all way "Depart you demons of contraception and abortion. The truth will set you free!" Homily ended.

> "I would advise those who practice, especially at first, to cultivate the friendship and company of others who are working in the same way. This is a most important thing, because we can help one another by our prayers, and all the more so because it may bring us even greater benefits." (St. Teresa of Avila)

Prayer to St. Michael the Archangel

St. Michael the Archangel, defend us in the day of battle; be our safeguard against the wiles and wickedness of the devil. May God rebuke him, we humbly pray, and do thou, O Prince of the heavenly host, by the power of God cast into Hell Satan and all the other evil spirits, who prowl through the world, seeking the ruin of souls. Amen

> "I pledge allegiance to the Flag of the United States of America, and to the Republic for which it stands, one Nation Under God, indivisible, with liberty and justice for all."

POTTER AND BERTHA PALMER—A REVERIE

The most successful Chicago entrepreneur during the BOOM years before the Chicago fire was a vast, profit-inspired building enterprise by one of its boldest speculators. Potter Palmer (1826-1902). He made his first millions with a dry-goods store. Among his innovations were "bargain days" (the first "sales"), money back guarantees (for any reason), the policy that the customer is always right, and free home delivery of all purchases. Palmer set out particularly to win female customers. His store was the one place in Chicago where women could go unescorted. Palmer imported high-quality merchandise from Europe and the Orient, taught clerks to remember customers' names and preferences, and instructed them never to pressure visitors into buying. In short, Potter Palmer created "shopping" as we know it.

In 1865, as a thirty-nine-year-old bachelor in poor health, he abruptly gave control of his business to the young Marshall Field and his partner Levi Z. Leiter, but remained their landlord. Then Palmer took a few years off to recuperate in Europe.

Back in Chicago in 1868, he built a ball field for the Chicago White Stockings baseball club (later the Cubs) and spent time at the horse races. When he wasn't enjoying the sporting life, however, he was developing a plan to reshape his city. Palmer had quietly bought up property on State Street, a narrow north-south thoroughfare parallel to the lakeshore. After he had acquired more than a mile of property, he asked the city council to widen the street to create a broad, Parisian-style boulevard. This was no simple task and many State Street neighbors refused to set their building back to accommodate a new street. The resulting street cut back and forth between the Palmer's new buildings and the older structures. After the Great Fire in 1871, however, the blocks were all regularized and State Street became wide enough to accommodate carriage parking and horse-drawn trolleys.

Potter Palmer had single handedly reoriented Chicago's downtown from Lake Street—an east-west road along the stinking canal—to the new, elegant boulevard that he virtually owned. A massive six-story structure on the corner of State and Washington was leased to Field and Leiter for a new Marshall Field's store.

But he was discontented. His discontentment vanished when he met Bertha Honore, 23 years younger than himself. It was love at first sight and they married in 1870. Thus began the happiest years of both their lives. Bertha was his loyal helper in all their ventures. As a wedding gift, he had presented her with a hotel. The Palmer House on State Street was, at eight stories, the tallest building in the city. Its 225 rooms were decorated with Italian marble and French chandeliers. Bertha always said she was very satisfied to be the wife of an innkeeper!

Mrs. Potter Palmer, as she was referred to in the style of her day, had both the requisites and the prerequisites for her unofficial title. These included family, education, and husband, and ultimately, charisma and self-confidence. She arrived in Chicago in 1855 at the age of six, a member of the prominent Honore family from Louisville. Miss Bertha was schooled at Chicago's Dearborn Seminary and then at the Convent of the

Visitation in Georgetown, Washington, D.C. There, she excelled, the school reported, "in the profane subjects."

Potter had started the store now known by the name of the man who bought it from him, Marshall Field. He had also developed State Street, drawing the city's attention away from the formerly exclusive Lake Street. He had almost finished constructing the Palmer House, the most sumptuous hotel in town. The Chicago Fire in 1871 destroyed both his new hotel and his State Street real estate, but he confidently and resolutely rebuilt them.

In addition to wealth and a successful husband, the place at the top of the city's social pecking order required Bertha to have the *sine qua non* of being a *grande dame*, the willingness at times to be preposterous and the ability to get away with it. And she did.

Her comments about art were an example. She was unquestionably the major American patron of the French Impressionists, as her subsequent contributions to the Art Institute of Chicago would prove. Yet, it was Bertha who said:

> What is art? I cannot argue with Loredo Taft who is a pundit, but in my limited conception it is the work of some genius credited with extraordinary proclivities not given to ordinary mortals. Speaking of art . . . my husband can spit over a freight car.

For simplicity, let's jump ahead to the 1880's and highlight some of the outstanding accomplishments of this outstanding Chicago family. When she and her husband moved in 1885 from the Palmer House to their North Side mansion Henry Ives Cobb designed for them on ground that had recently been an untenanted slough, they permanently altered the axis of Chicago society life, as years earlier Potter Palmer, the "Father of State

Street," had altered the city's commercial axis. By the turn of the century, to live on Potter Palmer's Gold Coast, far from the invasive industrial expansion that had set Prairie Avenue on its course of decline, was to reside at the center of Chicago elegance and social power.

Potter Palmer had bought this stretch of dune and marsh in the early 1880s, pumped in clean sand from the lake bottom as fill, strong armed the city to build a through street-later called Lake Shore Drive-and invited a group of his friends to form with him "a community where there had been wilderness."

It had taken three years to complete this imitation Rhinish Castle with the aid of an imported village of Italian craftsmen and at a cost so fabulous that a despairing Palmer asked the architects to stop showing him the bills. It had fantastic turrets, towers, and minarets and was easily the largest, most expensive residence in Chicago, Although Palmer himself never liked living in it, preferring the company of his race track cronies and the noisy lobby of his hotel. The massively defiant exterior was the architect's idea, but the interior mirrored the grandiose taste of Mrs. Palmer.

The interior centerpiece of her home was a spiral staircase that rose eighty feet into a tower and was completely unnecessary, it turned out, as there were two private elevators, the first ones installed in a Chicago residence. There was a Spanish music room, a Turkish parlor, a Flemish Renaissance library for Mr. Palmer, a Moorish bedroom of ebony and gold for Mrs. Palmer, an English dining room that seated fifty, a sixty-foot-long conservatory, a Louis XV drawing room, and a rooftop ballroom and picture gallery with an overhanging balcony. It was in this magnificent room in the sky that Bertha Palmer, a regally beautiful woman, dazzling in her Parisian gowns and diamond tiaras and collars, would host the most talked-about parties in Chicago.

In 1893, Bertha Palmer became the nation's, not just Chicago's, hostess, and many out-of-town guests responded to her invitations just to see the Palmer's art collection. Working through their agent Sara Tyson Hallowell, who introduced them to Mary Cassatt, Claude Monet, and the best Parisian dealers, she and her husband started their collection in 1889 with a Renoir and a Degas. They began buying in earnest two years later, when Bertha Palmer was named chairwoman of the Columbian Exposition's Board of Lady Managers, which was charged with overseeing the building of a pavilion in Jackson Park to display the accomplishments of women from all over the world. Young Sophia G. Hayden, the first woman graduate of MIT's architecture school, won the competition to design this, her first building. As it went up, Bertha Palmer sailed for Europe to encourage interest in the women's exhibition and while in Paris went on an art-buying spree, bringing back to Chicago for her private gallery, and to loan to the fair's Fine Arts pavilion, the most extensive collection of Impressionists in the new World, along with works from the Barbizon school. Her staggering collection soon included Pissarros, Corots, Sisleys, and over thirty Monets, paintings she could not bear to part with despite the good-natured solicitation of her friend Charles Hutchinson, who was not able to acquire them for the Art Institute until a year before his death through the terms of Mrs. Palmer's will.

Raised in a bright and lively southern family in which French was spoken and books and politics discussed, Bertha Palmer was bored with Prairie Avenue life. In her new castle on the lake, she opened the windows and let in a little of the modern world, inviting to her soirees settlement workers and labor leaders, journalists and politicians, struggling artists and new luminaries in town like Hamlin Garland. But Bertha Palmer also liked her privacy. On her instructions, there were no outside doorknobs on her home. One could enter only by presenting one's card, which had to pass through twenty-seven servants, maids, and social secretaries before coming under the censoring eyes of the mistress of the mansion.

In his most unusual will, Potter Palmer left a generous sum of money to his successor in the event his wife remarried. When asked why, Palmer quietly replied: "He'll need the money."

But the "Gold Coast Queen" had another outstanding quality. She was a dauntless do-gooder, and a feminist as well. She held meetings for female factory workers and women activists in her French parlor, helped millinery workers organize a strike, and pressed her son Honore to run for alderman in an immigrant ward, managing his campaign and hosting a reception for several hundred of his Italian supporters-including their neighborhood band-in the ballroom of her mansion.

The reforming energies of women like Bertha Palmer were channeled through the Chicago Woman's Club, "the Mother of woman's public work" in Chicago, Julian Ralph called it. By the mid-1880's, this club, with five hundred members, had progressed from a polite reading and self-study group to an aggressive organization for municipal betterment. Led by self-assured wives of autocrats like Ellen Martin Henrotin, wife of the president of the Chicago Stock Exchange, it became a force in the civic life of the city.

The club's work was directed toward the protection of women and children. In its path finding investigative work in asylums, hospitals, poorhouses, and prisons, the club always asked the disarming question "What are you doing with the women and children?" Not without struggle, it was successful in having a woman physician appointed to care for female patients in the county's primitive insane asylum, where the inmates were drugged by whiskey and sedatives, forced to eat pigs' heads with the bristles still on, and slept three to a steel bed. And club leaders pressured the city to put night matrons in police prisons to stop the practice of allowing the male inmates to sexually assault the women, some as young as twelve or thirteen, who were incarcerated with them.

The club's Protective Agency, headed by the wife of a Chicago banker, provided legal advice to mothers in danger of losing their children, to housemaids and shop girls defrauded of their wages, and to battered wives. It pushed for heavy sentences for rapists, found homes for foundlings, and set up offices in train stations to take care of "waifs" trying to get back home. Dressed in their rustling silks and jewels, its leaders tried to ensure, by their mere presence in the courtroom, that women received fair treatment at a time when it was commonplace to discredit a woman's testimony by showing her "bad character." Dr. Sarah Haskell Stevenson, president of the Woman's Club, and another crusading physician, Gertrude Gail Wellington, investigated conditions in the slums and got the city to build its first public bathhouse, arguing, disarmingly, that "the free public bath will inspire sweeter manners and a better observance of the law."

A number of Woman's Club reformers had been raised in homes in which care for the indigent was considered a religious obligation. "I had been brought up with the idea that some day I would inherit a fortune," recalled Louise de Koven Bowen, a Northern Trust banker's wife whose grandfather had lived in Fort Dearborn and whose mother was born inside its palisades, "and I was always taught that the responsibility of money was great, and that God would hold me accountable for the manner in which I used my talents." While still in finishing school, she taught a church class for deprived girls and later hired a Swedish woman to help her on charity rounds, work that brought her, in the early 1890's to Hull-House, where she became a lifelong associate of Jane Addams and a generous underwriter of her causes. It was to get support from just this class of women that Jane Addams had joined the Woman's Club when she arrived in Chicago in 1889 to open a social settlement, a new idea in America, in an immigrant neighborhood a mile west of State Street. Only twenty-nine years old, she struck a chord of sympathy with these privileged women because she was one of them, an educated, well-traveled "young girl," Mrs. Bowen said of her, who had been raised in a pious and prosperous Christian home and "had sympathy for her fellowmen," and the history of Hull-House began, but which is beyond the scope of this article.

Bertha is remembered for running the social event of the nineteenth century in the United States, the social side of the 1893 World's Columbian Exposition in Chicago. She was chairwoman of the Board of Lady Managers. As such, she chaired meetings and greeted visiting women professionals, writers and artists.

Perhaps many of you remember seeing the Palmer Mansion at 1350 N. Lake Shore Drive. This was a good example of how fortunes were increased by the entrepreneurs of Chicago via real estate during these boom times. Simply consider that the "Castle" land values increased from $160 a front foot in 1882 to $800 a front foot in 1892. The mansion or "Castle" was finally demolished in 1950 and replaced by a high rise apartment building.

Let's conclude this Reverie with a few thoughts on the members of the Chicago Women's Club. Most of us have read a lot about their material accomplishments but little about their spiritual accomplishments. So here goes. These women were first and foremost good wives and good mothers, loyal companions to their husbands, always dressed very modestly, had a deep respect for life, recognized the dignity of all people and were always respectful and charitable to all of God's people. No wonder the club was so successful in its many endeavors!!

If you wanted to continue this reverie by further readings, an excellent book to start with is Donald L. Miller's "City of the Century", published by Simon and Schuster in 1996.

Fittingly, the forever Queen of Chicago's Society is buried along with her family in the grandest tomb in Graceland Cemetery. No study of the history of Chicago would be complete without a tour of Graceland Cemetery.

Well, gentle readers, let's end this reverie by introducing the Chicago landscape architect O.C. Simonds (1855-1931) who designed Graceland Cemetery after it was established in 1860. Massive oaks, elms and maples stand in testament to the architecturally significant monuments and markers that cover nearly 120 acres of land. Simonds is the person responsible for the beauty of Graceland as we know it today. He served as the cemetery's superintendent and chief landscape architect from 1881 until 1898. He continued working at the cemetery until his death in 1930. During his tenure, Simonds transformed Graceland into a masterpiece of Midwestern landscape architecture for which the cemetery was awarded a medal of excellence at the Paris Exposition of 1900. Landscape historians regard Graceland Cemetery as one of the most remarkable park-like cemeteries of the Western world.

THE CHICAGO FIRE AND HAYMARKET AFFAIR— A REVERIE

There were two Chicago's disastrous events, the Fire in 1871 and the Haymarket riot or Haymarket massacre in 1886. Arguably they should be included in any book covering Chicago reveries. An excellent account of both was obtained from WIKIPEDIA the free encyclopedia.

The Great Chicago Fire was a conflagration that burned from Sunday October 8 to early Tuesday October 10, 1871, killing hundreds and destroying about four square miles in Chicago, Illinois. Though the fire was one of the largest U.S. disasters of the 19th century, the rebuilding that began almost immediately spurred Chicago's development into one of the most populous and economically important American cities.

Origin

The fire started at about 9 p.m. on Sunday, October 8, in or around a small shed that bordered the alley behind 137 DeKoven Street. The traditional account of the origin of the fire is that it was started by a cow kicking over a lantern in the barn owned by Patrick and Catherine O'Leary. Michael Ahern, the Chicago Republican reporter who created the cow story, admitted in 1893 that he had made it up because he thought it would make colorful copy.

The fire's spread was aided by the city's overuse of wood for building, a drought prior to the fire, and strong winds from the southwest that carried flying brands toward the heart of the city. The city also made fatal errors by not reacting soon enough and citizens were apparently unconcerned when it began. The firefighters were also exhausted from fighting a fire that happened the day before.

Spread of the blaze

The city's fire department did not receive the first alarm until 9:40 p.m., when a fire alarm was pulled at a pharmacy. The fire department was alerted when the fire was still small, but the guard on duty did not respond as he thought that the glow in the sky was from the smoldering flames of a fire the day before. When the blaze got bigger, the guard realized that there actually was a new fire and sent firefighters, but in the wrong direction. Soon the fire had spread to neighboring frame houses and sheds. Superheated winds drove flaming brands northeastward.

When the fire engulfed a tall church west of the Chicago River, the flames crossed the south branch of the river. Helping the fire spread were firewood in the closely packed wooden buildings, ships lining the river, the city's elevated wood-plank sidewalks and roads, and the commercial lumber and coal yards along the river. The size of the blaze generated extremely strong winds and heat, which ignited rooftops far ahead of the actual flames.

The attempts to stop the fire were unsuccessful. The mayor had even called surrounding cities for help, but by that point the fire was simply too large to contain. When the fire destroyed the waterworks, just north of the Chicago River, the city's water supply was cut off, and the firefighters were forced to give up.

As the fire raged through the central business district, it destroyed hotels, department stores, Chicago's City Hall, the opera house and theaters, churches and printing plants. The fire continued spreading northward, driving fleeing residents across bridges on the Chicago River. There was mass panic as the blaze jumped the river's north branch and continued burning through homes and mansions on the city's northside. Residents fled into Lincoln Park and to the shores of Lake Michigan, where thousands sought refuge from the flames.

Philip Sheridan, a noted Union general in the American Civil War, was present during the fire and coordinated military relief efforts. The mayor, to calm the panic, placed the city under martial law, and issued a proclamation placing Sheridan in charge. As there were no widespread disturbances, martial law was lifted within a few days. Although Sheridan's personal residence was spared, all of his professional and personal papers were destroyed.

The fire finally burned itself out, aided by diminishing winds and a light drizzle that began falling late on Monday night. From its origin at the O'Leary property, it had burned a path of nearly complete destruction of some 34 blocks to Fullerton Avenue on the north side.

Once the fire had ended, the smoldering remains were still too hot for a survey of the damage to be completed for days. Eventually it was determined that the fire destroyed an area about four miles long and averaging ¾ mile wide, encompassing more than 2,000 acres. Destroyed were more than 73 miles of roads, 120 miles of sidewalk, 2,000 lampposts, 17,500 buildings, and $222 million in property-about a third of the city's valuation. Of the 300,000 inhabitants, 90,000 were left homeless. The fire was said by The Chicago Daily Tribune to have been so fierce that it surpassed the damage done by Napoleon's siege of Moscow in 1812. Remarkably, some buildings did survive the fire, such as then-new Chicago Water Tower, which remains today as an unofficial memorial to the fire's destructive power. It was one of just five public buildings and one ordinary bungalow spared by the flames within the disaster zone. The O'Leary home and Holy Family Church, the Roman Catholic congregation of the O'Leary family, were both saved by shifts in the wind direction that kept them outside the burnt district.

After the fire, 125 bodies were recovered. Final estimates of the fatalities ranged from 200-300, considered a small number for such a large fire. In later years, other disasters in the city would claim more lives: at least 600 died in the Iroquois Theater fire in 1903; and, in 1915, 835 died in the sinking of the Eastland excursion boat in the Chicago River. Yet the Great Chicago Fire remains Chicago's most well-known disaster, for the magnitude of the destruction and the city's recovery and growth.

Land speculators, such as Gurdon Saltonstall Hubbard, and business owners quickly set about rebuilding the city. Donations of money, food, clothing and furnishings arrived quickly from across the nation. The first load of lumber for rebuilding was delivered the day the last burning building was extinguished. Only 22 years later, Chicago hosted more than 21 million visitors during the World's Columbian Exposition. Another example of Chicago's rebirth from the Great Fire ashes is the now famed Palmer House hotel. The original building burned to the ground in the fire just 13 days after its grand opening. Without hesitating, Potter Palmer secured a loan and rebuilt the hotel in a lot across the street from the original, proclaiming it to be "The World's First Fireproof Building."

In 1956, the remaining structures on the original O'Leary property were torn down for construction of the Chicago Fire Academy, a training facility for Chicago firefighters located at 558 W. DeKoven Street. A bronze sculpture of stylized flames entitled Pillar of Fire by sculptor Egon Weiner was erected on the point of origin in 1961.

Questions about the fire

Catherine O'Leary seemed the perfect scapegoat: she was a woman, an immigrant and Catholic, a combination which did not fare well in the political climate of the time in Chicago. This story was circulating in Chicago even before the flames had died out, and it was noted in the Chicgo Tribune's first post-fire issue. Michael Ahern, the reporter who came up with the story, would retract it in 1893, admitting that it had been fabricated.

More recently, amateur historian Richard Bales has come to believe it was actually started when Daniel "Pegleg" Sullivan, who first reported the fire, ignited some hay in the barn while trying to steal some milk. However, evidence recently reported in the Chicago Tribune by Anthony DeBartolo suggests Louis M. Cohn may have started the fire during a craps game. Cohn may also have admitted to starting the fire in a last will, according to Alan Wykes in his 1964 book The Complete Illustrated Guide to Gambling.

An alternative theory, first suggested in 1882, is that the Great Chicago Fire was caused by a meteor shower. At a 2004 conference of the Aerospace Corporation and the American Institute of Aeronautics and Astronautics, engineer and physicist Robert Wood suggested that the fire began when Biela's Comet broke up over the Midwest and rained down below. That four large fires took place, all on the same day, all on the shores of Lake Michigan, suggests a common root cause. Eyewitnesses reported sighting spontaneous ignitions, lack of smoke, "balls of fire" falling from the sky, and blue flames. According to Wood, these accounts suggest that the fires were caused by the methane that is commonly found in comets. This theory has been disputed by NASA.

Surviving structures

* St. Michael's Church, Old Town
* Chicago Water Tower

Related events

In that hot, dry and windy autumn, three other major fires occurred along the shores of Lake Michigan at the same time as the Great Chicago Fire. Some 400 miles to the north, a forest fire driven by strong winds consumed the town of Peshtigo, Wisconsin along with a dozen other villages, killing 1,200 to 2,500 people and charring approximately 1.5 million acres. Though the Peshtigo Fire remains the dealiest in American history, the remoteness of the region meant it was little noticed at the time. Across the lake to the east, the town of Holland, Michigan and other nearby areas burned to the ground. Some 100 miles to the north of Holland the lumbering community of Manistee, Michigan also went up in flames. Farther east, along the shore of Lake Huron, another tremendous fire swept through Port Huron, Michigan and much of Michigan's "Thumb".

HAYMARKET AFFAIR

The Haymarket affair (also known as the Haymarket riot or Haymarket massacre) on Tuesday 6 May 1886 in Chicago, began as a rally which became violent and was followed later by internationally publicized legal proceedings. An unknown person threw a bomb at police as they marched to disperse a public meeting in support of striking workers. The bomb blast and ensuing gunfire resulted in the deaths of seven police officers and an unknown number of civilians. Eight anarchists were tried for murder. Four were put to death, and one committed suicide in prison.

The Haymarket affair is generally considered to have been an important influence on the origin of international May Day observances for workers. In popular literature, this even inspired the caricature of "a bomb-throwing anarchist." The causes of the incident are still controversial, although deeply polarized attitudes separating business and working class people in late 19th century Chicago are generally acknowledged as having precipitated the tragedy and its aftermath. The site of the incident was designated as a Chicago Landmark on 25 March 1992. The Haymarket Martyrs' Monument in nearby Forest Park was listed on the National Register of Historic Places and as a National Historic Landmark on 18 February 1997.

Strife and confrontation

May Day parade and strikes:
In October 1884, a convention held by the Federation of Organized Trades and Labor Unions unanimously set May 1, 1886, as the date by which the eight-hour work day would become standard. When May 1, 1886 approached, American

labor unions prepared for a general strike in support of the eight-hour day. On Saturday, May 1, rallies were held throughout the United States. There were an estimated 10,000 demonstrators in New York and 11,000 in Detroit. In Milwaukee, Wisconsin some 10,000 workers turned out. The movement's center was in Chicago, where an estimated 40,000 workers went on strike. Albert Parsons was an anarchist and founder of the International Working People's Association (IWPA). Parsons, with his wife Lucy and their children, led a march of 80,000 people down Michigan Avenue. Another 10,000 men employed in the lumber yards held a separate march in Chicago. Estimates of the total number of striking American workers range from 300,000 to half a million.

On May 3, striking workers in Chicago met near the McCormick Harvesting Machine Co. plant. Union molders at the plant had been locked out since early February and the predominantly Irish-American workers at McCormick had come under attack from Pinkerton guards during an earlier strike action in 1885. This event, along with the eight-hour militancy of McCormick workers, had gained the strikers some respect and notoriety around the city. By the time of the 1886 general strike, strikebreakers entering the McCormick plant were under protection from a garrison of 400 police officers. Although half of the replacement workers defected to the general strike on May 1, McCormick workers continued to harass "scabs" who crossed the picket lines. Speaking to a rally outside the plant on May 3, August Spies advised the striking workers to "Hold together, to stand by their union, or they would not succeed." Well-planned and coordinated, the general strike to this point had remained largely nonviolent. When the end-of-the-workday bell sounded, however, a group of workers surged to the gates to confront the strikebreakers. Despite calls by Spies for the workers to remain calm, gunfire erupted as police fired on the crowd. In the end, six McCormick workers were killed. Spies would later testify, "I was very indignant. I knew from experience of the past that this butchering of people was done for the express purpose of defeating the eight-hour movement."

Outraged by this act of police violence, local anarchists quickly printed and distributed fliers calling for a rally the following day at Haymarket Square (also called the Haymarket), which at the time was a bustling commercial center near the corner of Randolph Street and Des Plaines Street. These fliers alleged police had murdered the strikers on behalf of business interests and urged workers to seek justice. One surviving flyer printed in both German and English contains the words Workingmen Arm Yourselves and Appear in Full Force.

Rally at Haymarket Square

The rally began peacefully under a light rain on the evening of May 4. August Spies spoke to the large crowd while standing in an open wagon on Des Plaines Street while a large number of on-duty police officers watched from nearby. According to witnesses, Spies began by saying the rally was not meant to incite violence. Historian Paul Avrich records Spies as saying "There seems to prevail the opinion in some quarters that this meeting has been for the purpose of inauguarating a riot, hence these warlike preparations on the part of so-called 'law and order.' However, let me tell you at the beginning that this meeting has not been called for any such purpose. The object of this meeting is to explain the general situation of the eight-hour movement and to throw light upon various incidents in connection with it."

The crowd was so calm that Mayor Carter Harrison, Sr., who had stopped by to watch, walked home early. Samuel Fielden, the last speaker, was finishing his speech at about 10:30 when police ordered the rally to disperse and began marching in formation towards the speakers' wagon. A pipe bomb was thrown at the police line and exploded, killing policeman Mathias J. Degan. The police immediately opened fire. Some workers were armed, but accounts vary widely as to how many shot back. The incident lasted less than five minutes. Several police officers, aside from Degan, appear to have been injured by the bomb, but most of the police casualties were caused by bullets, largely from friendly fire. In his report on the incident, John Bonfield wrote he "gave the order to cease firing, fearing that some of our men, in the darkness might fire into each other." An anonymous police official told the Chicago Tribune "a very large number of the police were wounded by each other's revolvers . . . It was every man for himself, and while some got two or three squares away, the rest emptied their revolvers, mainly into each other."

About sixty officers were wounded in the incident along with an unknown number of civilians. In all, seven policemen and at least four workers were killed. It is unclear how many civilians were wounded since many were afraid to seek medical attention, fearing arrest. Police captain Michael Schaack wrote the number of wounded workers was "largely in excess of that on the side of the police." The Chicago herald described a scene of "wild carnage" and estimated at least fifty dead or wounded civilians lay in the streets.

Trial, executions and pardons

Eight people connected directly or indirectly with the rally and its anarchist organizers were arrested afterward and charged with Degan's murder: August Spies, Albert Parsons, Adolph

Fischer, George Engel, Louis Lingg, Michael Schwab, Samuel Fielden and Oscar Neebe. Five (Spies, Fischer, Engel, Lingg and Schwab) were German immigrants while a sixth, Neebe, was a U.S. citizen of German descent. The other men, Parsons and Fielden, were born in the US. And England respectively. Two other individuals, William Seliger and Rudolph Schnaubelt, were indicted, but never brought to trial. Seliger turned state's evidence and testified for the prosecution, and Schnaubelt fled the country before he could be brought to trial.

The trial started on June 21 and was presided over by Judge Joseph Gary. The defense counsel included Sigmund Zeisler, William Perkins Black, William Foster and Moses Salomon. The prosecution, led by Julius Grinnell, did not offer evidence connecting any of the defendants with the bombing but argued that the person who had thrown the bomb and had been encouraged to do so by the defendants, who as conspirators were therefore equally responsible. Albert Parsons' brother claimed there was evidence linking the Pinkertons to the bomb.

The jury returned guilty verdicts for all eight defendants-death sentences for seven of the men, and a sentence of 15 years in prison for Neebe. The sentencing sparked outrage from budding labor and workers movements, resulted in protests around the world and made the defendants international political celebrities and heroes within labor and radical political circles. Meanwhile the press published often sensationalized accounts and opinions about the Haymarket affair which polarized public reaction. In an article titled "Anarchy's Red Hand", The New York Times, described the incident as the "bloody fruit" of "the villainous teachings of the Anarchists". The Chicago Times described the defendants as "arch counselors of riot, pillage, incendiarism and murder"; to other newspapers they were "bloody brutes", "red ruffians", "dynamarchists", "bloody monsters", "cowards", "cutthroats", "thieves", "assassins", and "fiends". Journalist George Frederic Parsons wrote a piece for The Atlantic Monthly articulating the fears of middle-class Americans concerning labor radicalism, asserting workers had only themselves to blame for their troubles. Edward Aveling, Karl Marx's son-in-law, remarked, "If these men are ultimately hanged, it will be the Chicago Tribune that has done it".

The case was appealed in 1887 to the Supreme Court of Illinois, then to the United States Supreme Court where the defendants were represented by John Randolph Tucker, Roger Atkinson Pryor, General Benjamin F. Butler and William P. Black. The petition for Certiorari was denied.

After the appeals had been exhausted, Illinois Governor Richard James Oglesby commuted Fielden's and Schwab's sentences to life in prison on November 10, 1887. On the eve of his scheduled execution Lingg committed suicide in his cell with a smuggled dynamite cap which he reportedly held in his mouth life a cigar (the blast blew off half his face and he survived in agony for six hours).

The next day (November 11, 1887) Spies, Parsons, Fischer and Engel were taken to the gallows in white robes and hoods. They sang the Marseillaise, the anthem of the international revolutionary movement. Family members including Lucy Parson who attempted to see them for the last time were arrested and searched for bombs (none were found). According to witnesses, in the moments before the men were hanged, Spies shouted, "The time will come when our silence will be more powerful than the voices you strangle today!" Witnesses reported that the condemned did not die when they dropped, but struggled to death slowly, a sight which left the audience visibly shaken.

Lingg, Spies, Fischer, Engel and Parsons were buried at the German Waldheim Cemetery (later merged with Forest Home Cemetery) in Forest Park, Illinois, a suburb of Chicago.

Schwab and Neebe were also buried at Walheim when they died, reuniting the "Martyrs." In 1893, the Haymarket Martyrs' Monument by sculptor Albert Weinert was raised at Waldheim. Over a century later it was designated a National Historic Landmark by the United States Department of the Interior, the only cemetery memorial to be noted as such.

The trial has been characterized as one of the most serious miscarriages of justice in United States history. Most working people believed Pinkerton agents had provoked the incident. On June 26, 1893, Illinois Governor John Peter Altgeld signed pardons for Fielden, Neebe and Schwab after having concluded all eight defendants were innocent. The governor said the real reason for the bombing was the city of Chicago's failure to hold Pinkerton guards responsible for shooting workers. The pardons ended his political career.

The police commander who ordered the dispersal was later convicted of corruption. The bomb thrower was never identified.

The Haymarket affair and May Day

The Haymarket affair was a setback for American labor and its fight for the eight-hour day. At the convention of the American Federation of Labor (AFL) in 1888 the union decided to campaign for it once again. May 1, 1890 was agreed upon as the date on which workers would strike for an eight-hour work day.

In 1889, AFL president Samuel Gompers wrote to the first congress of the Second International, which was meeting in Paris. He informed the world's socialists of the AFL's plans and proposed an international fight for a universal eight-hour work day. In response to Gomper's letter the Second International adopted a resolution calling for "a great international demonstration" on a single date so workers everywhere could demand the eight-hour work day. In light of the Americans' plan, the International adopted May 1, 1890 as the date for this demonstration.

A secondary purpose behind the adoption of the resolution by the Second International was to honor the memory of the Haymarket martyrs and other workers who had been killed in association with the strikes on May 1, 1886. Historian Philip Foner writes "there is little doubt that everyone associated with the resolution passed by the Paris Congress knew of the May 1st demonstrations and strikes for the eight-hour day in 1886 in the United States . . . and the events associated with the Haymarket tragedy."

The first international May Day was a spectacular success. The front page of the New York World on May 2, 1890 was devoted to coverage of the event. Two of its headlines were "Parade of Jubilant Workingmen in All the Trade Centers of the Civilized World" and "Everywhere the Workmen Join in Demands for a Normal Day." The Times of London listed two dozen European cities in which demonstrations had taken place, noting there had been rallies in Cuba, Peru and Chile. Commemoration of May Day became an annual event the following year.

The association of May Day with the Haymarket martyrs has remained particularly strong in Mexico. Mother Jones was in Mexico on May 1, 1921 and wrote of the "day of 'fiestas" that marked "the killing of the workers in Chicago for demanding the eight-hour day." In 1929 The New York Times referred to the May Day parade in Mexico City as "the annual demonstration glorifying the memory of those who were killed in Chicago in 1886." The New York Times described the 1936 demonstration as a commemoration of "the death of the martyrs in Chicago." In 1939 Oscar Neebe's grandson attended the May Day parade in Mexico City and was shown, as his host told him, "how the world shows respect to your grandfather." An American visitor in 1981 wrote she was embarrassed to explain to knowledgeable Mexican workers that American workers were ignorant of the Haymarket affair and the origins of May Day.

The influence of the Haymarket affair was not limited to the celebration of May Day. Emma Goldman was attracted to anarchism after reading about the incident and the executions, which she later described as "the events that had inspired my spiritual birth and growth." She considered the Haymarket martyrs "the most decisive influence in my existence." Alexander Berkman also described the Haymarket anarchists as "a potent and vital inspiration." Others whose commitment to anarchism crystallized as a result of the Haymarket affair included Voltairine de Cleyre and "Big Bill" Haywood, a founding member of the Industrial Workers of the World. Goldman wrote to Max Nettlau that the Haymarket affair had awakened the social consciousness of "hundreds, perhaps thousands, of people."

Your indulgence please as we conclude this Reverie, by once again quoting from Father Mitch Pacwa's "St. Paul, A Study Book Guide for Catholics."

St. Paul does not develop a teaching about the theological meaning of the Christian ministry of bishops, priests, and deacons. However, three passages discuss the qualifications he expects in ministers. He wrote all three passages in the epistles known as the "Pastorals." They addressed to St. Timothy and St. Titus, the men he had appointed as the bishops of Ephesus and Crete, respectively. The purpose of the instruction was to offer guidance on the kind of men whom Timothy and Titus should choose as bishops, priests, and deacons.

The first passage describes the virtues to seek and the vices to avoid in candidates for the offices of bishop and deacon: If any one aspires to the office of bishop, he desires a noble task. Now a bishop must be above reproach, the husband of one wife, temperate, sensible, dignified, hospitable, and apt teacher, no drunkard, not violent but gentle, not quarrelsome, and no lover of money. He must manage his own household well, keeping his children submissive and respectful in every way; for if a man does not know how to manage his own household, how can he care for God's church? He must not be a recent convert, or he may be puffed up with conceit and fall into the condemnation of the devil; moreover he must be well thought of by outsiders, or he may fall into reproach and snare of the devil.(1 Tim 3:1-7)

Deacons likewise must be serious, not double-tongued, not addicted to much wine, not greedy for gain; they must hold the mystery of the faith with a clear conscience. And let them also be tested first; then if they prove themselves blameless let them serve as deacons. The women likewise must be serious, no slanderers, but temperate, faithful in all things. Let deacons be the husband of one wife, and let them manage their children and their households well; for those who serve well as deacons gain a good standing for themselves and also great confidence in the faith which is in Christ Jesus. (1 Tim 3:8-13) St. Paul considers the aspiration to be a bishop as the desire for a good work. Being a bishop had little benefit except a good position and much confidence in faith in Christ (v.13). It would not be long before the position of bishop usually became a death sentence, because their prominence during times of persecution made them prime targets for government officials. Even during Paul's lifetime, the possibility of harassment and persecution of bishops was more likely than the acquisition of personal perks. In such a circumstance, eagerness for the role of bishop was a positive attitude commended by the apostle. Verse 2 sets the theme for the whole passage, as is confirmed in verse 7, the concluding line about the bishops: the bishop must be above reproach and not fall into reproach. St. John Chrysostom (Sermon X on First Timothy) wrote that being "above reproach" summarizes the whole list of virtues in this passage. The first qualification for being above reproach is that the bishop must be the husband of one woman. St. Justin Martyr (Dialogue with Trypho, chapter CXLI) mentioned that Jews in the Old Testament could have multiple wives and concubines; this passage forbids bishops from such. Also, the bishop must be faithful to the one wife he has, without any extramarital affairs. Finally, as interpreted frequently in the early Church, the bishop could not remarry if he were widowed. At the very least, a high level of marital ethics was required of the bishop (as well as of the deacon).

St. Paul mentions women in the context of teaching about the deacons. In fact, the deaconess Phoebe is mentioned in Romans 16:1. The early Fathers note that these deaconesses had specific roles with the female members of the Church, but, unlike the men, they were not ordained (St. Hippolytus, apostolic Traditions 10, 12).

The Christmas Season of our Liturgical year starts on Christmas Day. So let's wish each other a Merry Christmas and pray that we all enjoy a happy and holy Christmas Season.

REVERIE—YEAR OF ST. PAUL

The year of St. Paul ended June 29, 2009. We have read many things about St. Paul in many articles the past year. The following articles will hopefully add to your understanding, knowledge and appreciation of this great Apostle to the Gentiles. The following three articles were written by Dr. Scott Hahn for the Catholic New World in Chicago. Dr. Hahn is president and founder of the St. Paul Center for Biblical Theology (*www.salvationhistory.com*).

I (March 29-April 11, 2009) Despite challenges in the culture Paul dared to preach true love to all. We hear about love a lot in today's world. To marketers, it seems, love is a commodity. To true lovers, however, it is a mystery.

St. Paul's doctrine of human love is certainly mysterious—enigmatic, actually—to those for whom love is a commodity. But it's still more than that. It's a mystery in the traditional sense of the term.

In the Greek of the New Testament, "mysterion"—mystery—is equivalent to the English word "sacrament." It is an outward, material sign that points to an inward, spiritual reality.

There are people, of course, who dismiss St. Paul's notions of love as outdated, but I think he knew our world, and knew it, perhaps, better than we do.

In St. Paul's lifetime, Roman society was prosperous and at peace. People wanted to enjoy their leisure, without the impediment of a spouse or children.

Caesar Augustus feared that this situation would create a demographic and economic crisis for the empire, so he enacted legislation that penalized those who chose not to marry, and taxed and fined those who intentionally rendered their sex lives sterile. It didn't work. People weighed the cost of the fines against the pleasures of an unmoored lifestyle, and they decided they could afford it.

Though young people still held on to vestiges of ancient courtship customs, the culture was all about "hooking up"—casual encounters fueled by wine.

In such a climate, it's no wonder many people began to disdain and even condemn marriage. Some did it because they wanted free love instead. Others did it because they despaired of the possibility of human love.

Yet, St. Paul would have none of it. He reserved his strongest insults for those who would speak against human love: "Now the Spirit expressly says that in later times some will depart from the faith by giving heed to deceitful spirits and doctrines of demons, through the pretensions of liars whose consciences are seared, who forbid marriage" (1Tm4:1-3).

Demons and liars, with seared consciences! What is it about the degradation of human love that provokes such righteous anger in our apostle?

He's furious because he sees people desecrating a sacrament. In his extended discussion of marriage in Ephesians 5, St. Paul evokes the pristine goodness of the relationship between Adam and Eve in Eden. He praises the love of spouses for one another.

And he concludes by saying that "This mystery is a profound one, and I am saying that it refers to Christ and the church" (Eph 5:32).

Marriage that is complementary, monogamous, faithful and mutually self-giving is something more than domestic bliss. It is a mystery. It is a sacrament of something still greater: God's love affair with his bride, the church.

That sacramentality is the key to everything else St. Paul has to say about human love. It is the reason he condemns adultery and polyandry (Rom 5:3), divorce (1 Cor 7:10) and homosexual acts (Rom 1:26-27).

Against all these abuses of human potential, he dared to preach true love, which is patient and kind, not jealous or boastful, arrogant or rude, and does not insist on its own way (1 Cor 13:4-8).

This was diametrically opposed to the Greco-Roman way of "love," which was characteristically impatient and unkind, prone to rape and a gateway to abortion, infanticide and child neglect.

St. Paul was countercultural, then and now.

II (April 26-May 9, 2009) When Saul was a young Pharisee, he was zealous for the Torah. He studied in the most prestigious theological school in Jerusalem. He may have been a member of the Sanhedrin, Judaism's Supreme Court in the first century.

But he did all of this as a layman. He could never lay claim to priesthood—nor could he hope for a priestly "vocation"—as he was born into the tribe of Benjamin, and the priesthood of Israel was restricted to the tribe of Levi. For centuries, the Levitical priests alone had been responsible for carrying out the sacrificial rites in the Jerusalem Temple.

Yet, as an apostle, St. Paul clearly understood his role in priestly terms. In his magnum opus, his Letter to the Romans, he spoke of his calling as "the grace given me by God to be a minister of Christ Jesus to the Gentiles in the priestly service of the gospel of God, so that the offering of the Gentiles may be acceptable, sanctified by the holy spirit" (Rom 15:15-16).

Those are carefully crafted phrases, precise in their terms, each rich in evocative power. And what they evoke is priesthood.

By grace, Paul had become a "minister." In Greek, the word is "leitourgon," from which we get the English word "liturgy." In St. Paul's culture, this referred to a ritual role, a priestly role, not simply a job title for a religious administrator.

Thus, he goes on to say specifically that his work is a "priestly service"; and he further specifies that it is sacrificial. He speaks of the "offering of the Gentiles," and prays that it may be "sanctified."

For some people today this has become churchspeak, Christian jargon for bureaucratic functions. But in its time it was revolutionary. St. Paul was speaking of himself and his labors in terms that were off-limits to him because of his genetic make-up. To his fellow Jews, it would have seemed arrogant, if not insane.

Nevertheless, Paul employs it on many occasions. He spoke of his apostolate as a "ministry of reconciliation" (2 Cor 5:18). Again, in the Old Covenant, that role had been fulfilled by the priests, who brought about the forgiveness of sins through the expiating sacrifices of the Temple (see 1 Cor 8:13). Now, Paul can describe himself as a "steward of God's mysteries" (1 Cor 4:1), employing a common Greek term for religious rituals, "mysterion."

That is the very term that the church would use to describe its own essential rites. The ancient Romans translated "mysterion" as "sacramentum," fro which we have our English word "sacrament."

Paul was a steward of God's mysteries. He also identified himself repeatedly as an "ambassador of Christ" (2 Cor 5:20; Phlm 9). The ancient rabbis said that an ambassador was to be received as the dignitary whom he represented. And indeed that is how the churches received St. Paul-they "received me," he said, "as an angel of god, as Christ Jesus" (Gal 4:14).

With the coming of Jesus Christ, there was a "change in the priesthood" (Heb 7:12). Jesus himself was the high priest of the New Covenant. In fact, Paul spoke of Jesus as both sacrificial priest and sacrificial victim (see Eph 5:2).

But Jesus also shared his priesthood with men he designated as apostles, and he commanded them to offer the sacrifice of the New Covenant (see 1 Cor 11:25).

So close was the apostles' communion with Jesus that they represented him—they re-presented him. They were his ambassadors and more. When St. Paul forgave sins, he said he did so "en prosopo Christou" (2Cor 2:10). That Greek word "Prosopo" is very rich. It literally means face. It can also mean person or presence. In English, too, these words and their close relatives have overlapping meanings. If I am present, I am here in person. My persona is another word for the face I show you.

In the fourth century, St. Jerome translated that Greek phrase into Latin as "in persona Christi." Thus, tradition has always read that phrase: in the person of Christ.

That is how St. Paul understood his priesthood: to be the presence, the person and the face of Christ the High Priest. His is the face God showed to the Gentiles. Like Christ, St. Paul saw himself as a sacrificial victim, "poured as a libation upon the sacrificial offering of your faith" (Phil 2:17). The priesthood then, as now, was a call to self-giving.

By the rite of ordination, the apostle conferred the gift of priesthood on a new generation (see 2 Tm 1:6). And so it has passed through the millennia, to the priests who serve our parishes today. They may preach like Paul—or not. But, in all cases, we receive them as Christ, for so they are.

III (May 24-June 8, 2009) God Surpasses expectations. Our adoption as God's children is the deepest meaning of salvation. Trained as a Pharisee, young Saul of Tarsus knew well the expectations of his people. Saul studied in Jerusalem under Rabbi Gamaliel the Great, the most renowned scholar of his time. A normal part of Saul's education would be to ponder deeply the books of the prophets.

So Saul knew the promises God had made to his chosen people, and he knew that God would be faithful. Thus, like many Jews of the first century, Saul waited with longing for the promised Messiah, God's anointed deliverer. The Messiah would deliver Israel from its bondage and oppression. The Messiah would bring salvation from God.

Saul worked zealously to hasten the day of fulfillment-the day of salvation and deliverance.

DAY ALREADY HERE

Then Saul learned that the day had already arrived. The Messiah was Jesus. And deliverance had come in a way no one had expected. In fact, several lifetimes of study could not have prepared Saul—or anyone else—for the astonishing fulfillment of God's plan. Though the prophets had evoked images of suffering Messiah, the national tradition had dwelt instead upon the more abundant images of a conquering king, a military victor, who would expel the pagan rulers by the power of God and re-establish the order of divine law throughout the promised land. Such is the imagery we find in the Dead Sea Scrolls and other documents from the first century.

God had indeed fulfilled the expectations of Saul-and of Israel-but he did it in his own way, which was certainly not their way. God fulfilled every expectation and then surpassed them immeasurably.

Saul expected the Messiah to be a king who would restore the house of David. God sent his own eternal Son, incarnate as a Son of David.

Saul expected deliverance to bring peace, prosperity and freedom to obey the Law of Moses. But God's idea of salvation was far greater: he would deliver his people from sin; and, even more than that, he would deliver them from death; and, greatest of all, he would deliver them to share his own life. Salvation was not merely from something; it was for something. God delivered his people from sin so they might become his sons and daughters.

Saul of Tarsus became St. Paul the Apostle, and we should not be surprised to learn that he spent much of his time pondering and preaching about God's greatest surprises.

INADEQUATE LANGUAGE

When Paul spoke of deliverance, it was almost as if human language was inadequate to express what Jesus Christ had accomplished. He exhausted one metaphor after another. He used the terminology of the courtroom, saying that we have been justified—that is, acquitted—in a courts of law (see Rom 5:16-17). He drew analogies from the marketplace to make the point that we have been "redeemed": "You were bought at a great price" (1 Cor 7:23; see also 2 Titus 2:13-14). He drew military analogies, portraying us as the object of a divine rescue mission (2 Tim 4:18). Paul said we were "set free" from "slavery" (Gal 5:1).

But all the metaphors seem to lead to one that is his favorite: Our adoption as children of God. It would have been a grand thing if God had just delivered Israel from oppression. It would have been greater still if he had forgiven all the sins of a fallen world. But God did so much more in Jesus Christ. He brought about "redemption" for the sake of "adoption" (Rom 8:23)—"to redeem those who were under the law, so that we might receive adoption as sons" (Gal 4:5).

Our adoption as God's children is the deepest meaning of salvation. It encompasses redemption, justification and all the others. "But when the goodness and loving kindness of God our Savior appeared, he saved us, not because of deeds done by us in righteousness, but in virtue of his own mercy, by the washing of regeneration and renewal in the Holy Spirit, which he poured out upon us richly through Jesus Christ our Savior, so that we might be justified by his grace and become heirs in hope of eternal life" (Titus 3:4-7).

COVENANT BOND

Some non-Catholic interpreters would have us stop short of this reality. They put the focus instead on justification—and they interpret "justice" by the standards of the modern courtroom. But in doing so they are ignoring the cultural and religious context of St. Paul's many metaphors.

Supremely important for him (as for all first-century Jews) was the idea of covenant. It was the covenant with God that constituted Israel as God's chosen people. Covenant created a family bond; and with Jesus' "new covenant" (1 Cor 11:25) that family bond was made immeasurably stronger. Salvation has made us like Jesus—children of God in the eternal Son of God (see Gal 3:26)—"partakers of the divine nature" (2 Pt

1:4). Fidelity to the covenant is what Paul intends when he uses terms like justice and justification.

Paul knew that God was not content to be merely our judge. He wished to be our Father (see Eph 1:5). And that is the very essence of salvation in Christ.

"It is the children of god who are led by the spirit of God. You have not received a spirit that makes you fear returning to your former slavery; you have received the spirit of adopted sons that cries out Abba, Father! For it is the Spirit himself who gives testimony along with our spirit that we are children of God. And if children, also heirs: Together with Christ, God is our inheritance" (Rom 8:14-17). (End of Hahn's three articles.)

The following article was contributed by Sister Anne Flanagan, FSP to the Jan 4-17, 2009 Catholic New World.

HE PENNED A DARN GOOD LETTER

"Paul, Silvanus and Timothy to the church of the Thessalonians in God the Father and the Lord Jesus Christ-grace and peace be with you!" (1 Thes. 1:1).

This letter of St. Paul to the church in Thessalonica is probably the first of many other letters that he was to pen throughout his life. It is also considered to be one of the earliest Christian writings, coming at a time when the early church felt the need to set down its beliefs and its early story.

"According to a saying of the Fathers, Sacred Scripture is written principally in the church's ten principally in the church's heart rather than in documents and records" (Catechism of the Catholic Church, No. 113). What does this tell us about Paul the scriptural author? He was so in tune with the Body of Christ, that he was able to articulate the church's faith in a definitive way while writing under the insppriation of the Holy Spirit.

SPIRIT SHINES THROUGH

The Bible is fully human and fully divine, written under divine inspiration, but allowing the author's personality to shine through. Nowhere is this clearer than in the Pauline letters. Whether it is Paul's upbringing, his education, his overactive intellect or his personality, in the letters, these all become part of the enfleshing of the Word of God. We cannot avoid being struck by his delight in irony and paradox, his frustrations, his affection-and even his hurt feelings when his love is betrayed.

St. Paul was bilingual, fluent in Greek and Hebrew. His Greek was not just good, but cultured. But he was so intensely focused on presenting the Gospel that he sometimes made mistakes in grammar, or wove impossibly elaborate sentences, with one image or argument after another. The Bible admits that the letters may be a bit hard to understand: "Our beloved brother Paul wrote to you according to the wisdom given to him in all his letters.... Some things in them are hard to understand and the foolish distort them to their own destruction ... just as they do the other scriptures" (2 Pt 3:15).

MORE THAN JUST LETTERS

By the year 100, there was a collection of Pauline letters in circulation, not just among the Thesalonians, Corinthians and Philippians, but all the way to Egypt and France.

So St. Paul wrote "letters," but at the same time, they weren't only letters. They were a kind of real presence of Paul made available through the written word. Today we would call it a "virtual presence." Paul was expecting his letters to be read or "performed" in the assembly that was gathered for worship, in the same setting that the Christians joined to hear the Word of God in the Scriptures of Israel—since the early Christians adopted the synagogue prayer service with readings, instruction and intercessions.

In Colossians we read: "And when you've read this letter, have it read to the Laodicean church as well, and you should also read the letter from Laodicea" (4:16). Recent scholarship suggests that a few of the Pauline letters were written not directly by Paul but possibly by his disciples or by another generation of Christians who spoke in Paul's name to address issues they were facing.

Regardless of who exactly penned a letter, we recall what the Second Vatican Council II document on divine revelation explicitly said: "To compose the sacred books, God chose certain men who, all the time while he employed them in this task, made full use of their own faculties and powers so that . . . it was as true authors that they consigned to writing whatever he wanted written and no more" (Dei Verbum, No. 11). (End of Sister Flanagan's article)

The following letter dated December 2008, was written to benefactors by The Passionists of Holy Cross Province. Although the calendar year is changing, we are only halfway through the 2000th anniversary year of the birth of St. Paul the Apostle. I must tell you that I have looked to St. Paul, the spiritual giant of our early Church, for encouragement and strength on more than one occasion. I find it truly a blessing that as our country and our world faces great spiritual, economic and social challenges, we are celebrating a man who lived through an incredibly turbulent time and never gave up hope.

"Nothing, nothing, neither death, nor life, nor angels, nor principalities, nor things present, nor things to come, nor powers, nor height, nor depth, nor anything else in all creation will be able to separate us from the love of God in Christ Jesus" (Romans 9:38-39). (End of Passionist's letter)

Julie L. Rattey wrote a story with photos entitled "Discovering St. Paul's Greece" for the Catholic Digest April 2009 issue. Here are some excerpts from her article to further your understanding and appreciation of the great "Apostle to the Gentiles" in his missionary travels.

PHILIPPI:

After crossing the Aegean Sea, Paul arrived in Neapolis, an ancient port city now known as Kavala, and then, by the Egnatian Way, in Philippi, a Roman colony and leading city in Macedonia. One Sabbath day, Paul went down to the Gangitis River outside the city gates where, lacking a synagogue in their town, the local Jews gathered for prayer and ritual cleansing. Standing at the spot today, it's easy to imagine how the sound of the river gently rushing over mossy stones must have refreshed the beleaguered Apostle. His missionary efforts were soon rewarded by the conversion of Lydia, a wealthy local woman. Not only did she submit herself for Baptism in the river by Paul; she also offered her entire household for the sacrament and opened her home to him (Acts 16:13-15).

This kind of eager response to the Gospel is exactly what Paul would have hoped for when he took his message beyond the riverbanks to Philippi's agora, or marketplace. For the Greeks, the agora, an open square surrounded by covered passageways and public buildings (temples, shops, public baths, a library, administrative buildings, athletic facilities, etc.), was the local center of activity. Today the stone streets of Philippi's agora are sprouting with grass and scattered with large rubble and eroding columns, but during the first century they would have been bustling with people buying and selling wares and slaves, with the braying of donkeys bearing their masters' purchases, the clink of coins changing hands, the sizzle of early "fast food" being prepared for hungry shoppers, and with the sounds of public discourse and debate.

THESSALONIKI:

Paul and Silas now set out on the Egnatian Way for Thessaloniki, capital of the Roman province of Macedonia. On one side, Paul would have seen a seemingly endless expanse of sea-the Aegean-dropping away from the road; on the other, mountains rising toward the sky. He would have passed by alive and fruit trees, vineyards, fields of wheat and corn, small villages, and birdhouse-sized roadside shrines dedicated to mercury, the god of travelers. It would have taken Paul about two to three weeks to travel to Thessaloniki, an important port and cultural mecca, including small stops along the way.

About 2,000 years since Paul visited it, Thessaloniki is till an important city-the second-most populous in Greece after Athens, and celebrated as "the mother of Macedonia." Unfortunately, much of it has been destroyed over the years as a result of fires, earthquakes, and repeated bombing in World War II. Nevertheless, historic elements remain, including sections of the Byzantine city walls overlooking the Aegean Sea, a recently discovered (1978) corner of the agora where Paul preached for three Sabbaths to the people of the city, and the White Tower, a 16th century structure that has become the city's signature landmark. There are also many Orthodox churches to explore, including Ayios Dimitrios, built at the site where the patron saint of the city, St. Dimitrios, was imprisoned and executed in the year 304 for converting to Christianity and preaching the Gospel. Strolling by the waterfront at night, listening to the sounds of music and voices issuing from the many clubs and restaurants opposite the water, one can imagine that, many years ago, city dwellers of Paul's time made their way about the area on similar business-sharing a meal, discussing the gossip and business of the day, laughing, and toasting each other's health and prosperity.

When Paul arrived in the city, he preached the Good News to the local Jewish people. "Some of them," the Bible says, "were convinced and joined Paul and Silas; so, too, a great number of Greeks who were worshipers, and not a few of the prominent women" (Acts 17:4). In his later letter to the Thessalonians, Paul describes how he treated these new converts: "We were gentle among you," he writes, "as a nursing mother cares for her children. With such affection for you, we were determined to share with you not only the Gospel of God, but our very selves as well, so dearly beloved had you become to us" (1 Thessalonians 2:7-8). The converts in turn were dedicated to their newfound faith.

But Paul was not to share for very long the company of his new brothers and sisters in Christ. "The Jews," the Bible says, "became jealous and recruited some worthless men loitering in the public square, formed a mob, and set the city in turmoil" (Acts 17:4-5). Once again, Paul and Silas were forced to flee, slipping away during the night to meet Timothy at Beroea (today known as Veria), located in the foothills of Mount Vermio about 44 miles southwest of Thessaloniki. The Gospel was well received there, though once again, persecution from the local Jewish community stirred up trouble. Undaunted, Paul traveled down the coast toward what would be one of his biggest challenges: Athens, seat of the ancient Greek religion, home of the Parthenon and the Temple of Hephaistos, birthplace of democracy and, as Paul would have hoped, of a new Christian community. (End of Julie Rattey article)

Gentle readers, let's begin to end this reverie with some excerpts from Father Pacwa's latest book: St. Paul on the Power of the Cross by Fr. Mitch Pacwa, S.J. (Our Sunday Visitor Publishing Division, 2009). In his first letter to the Church at Corinth, St. Paul writes: "The message of the cross is foolishness to those who are perishing, but to us who are being saved it is the power of God" (1 Corinthians 1:18).

This little book is a study of an oft-repeated theme in Paul's letters: The centrality of the Cross of Jesus Christ for the salvation of souls. This theme reappears in a variety of contexts throughout the letters to explain the theology of salvation and the Church, his spirituality, and the dynamic of evangelization. In fact, most of the autobiographical material Paul wrote appears in those letters in which he speaks the most about his theology of the Cross. In these letters, he is usually confronting a pastoral problem caused by a variety of other evangelists bringing a changed form of the Gospel into the churches he had established. Therefore we not only learn his theology of the Cross but also the way it affected his life.

We will examine these themes as a Bible study for you. Before we begin, however, you might want to take a little time to understand just what the Cross and crucifixion would have meant in the time of Paul.

CRUCIFIXION—A MOST WRETCHED DEATH: Crucifixion was a common form of execution for treason, sedition, or rebellion in the ancient world. One form of this horrible death began with the Assyrians, who impaled their victims, driving a spiked pole through the pelvis and into the chest. The Persians changed this by sometimes tying or nailing victims to crosses or stakes. The Romans developed it to a science. Crucifixion served two main purposes: 1) to create a shameful, painful death for the victim and 2) to be a deterrent to anyone who might be considering similar action. A runaway slave might be crucified, for instance, as a clear sign to all other slaves that such action would not be tolerated. Traitors and insurrectionists were frequently crucified. Spartacus is one of the most famous of these. Crucifixion was frequently preceded by a scourging or beating intended to weaken the victim and hasten death since a healthy individual could live for several days hanging on a cross.

The condemned would carry his (rarely her) horizontal beam to the place of execution, where the upright would be permanently in place. Since crucifixion was the primary means of capital punishment in the Roman world, the process was streamlined as much as possible and having the vertical supports in place was more efficient than having to erect a new one each time. The victim was stripped naked, his hands and feet nailed or tied to the beams, and left to die.

The first century A.D. Jewish historian Josephus called crucifixion the "most wretched of deaths," and indeed, it was. Left exposed to the elements, to the derision of the crowds, and utterly helpless, the condemned suffered mercilessly. Death rarely came from loss of blood, but from muscle fatigue and exposure, which ultimately led to asphyxiation and heart failure. Victims exposure, which ultimately led to asphyxiation and heart failure. Victims usually died when they became too fatigued to push themselves up to take a breath; thus, in order to hasten death, the legs of the condemned would be broken-which is what happened to the thieves crucified with Jesus. In order to verify death, the centurion in charge of the execution would thrust a lance into the rib cage, administering the coup de grace. When this was done to Jesus, blood and water came from his side, indicating that he was truly dead.

In many parts of the ancient world, victims were often left hanging on the gibbet to be devoured by vultures and other wild beasts. Those who were removed were frequently discarded in common graves. In Palestine, however, Jewish law required the dead to be buried on the day of death, lest the land itself become polluted. For that reason the corpses of the crucified were not left hanging but buried according to Jewish law. This was done for Jesus, especially since he died on the eve of a great feast, the Passover.

THE MESSAGE OF THE CROSS, (1 Corinthians)

Paul's letters to the church at Corinth contain some of his most personal and intimate writings. 1 Corinthians, written while Paul was living in Ephesus, is the third of his letters. He wrote 1 and 2 Thessalonians while he was still dwelling in Corinth. 1 Corinthians was prompted because Paul had received word of problems that had arisen since he left; he wanted both to correct abuses and to encourage and instruct the church he had founded. In his letter, Paul gives us an inside look at some of the problems facing the nascent Christians, including factionalism, immorality, and liturgical abuses. The first issue that Paul addresses is the divisions that had developed within the young Christian community. These divisions were based on the Corinthians' ideas of the worth of certain apostles, evangelists, and teachers. Paul seeks to correct these views by highlighting the centrality of Jesus dying on the Cross. While the focus throughout these verses is on Paul's own preaching of the Cross, the Corinthians-and by extension, all of us-are intended to take the next step and see the need to proclaim the Cross as not only the center of our lives but also the central message for the evangelization of other people.

SUFFERING AND THE CROSS (2 Corinthians)

Paul frequently refers to his suffering for the sake of the Gospel, seeing his experiences as a living out the message of the Cross. Many modern Christians look to him as the source for their theology of salvation. They believe that being justified by faith in the death of Jesus Christ on the Cross leads to the comforting assertion that Jesus did all the suffering for me; I simply need to accept this free gift from God by faith alone. However, Paul disagrees, seeing his own suffering as an integral part of Christian growth. In fact, Paul's claim to be a servant of Christ is based, not on his own life of miracles and wonders-which, according to the Acts of the Apostles, would be reasonably easy for him to do-but on his suffering and persecution for Christ as his credentials. For Paul, the power of the Cross is the central source not only of faith, but power for living. In uniting with the cross, we die to self, only to live with Christ. The theology of salvation is known as soteriology. Soteriology examines how the merits of the incarnation, death, and Resurrection of Christ effect our salvation, as well as how we become righteous, holy, and sanctified. The thorniest issues concern the role of God's grace and its relationship to human free will.

2 Corinthians 1:1-2 Paul, an apostle of Christ Jesus by the will of God, and Timothy our brother: To the church of God which is at Corinth, with all the saints who are in the whole of Achaia: Grace to you and peace from God our Father and the Lord Jesus Christ. Paul opens his second letter to the Corinthians with a traditional greeting, which identifies the senders as Paul and Timothy and the recipients as the Church of God at Corinth. He identifies himself as "an apostle of Christ Jesus by the will of God." This title is connected to a chief concern of the letter-namely, that Paul's role and authority as an apostle had

been brought into question by some unnamed opponents who claim to be "super apostles" (11:5). This is quite different from his motivation for the first letter to the Corinthians, where he confronted issues of moral behavior and incorrect doctrine. In this letter, he defends himself against attacks on his authority as an apostle. More importantly, we can observe the development of his thought on the meaning of being a true apostle and apply it to our own lives and self-understanding. As we examine passages in this letter, we see how Paul defends his authority by developing a theology of the death and Resurrection of Christ. Through his personal struggles, we come to a clearer understanding of the real meaning and power of the Cross.

SAVED BY THE CROSS

(Galatians) Paul's letter to the growing faith community in the Roman province of Galatia contains some of his key teachings on the significance of the Law in relation to the Gospel of faith in Christ Jesus. This includes discussions of the curse of being crucified and an important answer to it, as well as Paul's own recognition of the need to be crucified with Christ. This epistle serves as an important explanation of the theme of the Cross in Paul's teaching This letter of Paul was addressed to the residents of the Roman province of Galatia, most likely the cities Perge, Iconium, Pisidian Antioch, Lystra, and Derbe, located in modern-day Turkey (Acts 13:13-14:27), Paul visited the area on his second and third journeys.

Galatians 1:1-5 Paul, an apostle-not from men nor through man, but through Jesus Christ and God the Father, who raised him from the dead-and all the brethren who are with me, to the churches of Galatia: Grace to you and peace from God the Father and our Lord Jesus Christ, who gave himself for our sins to deliver us from the present evil age, according to the will of our God and Father; to whom be the glory for ever and ever. Amen Paul begins by calling himself as an "apostle," one who is chosen by God to fulfill this role. The Church did not choose him, since a vocation is not bestowed by other people. God alone called him. Of special note is the fact Paul says that "grace and peace" come from God the Father and our Lord Jesus, indicating that God and Jesus are equal sources of grace and peace. At the same time the expression, "giving himself up" refers to Christ's death. Grace and peace flow from the fact that Jesus willingly gave himself up according to the Father's will to "deliver us from the present evil age." Greeks greeted each other with the word "grace" while the Jews greeted each other with the word "peace." Saying "Grace to you and peace" indicates Paul is addressing a community composed of both Gentiles and Jews.

DYING WITH THE CROSS

(Romans) Paul did not establish the church in Rome, as he did so many other churches. During his missionary travels, he longed to visit the Christians at Rome; unlike all his other letters, which were addressed to communities and individuals he already knew, he wrote his epistle to the Romans before he had ever met them. The book of Romans is a letter of introduction. Paul had planned to visit Rome after the spring of A.D. 58. However, his arrest in Jerusalem led to a nearly two-year imprisonment in Caesarea maritime. Only after a dangerous voyage in late A.D. 59 did he actually arrive in Rome. Acts of the Apostles ends by saying that Paul was under house arrest in Rome for two years, awaiting a trial that is never described. In this letter, Paul introduces the Roman community to his Gospel of salvation. He tends to be more systematic in the presentation because he is not answering a question, as in 1 Corinthians, nor responding to problems and opposition, as in 2 Corinthians and Galatians. Therefore understanding this letter does not entail reconstructing questions, objections, or opponents, as in the three preceding letters. The issues related to Paul's teaching on the Cross in Romans are especially associated with the themes of the first eight chapters of the letter-"the Gospel (as) the power of God for the salvation to every one who has faith, to the Jew first and also to the Greek" (Romans 1:16). The first three chapters set forth the problem: Because all people, whether Jew or Gentile, are "under the power of sin" (3:9), they are incapable of obtaining God's justice and they deserve God's wrath. Yet God has revealed the good news that he desires to save all people from the wrath by justifying them by faith in Jesus Christ who died on a cross to redeem the world.

Caesarea maritime was a harbor city built by Herod the Great between 25 and 13 B.C. The capital of Judea and the official residence of Pontius Pilate, it lies about halfway between the modern cities of Tel Aviv and Haifa. (Pilate had come to Jerusalem at the time of Jesus' death because it was the Feast of Passover.) At its height, Caesarea was home to nearly 125,000 people. Philip the Evangelist lived there (Acts 8:40), and Peter was sent there to baptize the centurion Cornelius (Acts 10). Peter also went there after being delivered from prison (Acts 12; 19), and King Herod Agrippa died there, having been "eaten by worms" (Acts 12:19-23).

CREATION AND THE CROSS

(Philippians and Colossians) These two letters of Paul contain many of the most poignant and moving passages written to the early Church. We are considering them together because the specific information relating to the importance and the power of the Cross is not as extensive as in his early writing, but still important enough that no examination of Paul's theology of the Cross would be complete without it. Philippians Paul wrote a very affectionate letter to the community at Philippi, indicating the close relationship he maintained with them over the years. Within this letter, he again addresses the central Christian theme of the cross, and, as in 2 Corinthians and Galatians, we learn important autobiographical information about St. Paul. The first autobiographical information appears in 1:12-20, where he tells them that he is again in prison for Christ. Paul probably founded the first Christian church in Europe at Philippi, in northeastern Greece. Named for Phillip of Macedon, Alexander the Great's father, the city became Roman in the second century B.C. Paul wrote his letter to the Philippians when he was imprisoned and under danger of death.

Philippians 1:21-30: For to me to live is Christ, and to die is gain. If it is to be life in the flesh, that means fruitful labor for me. Yet which I shall choose I cannot tell. I am hard pressed between the two. My desire is to depart and be with Christ, for that is far better. But to remain in the flesh is more necessary on your account. Convinced of this, I know that I shall remain and continue with you all, for your progress and joy in the faith. So that in me you may have ample cause to glory in Christ Jesus, because of my coming to you again. We cannot be absolutely positive about which imprisonment Paul is discussing when he writes to the Philippians. However, the mention of a Praetorian guard indicates an important Imperial city. Rome is one candidate, but Caesarea Philippi is more likely. This would place his letter between spring of A.D. 58 and late autumn of A.D. 59. During this imprisonment, some rival Christians tried to make Paul's situation more difficult.

Their apparent goal was to instigate worse treatment for Paul by making Christianity seem more contentious and perhaps even dangerous. Such action would make the charges against Paul look like a more serious threat to civil peace. However, Paul rejoices in their obnoxious behavior because he wants nothing better than to have Christ preached to more people. As far as he is concerned, life and death mean nothing in comparison to preaching the saving Gospel of Jesus Christ.

Only let your manner of life be worthy of the gospel of Christ, so that whether I come and see you or am absent, I may hear of you that you stand firm in one spirit, with one mind striving side by side for the faith of the gospel, and not frightened in anything by your opponents. This is a clear omen to them of their destruction, but of your salvation, and that from God. For it has been granted to you that for the sake of Christ you should not only believe in him but also suffer for his sake, engaged in the same conflict which you saw and now hear to be mine. In these verses, Paul now tries to explain his indifference to life and death. Death is "gain" because he has hope of being with Christ in heaven. However, he sees that continued life is fruitful in helping the Philippians and other Christians to progress in their faith. As it turns out, he believes that he will continue to live in this life in order to visit Philippi again and help them grow. Therefore, he gives some instruction on how to live until he returns to visit them. The first issue is to stand firm in their Christian unity. Second, he tells them to have no fear of their enemies, since that will be a sign of their coming destruction. Third, they are to accept the gift of suffering with Christ, just as they accept faith in him. Such suffering with Christ is Paul's lot, and it belongs to all Christians, a point Paul consistently teaches.

Colossians: This short letter to the Colossians is very tightly written to communicate a rich theology. It is addressed to the citizens of Colossae, which is located east of Ephesus in modern-day Turkey. The church had apparently been established by Epaphras of Colossae, who contacted Paul after certain problems concerning Christ's relation to the universe had arisen-issues quite different from the issues which had arisen in Paul's other communities. We will focus on the passages that present the Cross and its application to some of the local problems. (Colossians 1:13-18)

He has delivered us from the dominion of darkness and transferred us to the kingdom of his beloved Son, in whom we have redemption, the forgiveness of sins. He is the image of the invisible God, the first-born of all creation; for in him all things were created, in heaven and on earth, visible and invisible, whether thrones or dominions or principalities or authorities-all things were created through him and for him. He is before all things, and in him all things hold together. He is the head of the body, the church; he is the beginning, the first-born from the dead, that in everything he might be pre-eminent. The first part of this passage is a hymn to Christ and his power to redeem humanity and even the whole cosmos. The opening verses present the primary issue at stake in the redemption: humans exist within the dominion of darkness because they commit sin. Jesus redeems us by offering the forgiveness of sin and a consequent transfer from the dominion of darkness into the kingdom of Christ, God's beloved Son. The rest of the hymn describes Christ's credentials, by which he is empowered to affect the forgiveness of sins and gain our entrance into His kingdom.

This ends all of Pacwa's book as well as our Reverie.

CANAL AND RAILROAD (1848), UNION STOCK YARDS— A REVERIE

As early as 1674 Louis Jolliet foresaw that someday a canal between the Chicago and Des Plaines Rivers would connect the Great Lakes and the Gulf of Mexico. However, no practical steps were taken to realize his vision until the War of 1812 proved the need for a route over which forces and supplies could be transported to the northern frontier. In 1816 the Federal Government acquired title, from the Indians, to the land along the proposed waterway. During the 1820's Congress gave the State of Illinois the right to build the canal and made a grant of land to help defray the cost of construction. In 1835, when the legislature pledged the full credit of the state, the canal commissioners borrowed enough money to begin work.

Ground was broken on July 4, 1836. For a time the work proceeded rapidly. But the Panic of 1837 struck Illinois with devastating effect. Work on the canal slowed, then stopped. Not until 1845 could the state raise sufficient money to resume work, but this time the job was pushed through to the finish. On April 10, 1848, the first boat, the General Fry, passed through the canal to the lake. The Chicago Daily Democrat of April 11, described the occasion:

"The boat from Lockport, the General Fry, decorated with flags and crowded with ladies and gentlemen, was locked through the river at five o'clock, amid the cheers of the assembled crowds. The propeller, A. Rossiter, which took down a full load of passengers from the city, immediately after took her in tow, and at half past seven o'clock the General Fry was floating in Lake Michigan.

"As the boats passed through the city they were greeted with cheering, which was renewed at the different bridges, and points at which the citizens were collected. Altogether there was considerable excitement in the city, and all appeared rejoiced at the realization of the long-promised event-the opening of the Illinois and Michigan Canal."

The canal was a powerful factor in the development of Chicago. Population jumped from 20,000 in 1848 to 75,000 in 1854, and commerce expanded at the same rate. The produce of the Illinois Valley, formerly shipped to St. Louis, now poured into Chicago, while merchandise from the East passed down the canal to the river towns and from them to the interior settlements.

Yet the canal was doomed from the beginning. Six months after it was opened three sentences in the Chicago Daily Democrat for October 26, 1848, foretold its fate: "Yesterday the locomotive with cars attached, took its first start, and ran out a distance of five miles upon the road. A number of gentlemen rode out upon the cars. Everything worked well, and all parties appeared satisfied with the road so far."

The railroad was the Galena & Chicago Union, parent line of the present North Western system. When it first started to operate, its tracks extended only to what is now Oak Park.

In early January, 1850, they reached Elgin, and on August 2, 1852, Rockford. By that time the Illinois Central and the Chicago and Rock Island were both under construction. Before the end of the decade eleven trunk lines ran to or from Chicago and carried merchandise far exceeding in tonnage that carried on the canal. Already the city was the railroad center of the country-a position which it has held ever since.

The Union Stock Yard & Transit Co., or The Yards, operated in the New City community area of Chicago, Illinois for 106 years, helping the city become known as "hog butcher for the world" and the center of the American meat packing industry for decades. From the Civil War until the 1920's and peaking in 1924, more meat was processed in Chicago than in any other place in the world. Construction began in June 1865 with an opening on Christmas Day in 1865. The Yards closed at midnight on Friday, July 30, 1971 after several decades of decline during the decentralization of the meat packing industry. The Union Stock Yard Gate was designated a Chicago Landmark on February 24, 1972 and a National Historic Landmark on May 29, 1981.

HISTORY

Before construction, tavern owners provided pastures and care for cattle herds waiting to be sold. With the spreading service of railroads, stock yards were created in and around the city.

In 1848, small stockyards were scattered throughout the city along various rail lines. There was a confluence of reasons necessitating consolidation of the stockyards: westward expansion of railroads, causing great commercial growth in a Chicago that evolved into a major railroad center; the

Mississippi River blockade during the Civil War that closed the north-south river trade route; the influx of meat packers and livestock to Chicago. To consolidate operations, the Union Stock Yards were built on swampland south of the city. A consortium of 9 railroad companies (hence the "Union" name) acquired a 320-acre swampland area in southwest Chicago for $100,000 in 1864. The stockyards were connected to the city's main rail lines by 15 miles of track. Eventually, the 375-acre site had 2300 separate livestock pens in addition to hotels, saloons, restaurants, and offices for merchants and brokers. Led by Timothy Blackstone, a founder and the first president of the union Stock Yards and Transit Company, "The Yards" experienced tremendous growth. Processing two million animals yearly by 1870, the number had risen to nine million by 1890. Between 1865 and 1900, approximately 400 million livestock were butchered within the confines of the Yards. By the turn of the century the stock yards employed 25,000 people and produced 82 percent of the domestic meat consumption. In 1921, the stock yards employed 40,000 people. Two thousand of these worked directly for the Union Stock Yard & Transit Co., and the rest worked for companies such as meatpackers who had plants in the stockyards. By 1900, the 475-acre stock yard contained 50 miles of road, and had 130 miles of track along its perimeter. At its largest size, The Yards covered nearly a square mile of land, from Halsted Street to Ashland Avenue and from 39th (now Pershing Rd.) to 47th Streets.

At one time, 500,000 gallons a day of Chicago River water was pumped into the stock yards. So much stock yard waste drained into the South

Fork of the river that it came to bear the name Bubbly Creek due to the gaseous products of decomposition. The creek bubbles to this day.

When the City permanently reversed the flow of the Chicago River in 1900, the intent was to prevent the Stock Yards' waste products along with other sewage from flowing into Lake Michigan and contaminating the City's drinking water.

The meatpacking district was served between 1908 and 1957 by a short "L" line with several stops, devoted primarily to the daily transport of thousands of workers and even tourists to the site. The line was constructed when the City of Chicago forced the removal of surface trackage on 40th Street.

EFFECT ON INDUSTRY

The size and scale of the stockyards, along with technological advancements in rail transport and refrigeration, allowed for the creation of some of America's first truly global companies led by entrepreneurs such as Gustavus Franklin Swift and Philip Danforth Armour. The mechanized process with its killing wheel and conveyors helped inspire the automobile assembly line. In addition, hedging transactions by the stockyard companies played a key role in the establishment and growth of the Chicago based commodity exchanges and futures markets.

Numerous meatpacking companies were concentrated near the yards, including Armour, Swift, Morris, and Hammond. Eventually, meatpacking by product manufacturing of leather, soap, fertilizer, glue, imitation ivory, gelatin, shoe polish, buttons, perfume, and violin strings prospered in the neighborhood.

FIRE

The Chicago Union Stock yards Fire started on December 22, 1910, destroying $400,000 of property and killing twenty-one firemen, including the Fire Marshal James J. Horan. Fifty engine companies and seven hook and ladder companies fought the fire until it was declared extinguished by Chief Seyferlich on December 23. In 2004, a memorial to all Chicago firefighters who have died in the line of duty was erected at the location of the 1910 Stock Yards fire.

DECLINE AND CURRENT USE

The prosperity of the stockyards was due to both the concentration of railroads and the evolution of refrigerated railroad cars. Its decline was due to further advances in post-World War II transportation and distribution. Direct sales of livestock from breeders to packers, facilitated by advancement in interstate trucking, made it cheaper to slaughter animals where they were raised and excluded the intermediary stockyards. At first, the major meatpacking companies resisted change, but Swift and Armour both surrendered and vacated their plants in the Yards in the 1950's. In 1971, the area bounded by Pershing Road, Ashland, Halsted, and 47th Street became The Stockyards Industrial Park. The neighborhood to the west and south of the industrial park is still known as Back of the Yards, and is still home to a thriving immigrant population.

GATE

A remnant of the Union Stock Yard Gate still arches over Exchange Avenue, next to the firefighters' memorial, and can be seen by those driving along Halsted Street. This limestone gate, marking the entrance to the stockyards, survives as one of the few relics of Chicago's heritage of livestock and meatpacking. The steer head over the central arch is thought to represent "Sherman," a prize-winning bull named after John B. Sherman, a founder of the union Stock yard and Transit Company.

IN POPULAR CULTURE

* The Yards were a major tourist stop, with visitors such as Rudyard Kipling, Paul Bourget and Sarah Bernhardt.
* In 1906 Upton Sinclair published The Jungle, uncovering the horrid conditions in the stock yards at the turn of the 20th century.
* The stockyards are referred to in Carl Sandburg's poem Chicago: "proud to be Hog Butcher, Took Maker, Stacker of Wheat, Player with Railroads and Freight Handler to the Nation."
* Frank Sinatra mentioned the yards in his 1964 song "My Kind of Town."
* The stockyards receive a mention in the opening chapter of Thomas Pynchon's novel Against the Day.
* On January 9, 2007, a 3-alarm fire destroyed a large warehouse owned by the Rosebud Display and Packaging Company, on the north side of the Stockyards less than a mile from the memorial.
* The Skip James song "Hard Times Killing floor blues" refers to the nickname of the slaughter part of the stockyards during the great depression in the 1930's.

CHICAGO, by Carl Sandburg, 1916

HOG BUTCHER FOR THE WORLD,
TOOL MAKER, STACKER OF WHEAT,
PLAYER WITH RAILROADS AND THE
NATION'S
FREIGHT HANDLER;
STORMY, HUSKEY, BRAWLING,
CITY OF THE BIG SHOULDERS.

. . .

LAUGHING THE STORMY, HUSKY, BRAWLING
LAUGHTER OF YOUTH, HALF-NAKED,
SWEATING,
PROUD TO BE HOG BUTCHER, TOOK MAKER,
STACKER OF WHEAT, PLAYER WITH
RAILROADS AND FEIGHT HANDLER TO THE
NATION.

Let us conclude this Reverie with a brief introduction to Paul's Letter to the Philippians since we are now in the middle of the Jubilee Year dedicated to St. Paul. With this background, readers should understand and appreciate more Paul's Letter to the Philippians.

Philippi, in northeastern Greece, was a city of some importance in the Roman province of Macedonia. Lying on the great road from the Adriatic coast to Byzantium, the Via Egnatia, and in the midst of rich agricultural plains near the gold deposits of Mt. Pangaeus, it was in Paul's day a Roman town (Acts 16, 21), with a Greek-Macedonian population and a small group of Jews (see Acts 16, 13). Originally founded in the sixth century B.C. as Krenides by the Thracians, the town was taken over after 360 B.C. by Philip II of Macedon, the father of Alexander the Great, and was renamed for himself, "Philip's City." The area became Roman in the second century B.C. On the plains near Philippi in October 42 B.C., Antony and Octavian decisively defeated the forces of Brutus and Cassius, the slayers of Julius Caesar. Octavian (Augustus) later made Philippi a Roman colony and settled many veterans of the Roman armies there. This beautiful letter is rich in insights into Paul's theology and his apostolic love and concern for the gospel and his converts. In Philippians, Paul reveals his human sensitivity and tenderness, his enthusiasm for Christ as the key to life and death (1,21), and his deep feeling for those in Christ who dwell in Philippi. With them he shares his hopes and convictions, his anxieties and fears, revealing the total confidence in Christ that constitutes faith (3, 8-10). The letter incorporates a hymn about the salvation that God has brought about through Christ (2, 6-11), applied by Paul to the relations of Christians with one another (2, 1-5). Philippians has been termed "the letter of joy" (4, 4.10). It is the rejoicing of faith, based on true understanding of Christ's unique role in the salvation of all who profess his lordship (2, 11; 3, 8-12. 14.20-21).

Let us all try to spend a little more time this month reading Paul's Letter to the Philippians thereby growing deeper in our understanding of this apostle to the Gentiles.

CHICAGO BUILDINGS—
A REVERIE

In the year 1883 a prominent Chicago architect, W.L.B. Jenney, began to plan a building which the Home Insurance Company of New York intended to erect on the northeast corner of Adams and LaSalle streets. Without, perhaps, realizing the significance of what he was doing, Jenney decided upon a new method of construction. In all earlier buildings the walls had carried the weight of the entire structure. As buildings rose in height the piers at the ground level became ever thicker. Ten stories, the practical limit, called for walls four feet thick at the base-a thickness that reduced valuable rental space and cut down the amount of daylight admitted by the windows. Jenney, in the building on his drawing boards, proposed to erect an iron skeleton of columns, girders, and beams, and on that skeleton hang not only the floors and roof, but the walls themselves. Thus the walls would be no thicker at the base than at the roof. The owners could have as many windows as they wanted-could have, in fact, walls entirely of glass-and at the same time save valuable space formerly given over to heavy masonry. Jenney was planning the first skyscraper. The Home Insurance Building, completed in 1884, revolutionized the construction industry. As one eminent authority has put it: "The skyscraper is far and away the most important architectural achievement of America, her great gift to the art of building. In its train has come the most brilliant era of structural engineering that the world has ever known," the skyscraper also revoluntionized urban life. By enabling architects to build higher than they had ever dreamed of, it made it possible for far larger numbers of people to live and work in limited areas. The social consequences pose problems that have not yet been solved.

One of the things about living in Chicago—or anywhere, for that matter, I guess—is that unless you take the time to play tourist in your own city, there are things you miss. Particularly in Chicago, which—aside from being hog butcher to the world—is also one of the world's greatest architectural wonders. Even if you know it's there, you tend to walk right past it. Pomegranate Books, in conjunction with the Chicago Historical Society and the Chicago Department of Cultural Affairs, has come out with a series of guides to some of the remarkable things about Chicago. Jay Pridmore's Soldier Field (Pomegranate 2005) and John W. Stamper's North Michigan Avenue (Poemgranate 2005). The following was written by Robert M. Tilendis, who used these two guide books in his article. He pointed out something that people sometimes forget: as much as Chicago is prey to the whims of developers, it is a planned city. The Fire in 1871 completely destroyed everything in what was then "downtown," as well as the near north side—that is, the area from the Chicago River north to Fullerton Avenue (the only structures left standing were the Water Tower and the pumping station next to it). Afterwards, the city began rebuilding with a will, and there was strong awareness that the chance had come to develop a city that made sense. Frederick Law Olmstead gets the credit for the overall plan, but Chicago's own Daniel Burnham presented the City with a plan for North Michigan Avenue in 1909 that has largely been followed to the present day (although his restrictions on building height went by the board due to the demands of economics). The Magnificent Mile, as it was termed by developer Arthur Rubloff in his plan of the late 1940's, was to be a high-end retail area, a gracious boulevard lined with trees and providing the finest goods available for shoppers. In fact, North Michigan Avenue is today considered one of the premier retail areas in the world. It is also, as one might expect in this city, quite possibly the most architecturally distinguished. Anchored at the north side of the Chicago River by the Wrigley Building and the Tribune Tower, Michigan Avenue north of the river boasts the Hancock Center, a revolutionary building in its aesthetic use of structural steel, the Allerton Hotel (now the Crown Plaza), modeled on the architecture of medieval Italy; Water Tower Place, which combines a twelve-story commercial base with a 62-story hotel and residential tower, and was one of the earliest skyscrapers with a concrete frame; and the McGraw-Hill Building, a fine example of Art Deco architecture.

South of the river, the Avenue is anchored by the London Guarantee and Accident Building, with its strong classical references (generally considered—I would call it Hellenistic, with some touches of Italian Baroque in the top stories), and 333 North Michigan, influenced by Eliel Saarinen's second-place entry for the Tribune Tower competition, a study in verticality. Illinois Center, by the Office of Mies van der Rohe, demonstrates the importance of placement on the site: each component building is showcased, and there is room for an open plaza (we love our plazas almost as much as we love our parks). The Associates Building at 150 North Michigan, with its steeply raked, truncated and glazed top, stands across Randolph from the Chicago Cultural Center—our old Public Library, itself a prime example of Chicago's approach to the Beaux Arts style. (This is really just a random sample; looking through the book again, I'm amazed at the number of stunning buildings along what is not, really, a very long stretch—slightly over a mile. One thing that's very nice about this book is the chance to see the whole building—walking along at street level, you miss a few things. We don't think small in Chicago: thus, Soldier Field, which at its origin after World War I, was intended to be the largest open stadium in the country, seating 120,000. (It actually managed to accommodate 200,000 at the International Eucharistic Congress of 1926, and was big enough to contain ski runs for competitions.) The story of Soldier Field illustrates very well the kind of trade-offs that we always somehow manage here (well, almost always)—the land, which was mostly marsh, was part of the railroad right-of-way; South Lake Shore Drive ran right along the shore, and there was great concern that the lakefront be kept uncluttered and available for public use. Unlike other cities on the Great Lakes, or on waterfronts at all, Chicago's lakefront is a long stretch of parks and harbors that run from Hollywood Avenue in the north past Hyde Park in the south, and they are, believe it or not, all landfill and reclaimed marshland.

The Field Museum of Natural History was the anchor for what has become the Museum Campus, which now holds the Field Museum, the John G. Shedd Aquarium, the Adler Planetarium, and Soldier Field, rebuilt in 2002-2003 to accommodate new technology—everything from giant scoreboards to improved means of dispensing soft drinks—and the demands of multi-use stadium in the 21st century. (Keep in mind that the whole project over the years has involved rerouting Lake Shore Drive, dropping the railroad tracks down out of sight, and extensive landscaping that has introduced a rolling countryside into the heart of the city. Like I said, we don't think small.) The new Soldier Field has been more than a little controversial: many think it resembles nothing so much as a broken spaceship set down in the middle of a Roman temple. The original Soldier Field, a strongly classical structure modeled quite openly on Roman examples, was dedicated on its completion in 1925 as a memorial to the fallen of World War I. Today, it is perhaps even more significant as a monument, retaining the original bronze sculpture of a doughboy and adding a Memorial Wall that is reminiscent of the Vietnam Memorial in Washington, along with portions of the original facades that contrast and complement the new structure. Architecturally, it is really all about purity of form as seen from two viewpoints. The book shows the development of this site, the old Soldier Field (including pictures of the ski runs), and some stunning views of the new hybrid. Controversial it was (and the law suits continued along with the construction), but I think it will eventually be seen as one of Chicago's great works of architecture—it's beautiful, and it works.

These two guidebooks, because that is really what they are, are small treasures: they are beautifully produced and extensively illustrated with photographs and drawings both contemporary and from various archives that show their respective subjects in various stages of development. The texts are clear and concise and contain a wealth of information, supplemented by the timelines in the front of each book that give significant dates in the history of the subjects. It's this historical view that is most welcome, because we sometimes forget that architecture, of all the arts, exists in a context that ultimately involves all who have come in contact with it, which is just about everyone. I repeat this article was written by Robert M. Tilendis who used these two guidebooks in his article. Mr. Tilendis mentioned the International Eucharistic Congress of 1926 in his article. Since this was such an important event for the Catholics of Chicago as well as for the city, a little more background and information on this event should be of interest to our readers. It is beyond the scope of this reverie to do more than just mention the names and dates of the individuals associated with the Eucharistic Congress. You can find more information on them in most libraries; now back to the Eucharistic Congress.

A fleet of fishing smacks from the little Dutch town of Volendam went out to meet an ocean liner and to escort it into the harbor of Amsterdam. On board the liner was His Eminence Cardinal Willem Van Rossum, once a humble priest among the fishermen. Arrived at Amsterdam, the Cardinal acting as Legate (Plenipotentiary Representative of Pius XI), opened the 27th Eucharistic Congress of the Holy Catholic Church. Although Holland is predominantly Protestant, Amsterdam is largely Catholic and greeted with enthusiasm prelates from the world over. The central theme of the Conference was the "Holy Eucharist and Atone-ment" and special attention was given to the "spiritual advantages of frequent communion in combating materialism." The American section, headed by Bishop J. Henry Tihen of Denver, received with delight the decision to hold the next Congress in Chicago, in 1925. The newly-created Cardinal George Mundelein, from his famed red-brick residence, immediately designated the Sunday preceding the next Congress as general Communion Sunday in the archdiocese of Chicago.

May 31, 1926

"Holy Father, permit the celebration of the next Eucharistic Congress to take place in Chicago and I promise you a million communions as a spiritual bouquet to your august presence." So spoke His Eminence, George William Cardinal Mundelein to His Holiness, Pope Pius XI, nearly two years ago.

June 28, 1926

His Eminence, John Cardinal Bonzano, carried himself in Chicago last week as the most solemn man alive. He was the "most eminent Lord Cardinal Legate," chief deputy of the Vicar of Christ, come to Chicago for the XXVIII Eucharistic Congress. The purpose of these Eucharistic Congresses is to give Catholics opportunity to proclaim their faith . . .

The 1926 International Eucharistic Congress held in Chicago was a highpoint for Catholics. It signaled they had arrived in U.S. society. But in the midst of the euphoria as millions gathered, few realized how difficult the coming years would be for Catholics. When Al Smith, the popular Catholic governor of New York, ran for the presidency in 1928 against Herbert Hoover, the campaign reawakened every anti-Catholic smear imaginable. The situation provided Bishop Noll (Our Sunday Visitor) with an opportunity to respond with great force to the absurd anti-Catholic charges, but the paper, pledged to neutrality in the campaign, did not endorse Smith. As the Twenties came to a close, the Jazz Age reigned supreme: fast cars, easy money, loose morality. Our Sunday Visitor decried the trends. But readers soon faced a more immediate problem: The decade ended with a crash on Wall Street that brought the near-fatal blow of the Great Depression to the immigrant Catholics still working to gain a foothold in their new country. The 1930's were difficult times for Catholics, as for most Americans. The climb up the economic social ladder for the Catholic immigrants was temporarily halted by unemployment; Al Smith's resounding defeat had left them down in spirit. The pages of Our Sunday Visitor reflected the general malaise in the country. At the heart of the nation's economic woes, wrote Bishop Noll, was a simple fact: America had turned its back on spiritual values. The paper became more and more concerned with living one's faith in a secular society that was growing more lax every day. During the 1930s, Our Sunday Visitor strongly reflected its longstanding emphasis on rooting the lives of the laity in their Catholic identity. It was during the 1930s, too, that a name first appeared in Our Sunday Visitor that would soon be known worldwide: Fulton J. Sheen. The future bishop, already famous as a radio personality, discussed the problem of living the faith in an increasingly secularized world. A line from his 1938 article was all too prophetic; "The vision of the cross is fading.

George Mundelein, (from Wikipedia, The Free Encyclopedia)

George William Mundelein, later George Cardinal Mundelein, (July 2, 1872-October 2, 1939) was an American Prelate who served as the eighth bishop and third archbishop of the archdiocese of Chicago, serving in that post from 1915 to 1939. He was born on July 20, 1872 in New York city to a family of German ancestry, educated at La Salle Academy in New York, Manhattan College, St. Vincent Seminary in Rome, and ordained a priest on June 8, 1895 in the Diocese of Brooklyn. From 1895 to 1909, he served in various posts in the Brooklyn Diocese. On June 30, 1909, Pope Pius X appointed Mundelein Titular Bishop of Loryma and Auxiliary Bishop of the Roman Catholic diocese of Brooklyn, in Brooklyn, New York, where he was ordained a bishop on September 21, 1909. Pope Benedict XV appointed him Archibishop of Chicago, on December 9, 1915, and was installed February 9, 1916. He was elevated to Cardinal on March 24, 1924, and served as archbishop until his death at the age of 67. during his tenure at the Archdiocese of Chicago, Mundelein launched an effort to unify ethnic Catholic groups such as the Poles and Italians into territorial, instead of ethnic, parishes with mixed success. St. Monica's (Colored) parish, however, was endorsed by Mundelein as the city's sole black parish, leading to distaste for the Archbishop in both the early 1900's and today. After constructing the landmark Archbishop Quigley Preparatory Seminary in Chicago, Mundelein built St. Mary of the Lake Seminary in Area, now Mundelein, Illinois. Quigley Seminary was the site of Mundelein's 1937 "Paper hanger" speech, criticizing Adolf Hitler. The archdiocese greatly expanded its charity functions during the Great Depression, rivaling that of Chicago's Associated Jewish Charities. A city-wide network of St. Vincent de Paul Societies was established. He was a personal friend of Franklin Delano Roosevelt.

From what we read thus far we see that Secularism is not neutral. Pope Benedict XVI writes "the task of witness is not easy. There are many today who claim that God should be left on the sidelines, and that religion and faith, while fine for individuals, should either be excluded from the public forum altogether or included only in the pursuit of limited pragmatic goals. This secularist vision seeks to explain human life and shape society with little or no reference to the Creator. It presents itself as neutral, impartial and inclusive of everyone. But in reality, like every ideology, secularism imposes a world-view. If God is irrelevant to public life, then society will be shaped in a godless image, and debate and policy concerning the public good will be driven more by consequences than by principles grounded in truth."

Let us end this reverie by reading what Father Mitch Pacwa, S.J. writes about what St. Paul writes on Baptism and Reconciliation.

When St. Paul wrote this Letter to the Romans, he had not yet visited the city but had met some individual members, who are listed in a long series of greeting in chapter 16. This letter is Paul's personal introduction to a community he hoped to visit after his Pentecost pilgrimage to Jerusalem in the spring of A.D. 58. The epistle to the Romans treats many important issues, including some of the topics covered in Galatians on faith, righteousness, and the Torah ("the law"). Romans 6:1-2 begins with rhetorical questions that build upon St. Paul's earlier treatment of the greater power of grace to overcome sin. Though Adam's sin affected the whole human race by introducing death to everyone, Christ's redemption was more powerful in overcoming sin and death (Rom 5:12-21). He then poses rhetorical questions that could be asked by someone who argued through reduction ad absurdum: Are we to continue sinning more in order to make grace abound still more? Instead of answering rhetorically, Paul advances the argument with a discussion of the way Christians have died to sin and cannot continue in it. The next stage of the argument introduces Baptism as the means by which Christians die to sin:

> Do you not know that all of us who have been baptized into Christ Jesus were baptized into his death? We were buried therefore with Him by Baptism into death, so that as Christ was raised from the dead by the glory of the Father, we too might walk in newness of life. For if we have been united with Him in a death like His, we shall certainly be united with Him in a resurrection like His. We know that our old self was crucified with him so that the sinful body might be destroyed, and we might no longer be enslaved to sin. For he who has died is freed from sin. But if we have died with Christ, we believe that we shall also live with him. For we know that Christ being raised from the dead will never die again; death no longer has dominion over him. (Rom 6:3-9)

Here Paul teaches strongly that Baptism is the means by which Christians die to sin. The power of Baptism derives from the way it sacramentally unites a Christian to Jesus Christ's death, burial, and resurrection. Though Paul does not explicitly connect the action of entering the water with death and exiting the water with resurrection, this has been a common interpretation of the sacramental action in light of this passage. Paul asserts a great power to Baptism in the spiritual realm: it not only gives a person union with Jesus' death, but it offers hope for the resurrection of the body in the future, a topic St. Paul develops in Romans 8.

Romans 6:13 sets before the Christian the choice to use the members of their bodies as "weapons of wickedness" or "weapons of righteousness." Some translations (such as the RSV) use the more general term "instruments," but Greek word hoopla specifically refers to weapons. Furthermore, the mention of being slaves (Rom 6:16-18,20) or being set free (Rom 6:18,20,22) highlights the gladiatorial image, since most gladiators were slaves. These combats, unfortunately, were designated as "games," but the outcome was either life or death. Our combat for God's righteousness against sin, impurity, and iniquity is a struggle for eternal life or death.

Sure and I hope your dear eyes will be smiling when you view the green water of the Chicago River on St. Paddy's Day.

Erin Go Braugh
Bert Hoffman

ABRAHAM LINCOLN—
A REVERIE

This is certainly what Abraham Lincoln would have studied as he slowly prepared himself for his political career and in so doing slowly absorbed the different sentiments on various issues developing in our nation leading up to the Civil War. With the help of the "Review Text in American History" by Irving L. Gordon let us read about the events that led to the formation of the Republican Party, the election of Abraham Lincoln as President of the United States and finally to our Civil War.

FURTHER GROWTH OF ANTISLAVERY FEELING IN THE NORTH

1. The Fugitive Slave Law (1850), with its harsh treatment of suspected runaway slaves, aroused Northern resentment. The law authorized federal commissioners to try Negro suspects without allowing them to testify and without a jury. The commissioner received a double fee if he ruled the suspect a runaway slave rather than a free Negro. To prevent the enforcement of the Fugitive Slave Law, many Northern legislatures passed "personal liberty laws."

These laws prohibited state officials from cooperating in the capture of runaway slaves.
2. Harriet Beecher Stowe, an abolitionist and worker on the underground railroad, in 1852 wrote Uncle Tom's Cabin. This book, with its dramatic picture of Negro suffering in the South, swayed Northern sympathies. Abraham Lincoln supposedly called Mrs. Stowe the "little woman who made the big war."
3. Horace Greeley, founder of the New York Tribune, aroused Northern opinion by his vigorous antislavery editorials.

KANSAS-NEBRASKA ACT (1854)

1. Provisions. Stephen A. Douglas, Senator from Illinois, secured passage of a bill that repealed the Missouri Compromise and, in its place, (a) divided the remaining land of the Louisiana Purchase into the territories of Kansas and Nebraska, and (b) authorized the people in these territories to determine the status of slavery according to the principle of popular sovereignty.
2. "Bleeding Kansas." Slaveowners (especially from Missouri) and abolitionists (chiefly from New England) hurried to Kansas, each group seeking to gain control of the territory. These proslavery and antislavery men, resorting to armed violence, began a small-scale civil war. Missouri "border ruffians" attacked free-soil settlements. Abolitionist bands, notably one led by John Brown, raided proslavery centers. Reports from "Bleeding Kansas" kept sectional passions inflamed throughout the country.

FORMATION OF THE REPUBLICAN PARTY (1854)

Northern antislavery men were shocked by the passage of the Kansas-Nebraska Act. Displeased by the wavering stand on slavery of both the Whig and Democratic parties, antislavery political leaders, meeting in Wisconsin and Michigan, created the present-day Republican Party. They pledged to (1) oppose the extension of slavery into new territory, and (2) repeal the Kansas-Nebraska Act.

PRESIDENTIAL ELECTION OF 1856

As their first Presidential candidate, the Republicans in 1856 nominated the famed Western explorer and opponent of slavery, John C. Fremont. The Democrats, again seeking to evade the slavery issue, nominated a Pennsylvanian with southern sympathies, James Buchanan. (A short-lived third party, the American or Know-Nothing party, also ran a candidate.) The Whig party had disintegrated. Fremont carried 11 Northern states, but Buchanan triumphed in 5 other Northern states as well as in the South and won the election.

DRED SCOTT CASE

1. Issue. Dred Scott, a Negro slave, had been taken by his master into the Minnesota region, which according to the Missouri Compromise was free territory. He was then brought back to Missouri, a slave state. To create a test case, the abolitionists had Dred Scott sue for his freedom

on the grounds that his residence in free territory had made him a free man.
2. Supreme Court Decision (1857). The Supreme Court ruled against Scott. Chief Justice Roger B. Taney began the majority opinion by stating that a Negro could not be a citizen and that Scott could therefore not bring suit in a federal court. Taney then went beyond this point and ruled on the entire issue of slavery in federal territories. His further conclusions were labeled by antislavery men as an obiter dictum (Latin for "something said in passing") and therefore not legally binding. Taney stated that (a) slaves are property, (b) Congress may not deprive any person of the right to take property into federal territories, and (c) the Missouri Compromise, which prohibited slavery in part of the Louisiana Territory, was unconstitutional.

The dissenting opinions in the Dred Scott case pointed out that free Negroes had been considered as citizens in some states and that the Constitution granted Congress the power to make "all needful rules and regulations" for federal territories. The Dred Scott decision was applauded by the South, denounced by the North.

LINCOLN-DOUGLAS DEBATES (1858)

In 1858 Abraham Lincoln, a Republican relatively unknown nationally contested for the Senate seat from Illinois with the Democratic incumbent, the "Little Giant," Stephen A. Douglas. They engaged in a series of seven remarkable debates. In Freeport, Lincoln forced Douglas to state his view on slavery in the territories. Douglas said that the Dred

Scott decision made slavery legal in the territories in theory, but the people of a territory could keep slaves out in practice. Douglas was narrowly reelected Senator, but his Freeport Doctrine cost him Southern support for the Presidency in 1860. Abraham Lincoln meanwhile became known throughout the North.

JOHN BROWN'S RAID (1859)

John Brown, a fanatical abolitionist, led a band of some twenty men in a raid against the federal arsenal at Harper's Ferry in Virginia. Brown hoped to secure guns, arm the nearby Negroes, and lead a slave rebellion. He was caught, tried for treason, found guilty, and hanged. In the North, Brown was honored for having sacrificed his life for human liberty. In the South, Brown was despised as a dangerous criminal.

PRESIDENTIAL ELECTION OF 1860

1. Issues and Candidates

    a. The Democratic Party, unable to agree on a platform or a candidate, split into two parts. The Northern Democrats stood for popular sovereignty and nominated Stephen A. Douglas. The Southern Democrats demanded enforcement of the Dred Scott decision and chose John C. Breckinridge.
    b. The Republican Party opposed the extension of slavery to the territories but promised not to interfere with slavery in the states. The Republicans also appealed to Northern Businessmen and Western

settlers by pledging a protective tariff, federal aid for internal improvements, a transcontinental railroad, and free homestead farms. In selecting a candidate, the Republicans passed over the outspoken William H. Seward, who saw the struggle over slavery as an "irrepressible conflict." They nominated, instead, the more moderate Abraham Lincoln.
   c. The Constitutional union party, a third party, affirmed its support of the Union and nominated John Bell.

2. Results. Lincoln polled only 40 percent of the total popular vote but carried the North and West solidly. He won the election with a decisive majority in the electoral college.

THE SOUTH SECEDES

1. Southern Reaction to the Election.
   Southern leaders were outraged by the election of Lincoln, whom they called a "black Republican." Many Southerners ignored the facts that (a) the Republicans controlled neither the Senate nor the House of Representatives, and (b) pro-Southern judges dominated the Supreme Court.
2. Confederate States of America in December, 1860, South Carolina seceded from the Union. She was soon followed by six other Southern states. In February, 1861, the secessionist leaders met at Montgomery, Alabama, and established the Confederate States of America with Jefferson Davis as President. The Confederacy hastened military preparations in case it would have to use force to defend its independence.

3. Lincoln Takes Office.

In his Inaugural Address, Lincoln was both conciliatory and firm. He pledged not to interfere with slavery in the states where it existed, and he promised to enforce federal regulations, including the Fugitive Slave Law. However, he labeled secession as illegal and emphasized his solemn oath to "preserve, protect, and defend" the Constitution. He warned, "In your hands, my dissatisfied countrymen, and not in mine, is the momentous issue of civil war."

In April, 1861, Lincoln notified Southern authorities that unarmed ships would carry food to the federal troops at Fort Sumter in the harbor of Charleston, South Carolina. Nevertheless, Southern guns bombarded the fort and compelled its surrender. The Civil War had begun.

The first Republican Convention in 1860 deserves a few more sentences since it was held here in Chicago. Early in May, 1860, workmen hurried to finish a large, two-story frame building on the southeast corner of Lake and Market streets, now Lake Street and Wacker Drive. Already named the Wigwam, it was being built to house the Republican National Convention-the second to be held by that party and the first national political convention to meet in Chicago. The delegates, jostled by thousands of spectators, met for the first time on May 16. On the 18th came the nominations: for President, William H. Seward of New York, William L Dayton of New Jersey, Simon Cameron of Pennsylvania, Salmon P. Chase and John McLean of Ohio-and Abraham Lincoln of Illinois. On the first ballot Seward led with 173 ½ votes. Lincoln-considered only a favorite son-stood next with 102. With the second ballot Seward rose to 184 ½ votes; Lincoln jumped to 181. Before the third roll call was finished Lincoln had 231 ½ votes, with only 233 necessary for nomination. An Ohio delegate jumped on a chair and announced that his state was changing four votes from Chase to Lincoln. Cheers rocketed through the Wigwam, swelling to a roar so loud that the first guns of a salute, fired from a cannon on the roof, could hardly be heard. Outside the building men embraced each other, shouted for joy, formed impromptu parades, and crowded the barrooms. The Republican party had nominated its first president, and started a great American on the road to immortablity. It would take a lifetime to read all that was written about Abraham Lincoln but this brief summary of his life published by the free encyclopedia, Wikipedia, best serves the purpose for our month of February dedicated to "Honest Abe."

ABRAHAM LINCOLN
(February 12, 1809-April 15, 1865)

The sixteenth President of the United States, successfully led his country through its greatest internal crisis, the American Civil War, only to be assassinated as the war was coming to an end. Before becoming the first Republican elected to the Presidency, Lincoln was a lawyer, an Illinois state legislator, a member of the United States House of Representatives, and an unsuccessful candidate for election to the Senate.

As an outspoken opponent of the expansion of slavery in the United States, Lincoln won the Republican Party nomination in 1860 and was elected president later that year. During his time in office, he contributed to the effort to preserve the United States by leading the defeat of the secessionist Confederate States of America in the American Civil War. He introduced measures that resulted in the abolition of slavery, issuing his

Emancipation Proclamation in 1863 and promoting the passage of the Thirteenth Amendment to the Constitution, which passed Congress before Lincoln's death and was ratified by the states later in 1865.

Lincoln closely supervised the victorious war effort, especially the selection of top generals, including Ulysses S. Grant. Historians have concluded that he handled the factions of the Republican Party well, bringing leaders of each faction into his cabinet and forcing them to cooperate. Lincoln successfully defused a war scare with the United Kingdom in 1861. Under his leadership, the Union took control of the border slave states at the start of the war. Additionally, he managed his own reelection in the 1864 presidential election.

Opponents of the war (also known as "Copperheads") criticized Lincoln for refusing to compromise on the slavery issue. Conversely, the Radical Republicans, an abolitionist faction of the Republican Party, criticized him for moving too slowly in abolishing slavery. Even with these road blocks, Lincoln successfully rallied public opinion through his rhetoric and speeches; his Gettysburg Address is but one example of this. At the close of the war, Lincoln held a moderate view of Reconstruction, seeking to speedily reunite the nation through a policy of generous reconciliation. His assassination in 1865 was the first presidential assassination in U.S. history and made him a martyr for the ideal of national unity.

A brief mention should be made of the Lincoln-Douglas debates of 1858. The 1858 campaign featured the Lincoln-Douglas debates, a famous contest on slavery. Lincoln warned that "The Slave Power" was threatening the values of republicanism, while Douglas emphasized the supremacy of democracy, as set forth in his Freeport Doctrine, which said that local settlers should be free to choose whether to allow slavery or not. Though the Republican legislative candidates won more popular votes, the Democrats won more seats, and the legislature reelected Douglas to Senate. Nevertheless, Lincoln's speeches on the issue transformed him into a national political star.

Lincoln said "with malice toward none and charity for all let us bind up the wounds of our country" which shows the compassion and love he had for all his fellow Americans which became more apparent by his plan for the reconstruction of our nation.

Reconstruction began during the war as Lincoln and his associates pondered questions of how to reintegrate the Southern states and what to do with Confederate leaders and the freed slaves. Lincoln led the "moderates" regarding Reconstructionist policy, and was usually opposed by the Radical Republicans, under Thaddeus Stevens in the House and Charles Sumner and Benjamin Wade in the Senate (though he cooperated with these men on most other issues). Determined to fine a cause that would reunite the nation and not alienate the South, Lincoln urged that speedy elections under generous terms be held throughout the war in areas behind Union lines. His Amnesty Proclamation of December 8, 1863, offered pardons to those who had not held a Confederate civil office, had not mistreated Union prisoners, and would sign an oath of allegiance. Critical decisions had to be made as state after state was reconquered. Of special importance were Tennessee, where Lincoln appointed Andrew Johnson as governor, and Louisiana, where Lincoln attempted a plan that would restore statehood when 10% of the voters agreed to it. The Radicals thought this policy too lenient, and passed their own plan, the Wade-Davis Bill, in 1864. When Lincoln pocket-vetoed the bill, the Radicals retaliated by refusing to seat representatives elected from Louisiana, Arkansas, and Tennessee.

Near the end of the war, Lincoln made an extended visit to Grant's headquarters at City Point, Virginia. This allowed the president to visit Richmond after it was taken by the Union forces and to make a public gesture of sitting at Jefferson Davis's own desk, symbolically saying to the nation that the President of the United States held authority over the entire land. He was greeted at the city as a conquering hero by freed slaves, whose sentiments were epitomized by one admirer's quote, "I know I am free for I have seen the face of Father Abraham and have felt him." When a general asked Lincoln how the defeated Confederates should be treated, Lincoln replied, "Let 'em up easy." Lincoln arrived back in Washington on the evening of April 9, 1865, the day Lee surrendered at Appomattox Court House in Virginia. The war was effectively over. The other rebel armies surrendered soon after, and there was no subsequent guerrilla warfare.

One cannot help but be impressed with Lincoln's strong religious and philosophical beliefs in studying his life, his decisions, his Christian humanity. WIKIPEDIA wrote the following brief summary of these beliefs.

In March 1860 in a speech in New Haven, Connecticut, Lincoln said, with respect to slavery, "Whenever this question shall be settled, it must be settled on some philosophical basis. No policy that does not rest upon some philosophical public opinion can be permanently maintained." The philosophical basis for Lincoln's beliefs regarding slavery and other issues of the day require that Lincoln be examined "seriously as a man of ideas." Lincoln was a strong supporter of the American Whig version of liberal capitalism who, more than most politicians of the time, was able to express his ideas within the context of Nineteenth Century religious beliefs.

There were few people who strongly or directly influenced Lincoln's moral and intellectual development and perspectives.

There was no teacher, mentor, church leader, community leader, or peer that Lincoln would credit in later years as a strong influence on his intellectual development. Lacking a formal education, Lincoln's personal philosophy was shaped by "an amazingly retentive memory and a passion for reading and learning." It was Lincoln's reading, rather than his relationships, that were most influential in shaping his personal beliefs.

Lincoln did, even as a boy, largely reject organized religion, but the Calvinistic "doctrine of necessity" would remain a factor throughout his life. In 1846 Lincoln described the effect of this doctrine as "that the human mind is impelled to action, or held in rest by some power, over which the mind itself has no control." In April 1864, in justifying his actions in regard to Emancipation, Lincoln wrote, "I claim not to have controlled events, but confess plainly that events have controlled me. Now, at the end of three years struggle the nation's condition is not what either party, or any man devised, or expected. God alone can claim it."

As Lincoln matured, and especially during his term as president, the idea of a divine will somehow interacting with human affairs more and more influenced his public expressions. On a personal level, the death of his son Willie in February 1862 may have caused Lincoln to look towards religion for answers and solace. After Willie's death, in the summer or early fall of 1862, Lincoln attempted to put on paper his private musings on why, from a divine standpoint, the severity of the war was necessary:

> The will of God prevails. In great contests each party claims to act in accordance with the will of God. Both may be, and one must be, wrong. God cannot be for and against the same thing at the same time. In the

present civil war it is quite possible that God's purpose is something different from the purpose of either party-and yet the human instrumentalities, working just as they do, are of the best adaptation to effect his purpose. I am almost ready to say this is probably true-that God wills this contest, and wills that it shall not end yet. By his mere quiet power, on the minds of the now contestants, He could have either saved or destroyed the Union without a human contest. Yet the contest began. And having begun He could give the final victory to either side any day. Yet the contest proceeds.

Lincoln's religious skepticism was fueled by his exposure to the ideas of the Lockean Enlightenment and classical liberalism, especially economic liberalism. Consistent with the common practice of the Whig party, Lincoln would often use the Declaration of Independence as the philosophical and moral expression of these two philosophies. In a February 22, 1861 speech at Independence Hall in Philadelphia Lincoln said,

> I have never had a feeling politically that did not spring from the sentiments embodied in the Declaration of Independence . . . It was not the mere matter of the separation of the Colonies from the motherland; but that sentiment in the Declaration of Independence which gave liberty, not alone to the people of this country, but, I hope, to the world, for all future time. It was that which gave promise that in due time the weight would be lifted from the shoulders of all men. This is a sentiment embodied in the Declaration of Independence.

He found in the Declaration justification for Whig economic policy and opposition to territorial expansion and the nativist platform of the Know Nothings. In claiming that all men were created free, Lincoln and the Whigs argued that this freedom required economic advancement, expanded education, territory to grow, and the ability of the nation to absorb the growing immigrant population.

It was the Declaration of Independence, rather than the Bible, that Lincoln most relied on in order to oppose any further territorial expansion of slavery. He saw the Declaration as more than a political document. To him, as well as to many abolitionists and other antislavery leaders, it was, foremost, a moral document that had forever determined valuable criteria in shaping the future of the nation.

One of Chicago/s most famous landmark monuments is that of Abraham Lincoln found in Lincoln Park at North Dearborn Parkway, built in 1887. Augustus Saint-Gardens was the sculptor and Stanford White was the architect, designated a Chicago Landmark on December 12, 2001. One of the oldest and most important public sculptures in Chicago, this monument to America's sixteenth president influenced a generation of sculptors due to its innovative combination of a natural-looking Lincoln-depicted deep in thought as he is about to begin a speech-with a Classical-style architectural setting. It is the work of two nationally-important American designers and is widely considered to be the most significant nineteenth-century sculpture of Lincoln.

"Before ending this reverie, let us include some trivia for the many 'lovers' of trivia:"

* Lincoln was seeing the play "Our American Cousin" when he was shot.

* Lincoln was the first president to have a beard while in office.
* Lincoln, Nebraska was named after Abraham Lincoln.
* Abe Lincoln's mother, Nancy Hanks Lincoln, died when the family dairy cow ate poisonous mushrooms and she drank the milk.
* A plot was developed to steal Lincoln's body, so a secret society to guard his tomb was formed.
* During the Civil War, telegraph wires were strung to follow the action on the battlefield. But there was no telegraph office in the White House, so Lincoln went across the street to the War Department to get the news.
* Lincoln was the tallest president. He was 6 feet and four inches tall.
* Lincoln once had a dream right before the fall of Richmond that he would die. He dreamt that he was in the White House, he heard crying and when he found the room it was coming from he asked who had died. The man said the President. He looked in the coffin and saw his own face. A week later Lincoln died.
* Lincoln was shot on Good Friday.
* Robert Todd Lincoln arrived too late to stop three separate presidential assassinations. He met his father, president Abraham Lincoln, at the theatre after John Wilkes Booth had fired the shot. He went to a Washington train station to meet president Garfield, arriving only minutes after he was shot. And, he traveled to Buffalo, New York to meet President McKinley, but got there after the fatal shot had already been fired.
* Lincoln had a cat named "Bob," a turkey named "Jack," and a dog named "Jib."

- He was the first president to be photographed at his inauguration. John Wilkes Booth (his assassin) can be seen standing close to Lincoln in the Picture.
- Lincoln was the only president to receive a patent, for a device for lifting boats over shoals.
- Lincoln's brother, half-brothers, and brothers-in-law fought in the Confederate Army.
- Abraham Lincoln was shot while watching a performance of Our American Cousin at Ford's Theatre in Washington, D.C. The same play was also running at the McVerick Theatre in Chicago on May 18, 1860, the day Lincoln was nominated for president in that city.
- Lincoln's favorite sport was wrestling.
- Lincoln worked as a deck hand on a Mississippi flatboat.
- Lincoln had a wart on his right cheek, a scar on his thumb from an ax accident, and a scar over his right eye from a fight with a gang of thieves.
- Abraham Lincoln grew his beard out of a suggestion of an 11 year old girl.
- John Wilkes Booth's brother once saved Abraham Lincoln's son's life.
- Abe Lincoln is the U.S. president most frequently portrayed in films.
- The contents of his pockets on the night of his assassination weren't revealed until February 12, 1976. They contained two pairs of spectacles, a chamois lens cleaner, an ivory and silver pocketknife, a large white Irish linen handkerchief, slightly used, with "A. Lincoln" embroidered in red, a gold quartz watch fob without a watch, a new silk-lined, leather wallet containing a pencil, a confederate five-dollar bill, and news clippings of unrest in the Confederate

army, emancipation in Missouri, The Union party platform of 1864, and an article on the presidency by John Bright.
* He was named after his grandfather.
* Lincoln and his wife held seances in the White House. They had great interest in psychic phenomena.
* Lincoln loved the works of Edgar Allan Poe.
* Abraham Lincoln was the first president to be born outside of the original thirteen colonies. He was born in Kentucky.

Let us now end this reverie with the poem, Abraham Lincoln, composed by William Cullen Bryant, (1794-1878) American Poet and Editor.

Abraham Lincoln
April 26, 1865

Oh, slow to smite and swift to spare,
Gentle and merciful and just!
Who, in the fear of God, didst bear
The sword of power, a nation's trust!

In sorrow by thy bier we stand,
Amid the awe that hushes all,
And speak the anguish of a land
That shook with horror at thy fall.

Thy task is done; the bond are free:
We bear thee to an honored grave,
Whose proudest monument shall be
The broken fetters of the slave.

Pure was thy life; its bloody close
Hath placed thee with the sons of light,
Among the noble host of those
Who perished in the cause of Right.

O CAPTAIN! MY CAPTAIN!
Walt Whitman (1819-1892)

O CAPTAIN! My Captain! Our fearful trip is done;
The ship has weather'd every rack, the prize we sought is won;
The port is near, the bells I hear, the people all exulting,
While follow eyes the steady keel, the vessel grim and daring:
  But O heart! Heart! Heart!
    O the bleeding drops of *red*,
      Where on the deck my Captain lies,
        Fallen cold and dead.

O Captain! My Captain! Rise up and hear the bells;
Rise up-for you the flag is flung-for you the bugfle trills;
For you bouquets and ribbon'd wreaths-for you the shores a-crowding;
For you they call, the swaying mass, their eager faces turning;
  Here Captain! Dear father!
    This arm beneath your *head*;
      It is some dream that on the deck,
        You've fallen cold and dead.

My Captain does not answer, his lips are pale and still;
My father does not feel my arm, he has no pulse nor will;
The ship is anchor'd safe and sound, its voyage closed and done;
From fearful trip, the victor ship, comes in with object won;
  Exult, O shores, and ring, O bells!
    But I, with *mournful* tread,
      Walk the deck my Captain lies,
        Fallen cold and dead.

WORLD'S COLUMBIAN EXPOSITION—A REVERIE

In 1893 Chicago got the World's Fair which was supposed to go to either New York or Boston or Washington, D.C., but our representatives were too vocal and too positive on the advantages of Chicago especially on its location. They emphasized that 90 percent of all merchandise was made in an area enclosed by a circle with a 300 mile radius with Chicago as its hub which included St. Louis, Toledo, Indianapolis and almost Minneapolis. "Look at the attendance potential" they thundered. The New York Times who covered the meetings and listened to Chicago's spokesmen wrote an editorial after Chicago's selection in which they coined the phrase that "Chicago was the windiest city." They still call us the Windy City, but Corpus Christy in Texas is actually the windiest city in the United States.

The World's Columbian Exposition, 1893

As the year 1892 approached the feeling grew that the United States should commemorate the 400th anniversary of the discovery of America. Sentiment favored a great international exposition. But where? Spokesmen for Chicago descended on Congress. The city was the melting pot of the nation; it had hotel rooms to accommodate the visitors; in Jackson Park, as yet undeveloped, it had an unrivalled location. With a pledge of $10,000,000 to back up their arguments, the Chicagoans carried the day.

Daniel H. Burnham, Chicago architect, took charge of construction. Enlisting the aid of the most famous architects, sculptors, and landscape designers in the country, Burnham transformed a swamp into fairland. When the fair opened on May 1, 1893 an army of visitors saw great buildings of classic form in lustrous white, statues, fountains, and a sprawling and raucous amusement section. There were the caravels (replicas of course) in which Columbus had sailed to the new World, the giant Ferris Wheel, the Streets of Cairo and the Irish Village, 50,000 roses in bloom on the Wooded Island, Russian jades, Sevres vases, Chinese lacquer-products, inventions, and freaks assembled by forty-six foreign nations and most of the states of the Union. In the six months of its course the Exposition attracted 27,539,000 visitors-almost half the total number of people living in the United States. Overnight Chicago became the best known city in the world. On its visitors the Exposition had a profound effect: millions remembered a few days spent in the White City and on the Midway Plaisance as the greatest experience of their lives. The sight of new inventions, opening what seemed to be limitless avenues of progress, gave the entire world a lift of spirit. Perhaps the Exposition had its most far-reaching effect on architecture, for by reminding millions of the beauties of the classic form it started a trend that was to last for a generation.

The Columbian Exposition was one of the most spectacular construction efforts of the century. To help it pick a site for the exposition and prepare a ground plan, the Chicago committee commissioned Frederick Law Olmsted. The bent, white-bearded old master arrived in Chicago in August 1890 with Henry Codman, his young assistant, to begin work on the culminating achievement of his career on the very spot, eight miles south of the Loop, where he had prepared a park plan before the Great Fire. Jackson Park, with only a few improvements on its northern border, was a water-soaked flat, bare except for a scattering of oak trees stripped of their foliage by gales that swept in from Lake Michigan. But in its favor, it was on the lake, the most beautiful natural feature of the region, and was bordered on the west by the tracks of several major railroads, connecting it with the downtown area and, from there, with the country. It s very state of undevelopment provided Olmsted, an inspired "painter" of natural landscapes, a clean canvas to work with. That fall, Burnham and Root were named supervising architects of the exposition and began collaborating with Olmsted and Codman to sketch in pencil and on brown paper an American Venice of interlinked canals, basins, and lagoons, with all the major exposition halls touching water and with an architecture court-an obvious Parisian derivation-surrounding a reflecting basin decorated with symbolic fountains and statuary. The Court of Honor fronted the lake on an east-west axis and was to be the "entrance hall" to the exposition for travelers arriving by either boat or train, while Olmsted's canals and lagoons ran north from the court on an axis parallel to the lake. In the middle of the largest lagoon, Olmsted placed a wooden island, to be kept free of "conspicuous buildings," its natural landscaping supplying "an episode in refreshing relief" to the grandeur of the main exhibition halls. A quixotic combination of the stately and naturalistic, the landscape plan was a stunning visual achievement. Remembered best in history as a spectacular architectural show, the Columbian Exposition's most impressive design accomplishment was actually Olmsted and Root's artful reshaping of an unsightly split of sand and swamp water.

 The Ferris Wheel was one of the main attractions of the Fair. An excellent account of its origin is found in "The City of the

Century" written by Donald L. Miller: The crowds that lined the banks of the lagoons on these summer evenings were seeing more than an interesting entertainment. The show transported them to the Electric City of the approaching age, where "a blaze of lights" would banish the "fearful mysteries of darkness," one writer predicted, giving back the city's streets to decent folk. In the coming years, electricity would run America's factories and trains and heat its houses and businesses, said an engineer interviewed at the fair, clearing the air in its cities of grime and coal smoke.

This prophet was a thirty-four-year-old bridge designer from Pittsburgh named George Washington Gale Ferris. His big steel wheel on the Midway Plaisance, the expositions's commercially run entertainment strip, was the fair's only rival in popular appeal of the nighttime illumination and a foretaste of how technology would usher in a new industry of mass entertainment. "What on earth is that?" is the first astonished inquiry that every passenger on the Illinois Central, the 'L,' and the steamship liner on the lake makes as soon as he gets his first sight of the Ferris Wheel," said the Chicago Tribune. "And he asks it from afar off, for the wheel is the landmark of the Fair." Ferris got the inspiration for his invention from Daniel Burnham's challenge to American engineers to create something to outdo the Eiffel Tower, the chief exhibit at the Paris world's fair in 1889. Plans came in for a Tower of Babel forty stories high, with a different language spoken on each floor, for an aerial island supported by six giant hot-air balloons, for a replica of Dante's Hell, and for a range of manmade mountains, but Ferris was the only engineer to submit something both new and technically audacious, a proposal, as someone at the time described it, to put Eiffel's observatory on a pivot and set it in motion. He built his wheel in five months with his own money and assembled it in Jackson Park in June. When the

250-foot-diameter wheel was finished, it was ringed with three thousand electric bulbs. Ferris took the first ride with his wife, Mayor Harrison, Bertha Palmer, the entire city council, and a forty-piece band. At the top of the wheel's revolution, a point higher than the crown of the Statue of Liberty, they could see the gray Gothic buildings of the University of Chicago and, in the distance, the tops of the skyscrapers of Chicago rising out of the smog and smoke. "The World's Greatest Ride" was a carnival attraction to beat them all. More than 1.4 million riders paid fifty cents apiece for two revolutions in one of its thirty-six wood-veneered cabins, each larger than a Pullman Palace Car. But skeptics were persuaded of the wheel's strength and safety only when it withstood hurricane winds of a hundred miles per hour. Ferris, his wife, and a reporter rode out the gale in one of the cars. The windows shook, the blasts were deafening, but the wheel barely shivered as it made its slow, majestic orbit. When the fair closed, the Ferris wheel appeared at two other sites before it was dynamited and sold for scrap metal. The forerunner of all entertainment wheels, it helped usher in the age of the amusement park. After visiting the fair on his honeymoon, George C. Tilyou ordered a wheel half the size of Ferris's and built his Coney island Steeplechase Park around it. "We Americans," he told a journalist, "want either to be thrilled or amused, and are ready to pay well for either sensation."

Now, gentle readers, there were other notable attractions. The World's Columbian Exposition was the first world's fair with an area for amusements that was strictly separated from the exhibition halls. This area, developed by a young music promoter, Sol Bloom, concentrated on Midway Plaisance. It included carnival rides, among them the first Ferris wheel, built by George Ferris. This wheel was 264 feet high and had 36 cars, each of which could accommodate 60 people. One of the cars carried a band that played whenever the wheel was in motion. The Midway Plaisance introduced the term "midway" to American English to describe the area of a carnival or fair where sideshows are located.

What follows now are some notable "firsts" at the fair:

* The concert band of John Phillip Sousa played there daily.
* Another popular Midway attraction was the "Street in Cairo", which included the popular exotic dancer known as Little Egypt. She introduced America to the suggestive version of the belly dance known as the "hootchy-kootchy", to a tune improvised by Bloom (and now more commonly associated with snake charmers). The man who created it was American and never copyrighted the song, putting it straight into the public domain.
* Although denied a spot at the fair, Buffalo Bill Cody decided to come to Chicago anyway, setting up his Wild West show just outside the edge of the exposition. Historian Frederick Jackson Turner gave academic lectures reflecting on the end of the frontier which Buffalo Bill represented.
* The Electrotachyscope of Ottomar Anschutz, which used a Geissler Tube to project the illusion of moving images, was demonstrated.
* Louis Comfort Tiffany made his reputation with a stunning chapel designed and built for the Exposition. This chapel has been carefully reconstructed and restored. It can be seen in at the Charles Hosmer Morse Museum of American Art.
* Architect Kirtland Cutter's Idaho building, a rustic log construction, was a popular favorite, visited by an

estimated 18 million people. The building's design and interior furnishings were a major precursor of the Arts and Crafts movement.

* The John Bull locomotive was also displayed. It was only 62 years old, having been built in 1831. It was the first locomotive acquisition by the Smithsonian Institution. The locomotive ran under its own power from Washington, DC, to Chicago to participate, and returned to Washington under its own power again when the exposition closed. In 1981 it was the oldest surviving operable steam locomotive in the world when it ran under its own power again.

* Also on display in Chicago was an original frog switch and portion of the superstructure of the famous 1826 Granite Railway in Massachusetts. This was the first commercial railroad in the United States to evolve into a common carrier without an intervening closure. The railway brought granite stones from a rock quarry in Quincy, Massachusetts so that the Bunker Hill Monument could be erected in Boston. The frog switch is now on public view in East Milton Square, MA, on the original right-of-way of the Granite Railway.

* Norway participated with a replica of a Viking ship, a replica of the Gokstad ship. It was built in Norway and sailed across the Atlantic by 92 men, led by their helmsman Magnus Andersen. In 1919 this ship was moved to the Lincoln Park Zoo. It was recently taken to Good Templar Park in Geneva, Illinois, where it awaits renovation.

* The 1893 Parliament of the World's Religions, which ran from September 11 to September 27, marked the first formal gathering of representatives of Eastern and Western spiritual traditions from around the world.

* Forty-six nations participated in the fair, including Haiti, which selected Frederick Douglass to be its coordinator. The Exposition drew nearly 26 million visitors. It left a remembered vision that inspired the Emerald City of L. Frank Baum's Land of Oz and Walk Disney's theme parks. Disney's father Elias had been a construction worker on some of the buildings at the fair.

The Exposition gave rise to the City Beautiful movement, which began in Chicago. Results included grand buildings and fountains built around Olmstedian parks, shallow pools of water on axis to central buildings, larger park systems, broad boulevards and parkways and after the turn of the century, zoning laws and planned suburbs. Examples of the City Beautiful movement's works include the City of Chicago, the Columbia University campus, and the Mall in Washington D.C. After the fair closed, J.C. Rogers, a banker from Wamego, Kansas, purchased several pieces of art that had hung in the rotunda of the U.S. Government Building. He also purchased architectural elements, artifacts and buildings from the fair. He shipped his purchases to Wamego. Many of the items, including the artwork, were used to decorate his theater, now known as the Columbian Theatre. Memorabilia saved by visitors can still be purchased. Numerous books, tokens, published photographs, and well-printed admission tickets can be found. While the higher value commemorative stamps are expensive, the lower ones are quite common. So too are the commemorative half dollars, many of which went into circulation.

Let us end this Reverie with a brief overview of the history of fairs and the immense changes they ushered in the nations of the world, especially our own World's Columbian Exposition. This 1893 Fair was the last and the greatest of the nineteenth century's World's Fairs. Nominally a celebration of Columbus' voyages 400 years prior, the Exposition was in actuality a reflection and celebration of American culture and society—for fun, edification, and profit—and a blueprint for life in modern and postmodern America.

The Fair was immensely popular, drawing over 27 million visitors, including Frederick Douglass, Jane Addams, Paul Laurence Dunbar, Henry Blake Fuller, Scott Joplin, Walter Wyckoff, Edweard Muybridge, Henry Adams, W.D. Howells, and Hamlin Garland. It was widely publicized both nationally and internationally, and people traveled from all over the world to see the spectacle. Travelers came from the East by "Exposition Flyers"—Pullman coaches traveling at the amazing speed of 80 m.p.h.—which gave "many Americans their first look at the country beyond the Alleghenies . . ." (Donald Miller, 74) People left their factories, their farms, and their city businesses to participate in what was touted as the greatest cultural and entertainment event in the history of the world.

The goals of the management and the reactions of the public to this massive event reveal a great deal about the state of America at the close of the Gilded Age. The early 1890s were a time of considerable turmoil in America, and the conflicting interests and ideas found full play in the presentation and reception of the Fair. It was an age of increasing fragmentation and confusion, of self-conscious searching for an identity on a personal and on a national level. The industrial, and increasingly electrical, revolutions were transforming America; the American way of life was no longer based on agriculture, but on factories and urban centers, and the end of the Gilded Age signified the advent of what Alan Trachtenberg has called the "incorporation of America," the shift of social control from the people and government to big business. The accompanying shift from a producer to a consumer society and the incredible growth of these corporations led to financial instability. Recessions and the devastating Depression of 1893, the violent Homestead and Pullman labor strikes, and widespread unemployment and homelessness plagued the early years of the decade. The frontier was closing, immigration, technological advances, and the railroads had changed the face of the country, and suddenly "Americanness" was more and more difficult to define. Americans were at once confused, excited, and overwhelmed.

The World's Columbian Exposition was the perfect vehicle to explore these immense changes while at the same time celebrating the kind of society America had become. World's Fairs, by the end of the century, were an established cultural and entertainment form with immense international influence. From the first major nineteenth century exposition, the 1851 "Crystal Palace" fair in London to Philadelphia's 1876 Centennial Exhibition to Paris' Exposition Universelle of 1889, hundreds of millions of people around the world visited over 50 international fairs in the last half of the century, finding in them not only entertainment, but cultural enlightenment, commercial opportunity, and a reflection of their age.

Even as cultural producers and consumers of the time understood the importance of the Fair as a form, so modern scholars understand that as "cities within cities and cultures within civilizations, they both reflect and idealize the historical moments when they appear." (Gilbert, 13) We are able to learn a great deal about the culture and issues of the late nineteenth century by studying fairs as important social indicators. Robert Rydell has observed that Fairs, in short, helped to craft the modern world. They were arenas where manufacturers sought to promote products, where states and provinces competed for new residents and new investments, where urban spaces were organized into shimmering utopian cities, and where people from all social classes went to be alternately amused, instructed, and diverted from more pressing concerns. Memorialized in songs, books, buildings, public statuary, city parks, urban designs, and photographs, fairs were intended to frame the world view not only of the hundreds of millions who attended these spectacles, but also the countless millions who encountered the fairs secondhand.

The Columbian Exposition was very much a part of this tradition. It attempted to redefine America for itself and the world, and in doing so introduced many themes and artifacts still prevalent in American life: the connection between technology and progress; the predominance of corporations and the professional class in the power structure of the country; the triumph of the consumer culture; and the equation of European forms with "high culture", as well as the more pedestrian legacy of Juicy Fruit Gym, Pabst Blue Ribbon beer, ragtime music, and Quaker Oats. H.W. Brands, in his fascinating work on the 1890s, The Reckless Decade, points to the importance of studying this Fair and the age it informs and reflects.

> For Americans living in the 1990s, the events of the 1890s would be worth exploring even if they imparted no insight into the present. Life on the edge frequently evokes the best and worst in people and societies. It did so during the 1890s, when the United States produced more than its normal quota of demagogues and dedicated reformers, scoundrels and paragons of goodwill, when the American people lived up to their better selves and down to their worse . . .
>
> Yet the story of the 1890s also possesses significance beyond its inherent color and drama. How America survived the last decade of the nineteenth century—how it pursued its hopes, occasionally confronted and frequently fled its fears, wrestled its angels and

demons—reveals much about the American people. What it reveals can be of use to a later generation of those people, situated similarly on the cusp between an old century and a new one.

(Brands,5)

This project will focus on the message of this overwhelmingly popular Fair and its implications for contemporary and modern society. First, we will take a virtual tour of the Fair, pointing out its high and low points, and what they meant in the Official Fair's vocabulary, followed by a discussion of reactions to the Fair by its visitors—how, and how well, were the Fair's messages received? Finally, the focus shifts to the legacy of the Fair: the text and clues inferred by its spatial and ideological landscape, the messages that emerge with over a century of perspective, and the ramifications of its successes and failures.

So, take a step back in time, to an era when bicycles were a novelty, telephones a rarity, and phonographs an absolute revelation. To a time when the hustle and bustle of a consumer society, the immigration problem, economic instability, and feelings of cultural inferiority were foremost in Americans' minds. Does it sound familiar? Perhaps, in our investigation of this watershed event in American history—this celebration of early modernity—we can find ourselves in and learn from the messages of, and reactions to, the World's Columbian Exposition of 1893.

VALENTINE'S DAY MASSACRE— A REVERIE

For a city that is so filled with the history of crime, there has been little preservation of the landmarks that were once so important to the legend of the mob in Chicago. Gone are the landmarks like the Lexington Hotel, where Al Capone kept the fifth floor suite and used the place as his headquarters. But most tragic, at least to crime buffs, was the destruction of the warehouse that was located at 2122 North Clark Street. It was here, on Valentine's Day 1929, that the most spectacular mob hit in gangland history took place .... the St. Valentine's Day Massacre. The bloody events of February 14, 1929 began nearly five years before with the murder of Dion O'Banion, the leader of Chicago's north side mob. At that time, control of bootleg liquor in the city raged back and forth between the North Siders, run by O'Banion, and the south side Outfit, which was controlled by Johnny Torrio and his henchman, Al Capone. In November 1924, Torrio ordered the assassination of O'Banion and started an all-out war in the city. The North Siders retaliated soon afterward and nearly killed Torrio outside of his home. This brush with death led to him leaving the city and turning over operations to Capone, who was almost killed himself in September 1926. The following month, Capone shooters assassinated Hymie Weiss, who had been running the north side mob after the death of O'Banion. His murder left the operation in the hands of George "Bugs" Moran, a long-time enemy of Capone. For the most part, Moran stood alone against the Capone mob, since most of his allies had succumbed in the fighting. He continued to taunt his powerful enemy and looked for ways to destroy him. In early 1929, Moran sided with Joe Aiello in another attack against Capone. He and Aiello reportedly gunned down Pasquillano Lolordo, one of Capone's men, and Capone vowed that he would have him wiped out on February 14. He was living on his estate outside of Miami at the time and put in a call to Chicago. Capone had a very special "valentine" that he wanted delivered to Moran.

Now much has been written about the Saint Valentine's Day massacre and the Prohibition Era conflict between two powerful criminal gangs in Chicago. In the winter of 1929, the South Side Italian gang led by Al Capone and the North Side Irish/German gang led by Bugs Moran.

Former members of the Egan's Rats gang were also suspected to have played a large role in the massacre assisting Capone. What follows now was obtained from the WIKIPEDIA free encyclopedia.

On the morning of Thursday, February 14, 1929 St. Valentine's Day, four members of George 'Bugs' Moran's gang (some researchers believe five), a gang "follower", and a mechanic who happened to be at the scene were lined up against the rear inside wall of the garage of the SMC Cartage Company in the Lincoln Park neighborhood of Chicago's North Side. They were then shot and killed by the men, possibly members of Capone's gang, possibly "outside talent", most likely a combination of both. Two of the men were dressed as Chicago police officers, and the others were dressed in long trench coats, according to witnesses who saw the "police" leading the other men at gunpoint out of the garage (part of the plan). When one of the dying men, Frank Gusenberg, was asked who shot him, he replied, "I'm not gonna talk—nobody shot me." Capone himself had arranged to be on vacation in Florida at the time. The St. Valentine's Massacre resulted from a plan devised by a member or members of the Capone gang to eliminate Bugs Moran, the boss of the North Side Gang. Jack McGurn is the person most frequently cited by researchers as a suspected planner. The massacre was planned by the Capone mob for a number of reasons; in retaliation for an unsuccessful attempt by Frank and his brother Peter Gusenberg to murder Jack McGurn earlier in the year; the North Side Gang's complicity in the murder of Pasqualino "Patsy" Lolordo as well as Antonio "The Scourge" Lombardo, and Bugs Moran muscling in on a Capone-run dog track in the Chicago suburbs. Also, the rivalry between Moran and Capone for control of the lucrative Chicago bootlegging business led Capone to plan Moran's demise. The plan was to lure Moran and his men to the SMC Cartage warehouse on North Clark Street. It is assumed usually that the North Side Gang was lured to the garage with the promise of a cut-rate shipment of bootleg whiskey, supplied by Detroit's Purple Gang. However, some recent studies dispute this. All seven victims (with the exception of John May) were dressed in their best clothes, hardly suitable for unloading a large shipment of whiskey crates and driving it away. The real reason for the North Siders gathering in the garage may never be known for certain. A four-man team would then enter the building, two disguised as police officers, and kill Moran and his men. Before Moran and his men arrived, Capone stationed lookouts in the apartments across the streetfrom the warehouse. Wishing to keep the lookouts inconspicuous, Capone had hired two unrecognizable thugs to stand watch in rented rooms across the street from the garage. At around 10:30 a.m. on St. Valentine's day, four men arrived at the warehouse in two cars: a Cadillac sedan and a Peerless, both outfitted to look like detective sedans. Two men were dressed in police uniforms and two in street clothes. The Moran Gang had already arrived at the warehouse. However, Moran himself was not inside. One account states that Moran was supposedly approaching the warehouse, spotted the police car, and fled the scene. Another account was that Moran was simply late getting there. The lookouts allegedly confused one of Moran's men (most likely Albert Weinshank, who was the same height, build, and even physically resembled Moran) for Moran himself: he then signaled for the gunmen to enter the warehouse. The two phony police, carrying shotguns, exited the Peerless and entered the warehouse through the two rear doors. Inside they found members of Moran's gang, a sixth man named Reinhart Schwimmer who was not actually a gangster, but more of a gang (hanger-on) and a occasionally hired mechanic. The killers told the seven men to line up facing the back wall. There was apparently not any resistance, as the Moran men thought their captors were real police, and it was likely a "show" but merely to garner good press for the police department. Then the two "police officers" let in two men through the front door facing Clark Street. This pair riding in the Cadillac, were dressed in civilian clothes. Two of the killers starting shooting with Thompson sub-machine guns. All seven men were killed in a volley of seventy machine-gun bullets and two shotgun blasts according to the coroner's report. To show bystanders that everything was under control, the men in street clothes came out with their hands up, prodded by the two uniformed cops. The only survivor in the warehouse was John May's German Shepherds, Highball. When the real police arrived, they first heard the dog howling. On entering the warehouse, they found the dog trapped under a beer truck and the floor covered with blood, shell casings, and corpses.

The seven men killed that morning were:

* Peter Gusenberg and his brother Frank Gusenberg were both front line enforcers for the Moran organization. Frank was miraculously still alive when police first arrived on the scene. He died three hours later at 1:40, saying only, "Nobody shot me" or "Cops did it."
* Albert Kachellek, alias "James Clark", Moran's second-in-command.
* Adam Heyer, the bookkeeper and business manager of the Moran gang.
* Reinhard Schwimmer, an optician who had abandoned his practice to gamble horse racing (unsuccessfully) and associate with the Moran gang. He would, in contemporary parlance, be referred to as a "gang groupie". Though Schwimmer called himself and "optometrist" he was actually an optician (an eyeglass fitter) and he had no medical training.
* Albert Weinshank managed several cleaning and dyeing operations for Moran. His physical and even clothing resemblance to Moran is what allegedly set the massacre in motion before Moran actually arrived.
* John May, an occasional car mechanic for the Moran gang, though not a gang member himself. May had two earlier arrests for safe blowing (no convictions) but was attempting to work legally. However, his desperate need of cash, with a wife and seven children, caused him to accept jobs with the Moran gang as a mechanic.

The slaughter exceeded anything yet seen in the United States at that time. At first, it was thought that police may have indeed been responsible for the killings, but 255 detectives were soon cleared. Chicago Police scrambled to figure out who had been responsible. Since it was common knowledge that Moran was hijacking Capone's Detroit-based liquor shipments, police focused their attention on the Purple Gang. Mug shots of Purple members George Lewis, Eddie Fletcher, Phil Keywell and his kid brother Harry, were picked out by the landlady across the street as the phony roomers. Later, the women who identified them wavered, and, Fletcher, Lewis, and Harry Keywell were all questioned and cleared by Chicago Police. Nevertheless, the Keywell brothers (and by extension the Purple Gang) would remain ensnared in the massacre case for all time. A week after the massacre, a 1927 Cadillac sedan was found disassembled and partially burned in a garage on Wood Street. It was determined that the car was used by the massacre killers. The garage was located two blocks from the Circus Café, which was operated by Claude Maddox, a former St. Louis gangster and member of the Capone mob. Detectives checking leads in St. Louis discovered that former members of the Egan's Rats mob may have played a part. They soon announced they were seeking Fred "Killer" Burke and James Ray as the two uniformed police officers in the garage. Burke and other members of the mob had been known to use police uniforms to lull victims. Police also proposed that Joseph Lolordo may have been one of the machine gunners, mostly likely because his brother Pasqualino had recently been murdered by the North Side Gang.

Police also announced they suspected Capone gunmen John Scalise and Albert Anselmi, as well as Jack McGurn himself, and Frank Rio, a Capone bodyguard. Police eventually charged McGurn and Scalise with the massacre. John Scalise was murdered before he went to trial and the charges against Jack McGurn were downgraded to a violation of the Mann Act, stemming from taking the main witness against him, girlfriend Louise Rolfe (who became known as the "Blonde Alibi"), across state lines to marry.

The case stagnated until December 14, 1929, when Berrien County sheriffs raided the St. Joseph, Michigan bungalow of "Frederick Dane". Dane had been the registered owner of a vehicle driven by Fred "Killer" Burke. Burke had been drinking and rear-ended another vehicle in front of the police station. Officer Charles Skelly ran outside to investigate. When Burke attempted to drive away, Officer Skelly hopped on the running board and was shot off. He died of his wounds a short time later.

When police raided Burke's bungalow, they found a bulletproof vest, bonds recently stolen from a Wisconsin bank, two Thompson submachine guns, pistols, and thousands of rounds of ammunition. Both machine guns were determined to have been used in the massacre. Unfortunately, no further concrete evidence would surface in the massacre case. Burke would be captured over a year later on a Missouri farm. As the case against him in the murder of Officer Skelly was strongest, he was tried in Michigan and would be sentenced to life imprisonment. Fred Burke would die in prison in 1940.

Public outrage over The St. Valentine's Day Massacre marked the beginning of the end to Moran's power. Although Moran suffered a heavy blow, he still managed to keep control of his territory until the early 1930's, when control passed to the Chicago Outfit under Frank Nitti. The massacre also brought the belated attention of the federal government to bear on Capone and his criminal activities. In 1931, Capone was convicted of income tax evasion and was imprisoned for 11 years. The massacre ultimately affected both Moran and Capone and left the war they had with each other a stalemate. The massacre did severely cripple the North Side gang, a blow from which they never fully recovered. But the primary target of the massacre, Moran, escaped, and the public and police pressure brought to bear on the Capone organization hampered their operation almost as badly. Though Jack McGurn would beat the massacre charges, he would be murdered himself on February 15, 1936. The two most widely accepted theories credit either Bugs Moran or the Chicago Outfit itself under Frank Nitti with the killing, as McGurn had become a public relations liability to the Outfit.

Over the years, many mobsters, in and out of Chicago, would be named as part of the Valentine's Day hit team. Two prime suspects are Capone hit men John Scalise and Albert Anselmi; both men were lethal killers and are frequently mentioned as possibilities for two of the shooters. In the days after the massacre, Scalise was heard to brag, "I am the most powerful man in Chicago." He had recently been elevated to the position of vice-president in the Unione Siciliana by its president, Joseph Guinta. Nevertheless, Scalise, Anselmi, and Guinta would be found dead on a lonely road near Hammond, Indiana on May 8, 1929. Gangland lore has it that Al Capone had discovered that the pair was planning on betraying him. At the climax of a dinner party thrown in their honor, Capone produced a baseball bat and beat the trio to death. One recent addition to the roll of suspects is Tony Accardo, then a twenty-two year old gangster and driver for Jack McGurn. Many years later, Accardo would boast to his fellow gangsters that he had taken part (FBI agent William Roemer overheard him on a wiretap.) Most historians believe that while Accardo may have played a peripheral role in the murders, he was probably not one of the actual shooters. Another suspect was future mob boss Sam Giancana, then a twenty-year old member of the 42 Gang. Giancana was arrested in the days after the massacre on a charge of general investigation, and those most familiar with the case don't believe he played a major role. New York mob informant Dominick Montiglio would later claim in the book Murder Machine that his uncle Anthony 'Nino' Gaggi, intimated that his uncle Frank Scalise had been one of the killers in the massacre. While not likely, this shows how the massacre continues to captivate people to this day. Some people today speculate that perhaps Capone really was innocent after all. Maybe it was a bunch of crooked cops or an internal beef amongst the Moran Gang. One historian suspects a bunch of "hillbilly gangsters." The true identities of the shooters may never be known with certainty.

The garage, which stood at 2122 N. Clark Street, was demolished in 1967; the site is now a landscaped parking lot for a nursing home. There is still controversy over the actual bricks used to build the north inside wall of the building where the mobsters were lined up and shot. They were claimed to be responsible, according to stories, for bringing financial ruin, illness, bad luck and death to anyone who bought them. The bricks from the bullet-marked inside North wall were purchased and saved by Canadian businessman George Patey in 1967. His original intention was to use it in a restaurant that he represented, but the restaurant's owner didn't go for the idea. Patey ended up buying the bricks himself, outbidding three or four others. Patey had the wall painstakingly taken apart and had each of the 414 bricks numbered, then shipped them back to Canada. There are various different reports about what George Patey did with the bricks after he got them. In 1978, Time Magazine reported that Patey reassembled the wall and put it on display in a wax museum with gun-wielding gangsters shooting each other in front of it to the accompaniment of recorded bangs. The wax museum later went bankrupt. Another source, an independent newspaper in the UK, reported in February 2000 that the wall toured shopping malls and exhibitions in the United States for a couple of decades. In 1968 Patey stopped exhibiting the bricks and put them into retirement. Patey opened a nightclub called the Banjo Palace in 1971. It had a Roaring Twenties theme. The famous bricks were installed inside the men's washroom with Plexiglas placed right in front of it to shield it, so that patrons could urinate and try to hit the targets painted on the Plexiglas. In a 2001 interview with an Argentinian journalist, Patey said, "I had the most popular club in the city. People came from high society and entertainment, Jimmy Stewart, Robert Mitchum." The bricks were placed in storage until 1997 when Patey tried to auction them off on a website called Jet Set On The Net. The deal fell through after a hard time with the auction company. In 1999, Patey tried to sell them brick by brick on his own website. The last known substantial offer for the entire wall was made by a Las Vegas casino but Patey refused the $175,000 offer. Patey died on December 26, 2004, having never revealed how much he paid to buy the bricks at auction.

Well, this was quite an unusual reverie, one of real evil. But why stop here? Let us end our own reverie in the silence of our own thoughts about the lives of the people we have just read about including (1.) The last four things, death, judgment, heaven and hell, and (2.) "There but for the grace of God, go I." Jesus, have mercy on me, a sinner.

CENTURY OF PROGRESS— A REVERIE

Most of the following information was obtained from Wikipedia, The Free Encyclopedia. A Century of Progress International Exposition was held to commemorate the 100th anniversary of the incorporation of the City of Chicago. Its theme, as given in A Century of Progress Chicago International Exposition of 1933, Statement of its Plan and Purposes and of the Relation of States and Foreign Governments to Them (Chicago, 1933) was to "attempt to demonstrate to an international audience the nature and significance of scientific discoveries, the methods of achieving them, and the changes which their application has wrought in industry and in living conditions." This was done through exhibits that appeal to the public in general, often with miniaturized or replicated processes. The fair was held on 427 acres (much of it landfill) on Lake Michigan, immediately south of Chicago's downtown area, from 12th Street to 39th Street (now Pershing Road). Today, Meigs Field and McCormick Place occupy this site. A Century of Progress officially opened on May 27, 1933 and closed on November 12 of that year. Although originally planned for the 1933, season only, it was extended for another year, reopening on May 26, 1934, and closing on October 31, 1934. This extension was due in part to the fair's public popularity, but mainly as an effort to earn sufficient income to retire its debts.

A Century of Progress International Exposition was the name of the World's fair held in Chicago, Illinois from 1933 to 1934 to celebrate the city's centennial. The theme of the fair was technological innovation. Its motto was "Science Finds, Industry Applies, Man Conforms" and its architectural symbol was the Sky Ride, a transporter bridge perpendicular to the shore on which one could ride from one end of the fair to the other. A Century of Progress was organized as an Illinois not-for-profit corporation in January, 1928 for the purpose of planning and hosting a World's Fair in Chicago in 1934. The site selected was the land and water areas under the jurisdiction of South Park commissioners lying along and adjacent to the shore of Lake Michigan, between 12th and 39th Streets. Held on a 427 acre plot of land in Burnham Park, much of which was landfill, and boarding Lake Michigan, the Century of Progress opened May 27, 1933. The fair was opened when the lights were automatically activated when the light from the ray of the star Arcturus was detected. The star was chosen as its light had started its journey at about the time of the previous Chicago world's fair—the World's Columbian Exposition—in 1893. The rays were focused on photo-electric cells in a series of astronomical observatories and then transformed into electrical energy which was transmitted to Chicago.

The fair buildings were multi-colored, to create a "Rainbow City" as opposed to the "White City" of the World's Columbian Exposition. The buildings generally had a linear Art Deco design to them in contrast to the Grecian aspect of the earlier fair. One of the more famous aspects of the fair were the performances of fan dancer Sally Rand. Other popular exhibits were the various manufacturers, the Midway (filled with nightclubs such as Old Morocco, where featured stars Judy Garland, The Cook Family Singers and The Andrews Sisters performed), and a recreation of important scenes from Chicago's history.

The fair also contained exhibits that would seem shocking to contemporary audiences, including offensive portrayals of African-Americans, a "Midget City" complete with "sixty Lilliputians", and an exhibition of incubators containing real babies. One of the highlights of the 1933 World's Fair was the arrival of the German airship a Graf Zeppelin on October 26, 1933. After circling Lake Michigan near the exposition for two hours, Commander Hugo Eckener landed the 776-foot airship at the nearby Curtis-Wright Airport in Glenview. It remained on the ground for twenty-five minutes (from 1 to 1:25 p.m.) then took off ahead of an approaching weather front bound for Akron, Ohio. For some Chicagoans, however, the appearance of the Graf Zeppelin over their fair city was not a welcome sight, as the airship had become a prominent reminder of the ascendancy of Adolf Hitler to power earlier that same year. This triggered dissention in the days following its visit, particularly within the city's large German—American population. The "dream cars" which American automobile manufactures exhibited at the fair included Cadillac's introduction of its V-16 limousine; Nash's exhibit had a variation on the vertical (i.e. paternoster) parking garage—all the cars were new Nashes; Lincoln presented its rear-engined "concept car" precursor to the Lincoln-Zephyr, which went on the market in 1936 with a front engine; Pierce-Arrow presented its modernistic Silver arrow for which it used the byline "Suddenly it's 1940!" But it was Packard which won the best of show. One interesting and enduring exhibit was the 1933 Homes of Tomorrow Exhibition that demonstrated modern home convenience and creative practical new building materials and techniques with twelve model homes sponsored by several corporations affiliated with home décor and construction. The first Major League Baseball All-Star Game was held at Comiskey park (home of the Chicago White Sox) in conjunction with the fair. In May 1934 the Union Pacific

Railroad exhibited its first streamlined train, the M-10000, and the Burlington Route its famous Zephyr, which made a record-breaking dawn-to-dusk run from Denver, Colorado, to Chicago in 13 hours and 5 minutes. To cap its record-breaking speed run, the Zephyr arrived dramatically on-stage at the fair's "Wings of a Century" transportation pageant. The two trains launched an era of industrial streamlining. Both trains later went into successful revenue service, the union Pacific's as the City of Salina, and the Burlington zephyr as the first Pioneer Zephyr. The Zephyr is now on exhibit at Chicago's Museum of Science and Industry. The site of the fair is now home to Northerly island park (since the closing of Meigs Field) and McCormick Place. A column from the ruins of a Roman temple in Ostia given to Chicago by the Italian government to honor General Italo Balbo's 1933 trans-Atlantic flight still stands, although now by itself, not too far from Soldier Field. The city added a third red star to its flag in 1933 to commemorate the Exposition. (The fourth star of Chicago's flag was added five years later in 1939.)

Originally, the fair was scheduled only to run until November 12, 1933, but it was successful that it was opened again to run from May 26, to October 31, 1934. The fair was financed through the sale of memberships, which allowed purchases of a certain number of admissions once the park was open. This was done so the fair would not be subsidized by the government. More than $800,000 was raised in this manner as the country came out of the Great Depression. A $10 million bond was issued on October 28, 1929, the day before the stock market crashed. By the time the fair closed in 1933, half these notes had been retired, with the entire debt paid by the time the fair closed in 1934. For the first time in American history, an international fair had paid for itself. In its two years, it had attracted 48,769,227 visitors. According to James Truslow Adam's *Dictionary of*

American History, during the 170 days beginning May 27, 1933, there were 22.565,859 paid admissions; during the 163 days beginning May 26, 1934, there were 16,386,377; a total of 39,052,236.

Now gentle reader, let us begin to end this Reverie, by making use of articles obtained from the third edition of The American Nation written by John D. Hicks, the University of California, Berkeley, published by the Riverside Press Cambridge, Massachusetts 1941, 1949, 1955. During these years (1950, I attended graduate school at Cal earning a Master of Science degree (1952). It is felt that these articles could be of significant usefulness and assistance in understanding this Reverie and its impact on Chicago. The stock-market collapse came in October, 1929, when English interest rates were raised to six and one half percent in order to bring home needed capital that had been attracted to the United States by the high speculative profits. As a result many European holdings were thrown on the market, and prices began to sag. Frightened at the prospect, and no longer able to borrow at will, American speculators also began to unload. On Thursday, October 24, 1929, 12,800,000 shares changed hands, and until October 29, when the sales reached 16,410,030 shares, the frantic selling continued. During the month of October the value of stocks listed on the New York Stock Exchange declined from eight-seven billion to fifty-five billion dollars, or about thirty-seven percent. And this, it developed was only the beginning. In spite of repeated assurances from high authorities, both in government and in finance, that prosperity lay "just around the corner," no less than nine similar declines to "new low levels" were recorded within the next three years. By the first of March, 1933, the value of all stocks listed on the New York Stock Exchange was set at only nineteen billion dollars, less than one fifth the inflated figures of October 1, 1929. In spite of optimistic efforts to maintain that the stock-market collapse was purely a paper loss which would not seriously undermine the fundamental soundness of American business, it was soon evident that a period of unparalleled depression had begun. Prices dropped sharply; foreign trade fell off; factories curtailed production, or in many cases closed their doors never to reopen them; real estate values (but not mortgages) declined; new construction, except on governmental works, practically ceased; banks went under; worst of all, wages were cut drastically and unemployment figures began to mount. By the end of 1930 about six or seven million workers were out of jobs; two years later the number had doubled. Nor was the United States alone in its distress. No longer able to secure American loans, foreign nations fell likewise into the abyss of depression; indeed, many of them, like Germany, had not far to fall. Once again the isolationist-minded people of the United States were to learn by experience that whatever seriously affected one great nation was bound to affect all. Efforts to account for the plunge from prosperity to adversity soon demonstrated conclusively that no one factor alone, but only a great number of factors working together, could have produced such startling results. Economists were also able to reach substantial agreement as to the principal causes of the depression, although they were by no means in harmony as to the degree of responsibility to be assigned to each cause. Among other disturbing influences they cited the following:

1. Agricultural overexpansion, both in the United States and elsewhere. American farmers produced more wheat, cotton, corn, livestock, and other commodities than they could sell at satisfactory prices, and to some extent the same condition existed in much of the rest of the world. Agricultural surpluses piled up at home and abroad with devastating effect on the price of each new crop. Farm

purchases steadily declined, for the farmers had less and less with which to buy. Payments on the heavy mortgage burden assumed in more prosperous times still further curtailed the farmers' buying power, and drove many of them to tenancy.
2. Industrial overexpansion. The American industrial plant had been overbuilt during the period of the boom, and could not be operated at maximum capacity. There were too many factories, and too much machinery. American industry was geared to produce far more than it could sell. Automobiles, for example, had been turned out in steadily increasing numbers during the twenties to supply a new market. But the time came when every American family that could afford to own an automobile (and many who could not) had one or sometimes more than one. With twenty-six and one half million motor cars in operation by 1929, the market for automobiles was confined largely to replacements. The same condition existed in the housing industry. Rapid building during the twenties had over expanded the lumber industry and others concerned with the production of building new houses had built them, and plants that had once flourished stood idle.
3. The increasing effectiveness of machines. Ingenious labor-saving devices made possible greater production with comparatively less labor. Fewer and fewer men produced more and more goods. "Technological unemployment" might not be permanent, but at least the men who were thrown out of work by the new machines had to seek other jobs, and they sometimes failed to find them. Thus the buying power of labor was diminished. The new machines might make more goods, but whose wages were to pay for them? Introduction of these

labor-saving devices might well have been paralleled by increased wages, a shortening of the labor day and the labor week, and a diminishing use of women and children in industry. But only occasionally were such accompaniments recorded.
4. Capital surpluses were too high; as a prominent banker, Fran A. Vanderlip, expressed it, "Capital kept too much and labor did not have enough to buy its share of things." This was the more easily possible because of the monopolistic nature of much American business, which so greatly facilitated the control of prices. Throughout the boom years the tendency of business was to take too long profits, and to reinvest the capital thus accumulated in order to produce still more profits. A wider distribution of earnings, particularly if paid out in the form of high wages, might well have stimulated purchasing power and diminished the danger of ultimate collapse.
5. The overexpansion of credit, both for productive and consumptive purposes. Money was plentiful and cheap throughout the twenties, and the policy of the Federal Reserve Board was definitely to keep it so. It was too easy to borrow, whether for business expansion, for speculation, or for the satisfaction of personal desires. There was too much installment buying, and too much of the national income was diverted into interest payments. In keeping with the speculative spirit of the time, purchasers cheerfully mortgaged their futures to obtain goods that would often be consumed before they could be paid for.
6. International trade was out of balance, European nations, with their economics badly shattered by the war, had depended mainly on funds borrowed from American investors to pay for imports and to stabilize foreign

exchange. The only way they might have repaid these obligations was by shipping goods to the United States. But the Fordney-McCumber Act of 1922, followed by the Hawley-Smoot Act of 1930, definitely forestalled any such possibility. The debtor nations of Europe in self-defense were obliged to adopt high-tariff policies, and by various other expedients to stimulate whatever industries were necessary to cut down their reliance on foreign goods. During the years of 1922-27 the production of British-made automobiles, for example, was increased from forty-nine per cent of the domestic supply to eighty-six per cent. Thus the United States, blindly committed to the protective principles of an earlier age, stood to lose both its export business and a good share of the money by which this business had been sustained. Many manufacturers understood the situation, and did their best to prevent the adoption of tariffs that in the long run were certain to bring disaster, but most Americans were slow to recognize that international trade was a "two-way street," and were quite unprepared for the collapse that followed the withdrawal of American credits.

7. Political unrest throughout the world, particularly in Europe, Asia, and South America, added to the difficulties in the way of a sustained prosperity. The intergovernmental debts, whether funded or not, constituted a continuing threat both to trade and to international good feelings. The reparations problem remained unsettled. Most countries were overburdened with governmental debts, and few national budgets were in balance. Agitation for independence was chronic in India, the designs of Japan toward china were abundantly clear, and warfare soon broke out between Bolivia and Paraguay over the Chaco.

Altogether the international skies seemed dark, and the prospects of a return to "normalcy" as far away as ever.

Of tremendous interest in revealing the trend away from traditionalism in architecture toward the new ideal of "functionalism" was the Century of Progress Exposition which opened in Chicago during the spring of 1933, just forty years after Chicago's earlier world's fair had first startled the nation. From an architectural point of view the two expositions could hardly have stood in greater contrast. Visitors of 1893 saw a dream of classical beauty done in the purest white; visitors of 1933 saw huge, strangely shaped structures, painted with the boldest colors, and suggestive of nothing they had ever seen before. Only after nightfall, when the floodlights were loosed, could the ordinary observer appreciate the setting. But the buildings, windowless and curiously shaped as they were, served well the purposes for which they were built, a lesson that was by no means lost on the millions who saw them. Soon "modernistic" structures appeared all over the nation as architects vied with one another in the effort to make an honest adjustment of their materials to the needs they were meant to serve. The location of the Exposition also taught a lesson.

The land on which it stood was all "made land," dredged up from the bottom of Lake Michigan to provide a wide approach to the waterfront. After the fair was over the area was made into a city park, and still more dredged-up land was used to facilitate the construction of an elaborate system of automobile highways bordering upon the lake. City planning had made much progress since 1893, and the example of Chicago in taking better advantage of its natural setting was followed by many other cities. The Fair, in spite of the hard times, was no less successful financially than its predecessor of forty years before, and was held over for the following year. Six years later two other American cities, San Francisco and New York, held fairs. The setting for the Golden Gate Exposition was a four-hundred-acre man-made island in San Francisco Bay, and its purpose was to show how completely civilized western America and the Pacific Basin had become. The buildings essayed a blend of Mayan, Incan, Malayan, and other Pacific forms. In New York the "World of Tomorrow" was the principle theme of the most elaborate fair ever staged in America. The exposition grounds occupied nearly two square miles of territory in Flushing Meadows, at the very heart of Greater New York, and the project involved an expenditure of over one hundred and fifty million dollars. The buildings showed that the search for architectural innovations had by no means ceased, but the garish colors and angular lines of the Century of Progress were much toned down. Both the Golden Gate Exposition and the World of Tomorrow were reopened the succeeding year, but in spite of large attendances neither was able to duplicate the financial success of the Century of Progress. These three world's fairs, quite apart from the revolt they registered against architectural traditions, made significant contributions to American life. The millions who visited them came away with a better understanding of the intricate processes by which the scientific advancement of their age had been attained, and with a conviction that the wonders of the future would far surpass anything they had yet seen. They learned much, too, about the rest of the world that schoolroom lessons in geography could never have been taught them, and in consequence were better prepared for the era of international change so soon to burst upon them. And whether they traveled to the East or to the West or to both, by automobile or by streamlined train or by airplane, they could hardly fail to observe the limitless resources with which their country was blessed, and the anachronism of poverty and unemployment in a land so rich.

Now again, gentle readers, let us end this Reverie, with a few thoughts on the Depression and War (1929-1945). The depression that began during the first years of the Hoover administration lasted on in varying degrees of intensity until the outbreak of the Second World War. Hoover as President bent every effort to restore normal times, a radical departure from the behavior of most earlier Presidents, to whom a downward turn of the business cycle was a matter for business itself to handle, rather than the government. But Hoover soon realized that without governmental intervention the whole economic structure of the nation would collapse. For the banks, the railroads, the insurance companies, and a vast number of other great business corporations to be forced into bankruptcy was a greater calamity than the government could sit idly by and permit. Furthermore, as the needs of the unemployed outran the resources of state and local authorities, the national government had to assume an increasing responsibility for the problem of relief.

The measures taken by the Hoover administration thus served as a kind of springboard for the new Deal. Under Franklin D. Roosevelt the government went much further than Hoover had contemplated in its efforts to cure the depression, but the methods of the two administrations differed more in degree than in kind. The New Deal was not nearly as revolutionary as radical theorists wished it to be, or as thorough going conservatives have portrayed it. It sought to preserve, not to destroy, the capitalist system, but to achieve this end it was ready to make startling innovations. Roosevelt himself was less the theorist than the man of action, willing to try almost anything once that seemed to give promise of help, and totally unembarrassed by contradictions and inconsistencies. He hoped by economic planning and the use of governmental authority to put an end to the business cycle, to maintain full employment, and to better the lot of the underprivileged, but it was principally reform that he had in mind, not revolution. By the end of his second administration, he had achieved a great deal, but at a cost in governmental indebtedness that then seemed colossal.

The international background of the New Deal was the breakdown of world peace. While the United States had turned aside from the main currents of world affairs to enjoy the prosperity of the 1920's and to struggle against the adversity of the 1930's, the makers of national policy both in Europe and in Asia had pursued courses that could lead only to war. Russian Communism, Italian Fascism, German Naziism, and Japanese stateism all had their predatory sides; each planned to expand its system and interests at the expense of the futile gestures, while in the United States the number of those who were willing to risk anything by way of collective action against the potential aggressors was small indeed. The isolationists were in the saddle; the rest of the world could have its war if it wished, but the United States would keep out. It was apparent that Roosevelt leaned toward the side of collective security, but he was not able to secure a substantial following until war in Europe had actually broken out; then, as far as keeping the peace was concerned, it was too late. But it was not too late to show a united front toward the aggressors, and the danger to the United States involved in a complete Axis victory brought many belated conversions. With the defeat of France, the control of the Atlantic was imperiled, while in Asia Japanese conquests at the expense of China, and will for other conquests elsewhere, made Americans realize the danger to their Pacific outposts. No doubt Roosevelt saw well in advance of most Americans the inevitability of American participation in the war, and he did what he could to prepare his countrymen for it. With the attack on Pearl Harbor, "measures short of war" gave way to war measures on a more prodigious scale than the nation had ever known before.

The war was fought through to a complete victory, both in Europe and in Asia. In the Pacific theater the United States had the chief responsibility, but chose to fight a holding war until the defeat of the Axis powers in Europe. In required for the invasion of North Africa and Italy, and for the cross-channel attack from England that led to Germany's defeat. For all Allied participants American supplies were of fundamental importance. To carry on these vast undertakings, the American economic machine, lagging during the depression, went at last into high gear.

THE APOSTLE OF FREEDOM— A REVERIE

April 4th is a day of remembrance for Martin Luther King (1929-1968). All of us here at RRC should remember the 50's and 60's and those turbulent years in the history of our country. It is good for us to reflect on the struggle that our fellow black Americans made to obtain true freedom. It is easy to forget those days, hence this reverie to help us remember those days and the impact they had on our country. I again turn to my friend Robert Ellsberg and his reflection on Martin Luther King in his book "All Saints." The cross is something that you bear and ultimately that you die on.

"In a church in Montgomery, Alabama, on December 2, 1955, a young Baptist minister named Martin Luther King, Jr., at the time only twenty-six and fresh from graduate school in Boston, stood up before a packed audience of protesters. The previous day Mrs. Rosa Parks, a black seamstress, had been arrested after refusing to yield her seat on a bus to a white man. The incident immediately sparked a bus boycott by the city's black population. King, only newly arrived in Montgomery for his first pastoral assignment, had been drafted to lead the protest committee. As he faced the expectant crowd before him that evening he began, "As you know, my friends, there comes a time when people get tired of being trampled over by the iron feet of oppression." The church erupted with applause and cries of "Yes!" "If we are wrong-God Almighty is wrong! If we are wrong," he continued, "Jesus of Nazareth was merely a utopian dreamer and never came down to Earth! If we are wrong, justice is a lie!"

It was an extraordinary speech that galvanized the struggle in Montgomery as surely as it launched King's career as a leader of the black freedom struggle in America. When at last the campaign in Montgomery was won, the tactics of nonviolent resistance tested there were applied and extended throughout the South. King proved to be a gifted political strategist, as well as a brilliant orator. But he was more. He was a prophet, in the truest biblical sense, who proclaimed to his generation the justice and mercy of God, remaining true to his mission even to the laying down of his life.

A critical moment of doubt came early in his journey. One night in 1957 a death threat was delivered over the phone. He had already faced plenty of violence and hatred. But somehow the strain of the moment and the implicit threat not only to himself but to his family brought him to the limit of his strength. He went into the kitchen and as he sat there with a cup of coffee he turned himself over to God. "Almost out of nowhere I heard a voice. 'Martin Luther, stand up for righteousness. Stand up for justice. Stand up for truth. And lo, I will be with you, even until the end of the world.'" Afterward, he said, "I was ready to face anything."

His house was bombed. He was repeatedly jailed. On one occasion he was nearly fatally stabbed. But he was never again tempted by doubt or despair. All the while he continued to grow in his commitment to nonviolence, not simply as a political tactic, but as a thoroughgoing principle of life, a means appropriate to his constant goal-what he called the Beloved

Community. In 1963 at the Lincoln Memorial in Washington, D.C., he delivered his famous "I Have a Dream Speech." That speech summarized his most hopeful image of an America Redeemed by the transforming power of love: "When we allow freedom to ring, when we let it ring from every village and every hamlet, from every state and every city, we will be able to speed up that day when all of God's children, black men and white men, Jews and Gentiles, Protestants and Catholics, will be able to join hands and sing in the words of the old Negro spiritual: "Free at last, Free at last. Thank God Almighty, we are free at last.""

King's popularity was never higher. Within a year he had won the Nobel Peace Prize. But he did not cling to the safety of honor. Instead he continued to grow, to delve deeper into the roots of American racism and violence, to plumb deeper into the challenge of his vocation as a minister of God. In 1967 he broke with many of his colleagues and supporters by publicly speaking out against the Vietnam War. He became increasingly critical of the structures of power in the United States, and he began to forge the bonds of a radical alliance that would unite poor people of all colors in the struggle for social change. J. Edgar Hoover, director the FBI, who had for many years waged a covert effort to destroy King, publicly called him the most dangerous man in America.

But the roots of King's challenge and hope lay not in any political philosophy. They were based on his faith in the promise of God-the faith, expressed in his maiden speech, that God is not a liar. As he said in 1965,

> Truth crushed to earth will rise again. How long? Not long! Because no lie can live forever. How long? Not long? Not long! . . . Truth forever on the scaffold, wrong forever on the throne. Yet that scaffold sways

the future and behind the dim unknown standeth God within the shadow, keeping watch over his own. How long? Not long! Because the arc of the moral universe is long but it bends toward justice.

By that time King's days were already numbered. In April 1968 he was in Memphis to lend support to the city's striking sanitation workers. He seemed increasingly to anticipate his appointment with destiny. On the evening of April 3 he addressed a rally and ended with these words:

> Well, I don't know what will happen now. We've got some difficult days ahead. But it doesn't matter with me now. Because I've been to the mountaintop. And I don't mind. Like anybody, I would like to live a long life. Longevity has its place. But I'm not concerned about that now. I just want to do God's will. And he's allowed me to go up to the mountain. And I've looked over. And I've seen the promised land. I may not get there with you. But I want you to know tonight that we, as a people, will get to the promised land. And I'm happy tonight. I'm not worried about anything. I'm not fearing any man. Mine eyes have seen the glory of the coming of the Lord.

He was assassinated the next day.

King did not represent himself as a saint. Posthumous revelations of some of his weaknesses underscored the fact that King, at the time of his death, was still evolving, still on the way to reconciling the logic of his faith with his personal conduct. But nothing detracts from his role as a "drum major of freedom." He said of himself, "I want you to know . . . that I am a sinner like all God's children. But I want to be a good man.

And I want to hear a voice saying to me one day, 'I take you in and I bless you, because you tried.'" King struggled to be more than his weakest qualities. He challenged the church and all Americans to do the same."

UNIVERSITY OF ST. MARY OF THE LAKE MUNDELEIN SEMINARY—A REVERIE

The University of St. Mary of the Lake/Mundelein Seminary is the major seminary and school of theology for the Archdiocese of Chicago. Many of the students will serve dioceses in the United States and abroad. The University of St. Mary of the Lake had its beginnings as Saint Mary's College. In 1844, the first bishop of Chicago, the Right Reverend William J. Quarter, D.D. received from the State of Illinois a charter giving the university the power "to confer . . . such academic or honorary degrees as are usually conferred by similar institutions." Chicago welcomed Saint Mary's as the first institution of higher education in the city. The University of St. Mary of the Lake flourished until 1866, when financial difficulties forced it to close. In 1921, Archbishop George Mundelein opened a new seminary forty-five miles northwest of the original campus. Saint Mary of the Lake Seminary would operate under the same charter originally granted to the University of St. Mary of the Lake, making it the longest continuous academic charter in the State of Illinois. In 1926, the new seminary was host to the world, as one of the sites of the International Eucharistic Congress. The campus made transportation history with that event for it required the largest movement of people by rail in the history of the country. In September of 1929, the seminary received a second charter, this time from the Holy See. Cardinal Mundelein obtained from the Sacred Congregation for Seminaries and Universities the authority to grant the international academic degrees of the Holy See. In 1934 the Ecclesiastical Faculty of Theology at Mundelein was honored with a permanent grant of this authority. The seminary became the first American institution to be honored as a pontifical theological faculty under the Apostolic Constitution Deus Scientarium Dominus. Under the leadership of Albert Cardinal Meyer, in 1961 the seminary opened a second campus in Niles, Illinois. The Niles campus became the site for the two-year liberal arts program. The Mundelein campus included the upper class college studies in philosophy followed by a four year theology curriculum. Under Cardinal Meyer's successor, John Cardinal Cody, the undergraduate program was affiliated with Loyola University of Chicago and became Niles College of Loyola University. Saint Mary of the Lake Seminary was now strictly a graduate school of theology. The program which resulted from that revision continued to be implemented for more than a decade, its academic, formation/spiritual and pastoral aspects guided by the Program of Priestly formation of the National Conference of Catholic Bishops and the directives of the Sacred Congregation of Education.

In 1971, Saint Mary of the Lake Seminary became affiliated with the Association of Theological Schools of the United States and Canada, which is the accrediting body for theological seminaries and divinity schools. 1976 saw two milestones in the seminary history. In cooperation with the Center for Pastoral Ministry, the Archdiocese of Chicago's continuing education school, the seminary began a program of studies leading to the new doctor of ministry degree. Also in 1976, the seminary celebrated the 50th anniversary of the first ordinations held in the Chapel of the Immaculate Conception. In the fall of 1982, under the direction of Archbishop Joseph Bernardin, the seminary faculty initiated a thorough revision of the program which had been in place for ten years. The changes had as their goal the better implementation of the objectives set forth in the third edition of the Program of Priestly Formation. Cardinal Bernardin announced a new and exciting development in April of 1986. The University of St. Mary of the Lake would be revived with the addition of the continuing education school, renamed the Center for Development in Ministry, to the campus. The new center would continue the work of continuing education for priests, which was the mission of the Center for Pastoral Ministry, but would now expand to offer continuing education to all those in ministry, clergy, religious and laity. Saint Mary of the Lake Seminary again adopted the name on its original 1844 charter, the University of St. Mary of the Lake, and honored its second founder by renaming the graduate school as Mundelein Seminary.

During the spring of 1996, Mundelein Seminary was visited by members of the Bishops' Committee on Seminaries. After an extensive series of meetings with faculty and students, the members of the committee gave a strong recommendation to the seminary program. Francis Cardinal George continued this development of the university in February 2000 by transferring the archdiocese of Chicago's programs of ministry formation to the seminary. Three former agencies of the Pastoral Center were transferred here to become programs of Mundelein Seminary. Joining USML that year were the Lay Ministry Formation Program, the Diaconate formation Program and the Instituto de Liderazgo Pastoral. While remaining separate and distinct from the priestly formation program, all are to cooperate under the seminary aegis in advancing the efforts of ministry preparation and formation for all those involved in pastoral ministry. Plans were also begun to separate the continuing education programs of the Center for Development in Ministry from the university and to relocate them as an agency of the Pastoral Center. These same plans included the continued operation of a Conference Center at the University of Saint Mary of the Lake. This would make Mundelein Seminary the center for all basic formation for ministry, while leaving continuing formation to other agencies. To reflect this evolution, the board of Advisors decided to adopt a compound name, The University of St. Mary of the Lake/Mundelein Seminary. This follows the style of most of the pontifical universities which have a formal name and a common name which become interchangeable. Also, in 2000, Cardinal George established the Liturgical Institute at the University of St. Mary of the Lake/Mundelein seminary. This is the first step in a new vision of the cardinal to expand the university to include specialized institutes to support the major ministries of the archdiocese. The Liturgical Institute has its own faculty and is dedicated to training, research and publication in the fields of sacramental theology and liturgy. The Institute offers a professional master of arts in liturgy, an academic master of arts (liturgical studies), and a licentiate in sacred theology. All degrees are awarded by the University of St. Mary of the Lake/Mundelein Seminary. Other specialized institutes are planned for the near future along these same lines.

Of particular note is the Feehan Memorial Library. This specialized library has over 180,000 volumes. It is one of the outstanding libraries in the country in the fields of patristics and church history. The library maintains subscriptions to over 500 American and foreign language serial publications related to theology. Through its membership in the Association of Chicago Theological Schools, an ecumenical consortium of ten seminaries, students have further access to 1.5 million books and 5,000 periodicals. Plans are currently underway for a major expansion of the library with the addition of Theological Resource Center. This will double the capacity and study space of the Feehan Memorial Library. The original structure will be kept and renovated and the new Theological Resource Center integrated into it.

Let us end this reverie with three remarks on Mundelein from Cardinal George. The first remark concerns the Benedictine Convent of Perpetual Adoration (Marytown, Libertyville, Illinois). The Marytown site in Libertyville, Illinois has been home to a convent, monastery, retreat center and shrine. After the International Eucharistic Congress in 1926 which took place at St. Mary's Seminary in Mundelein, George Cardinal Mundelein invited the Benedictine Sisters of Perpetual Adoration from Clyde, Missouri to establish a permanent sanctuary of adoration. Perpetual Adoration of Jesus in the Blessed Sacrament has taken place here since June 7, 1928. The chapel and convent were completed in 1932. In 1977 the Benedictine sisters left, and the ministry was taken up by an order of Conventual Franciscan Friars who relocated here from Kenosha in 1978. In 1998 a retreat center was added to the site for personal or group retreats and conferences. In 2000 the National Conference of Catholic Bishops designated the site as the national Shrine of St. Maximillian Kolbe who was canonized in 1982 by Pope John Paul II as a "martyr of charity." Father Maximilian was killed at Auschwitz in 1941.

The second remark concerns Mundelein's first fire truck is headed home as written by Diana Newton on October 2, 2008 for PIONEER PRESS. Cardinal George Mundelein gave the truck to the village in 1925, and now it will figure prominently in the village's 100 year anniversary celebrations next year. The Village Board voted September 22 to purchase the 1925 Stoughton fire truck from Jim Carew for $11,000. Carew, who retired as a Mundelein fire lieutenant in 1993, restores old fire trucks at his shop in Bristol, Wis. He bought the truck 15 years ago after a friend located it just days before it was headed for the scrap heap. "I'm going to be tickled pink to see it on the road again," Carew said. "They only made 21 of them." "We're really looking forward to bringing the fire truck home and presenting it to all the residents of Mundelein," said Bob Stadlman, chair of the centennial fire truck committee. The village's Centennial Committee must raise another $50,000 or $60,000 in private funds to restore the truck, said Mayor Kenneth Kessler, who promised to help raise the first $5,000. "I'm very optimistic there will be a great deal of interest," Kessler said.

"We have body shops in town and hundreds of people who love cars and antique vehicles. There is a great deal of talent around that will rally around this project." "I think it's a fabulous idea," said Wendy Frasier, chairman of the Centennial Committee. "There aren't a lot of old things that Mundelein has. It's very exciting to know that we are going to be able to restore something from when Mundelein was named Mundelein."

Cardinal Mundelein was stationed at what is now called University of St. Mary of the Lake/Mundelein Seminary. The cardinal was part of another historic moment. He organized the XXVII International Eucharistic Congress in Mundelein in 1926, the first of its kind in the United States, drawing 500,000 people. "Cardinal Mundelein had tremendous vision," said Dottie Watson, a volunteer with the Historical Society of the Fort Hill Country, the Fort Hill Heritage Museum and the Centennial Committee. "People came together and felt that because of what he was doing at the seminary, the name of the village should be changed from Area to Mundelein. At first, he was reluctant. But he gave it some thought and was very appreciative. He, in turn, gave the village its first fire truck." "We had not trucks, only a horse-drawn fire wagon," Kessler said. "The Centennial Committee said, "Wouldn't it be cool to get this historical piece representing Mundelein back in our possession?" The name Area came from the principles of a business school that was located where the seminary is now. Area stood for ability, reliability, endurance and action, Watson said. The village also has been named Mechanics Grove. Holcomb and Rockefeller (not after John D., but his brother William), she said. Carew will oversee the restoration of the truck. He already had rebuilt the engine and pump, but it needs substantial work. "I carried it home in milk crates and bushel baskets," Carew said. "The tires, engine and chassis were the only things I rolled." The restoration job normally would take two to three years, but it has been put on the fast track. Carew said a friend will help him, but Stadiman said others may be needed. "We're hoping some of the repair shops in town might show an interest in fabricating parts or perhaps doing some painting or mechanical repairs," Stadiman said. "They might be very proud to know that they were involved in the project in some small way." After the centennial, the truck will be used for education and in other ceremonies. For more information on the Centennial Committee or to volunteer, go to the village Web site at *www.mundelein.org* and click on the centennial link. "We're asking people to be very interactive with the Web site," Stadiman said. "If anyone has a memory of Mundelein, we want them to go to the Web site and put in their memory. They also can upload pictures."

The third remark concerns our American cardinal, George Mundelein. He was born July 2, 1872 in New York, and died October 2, 1939 in Mundelein, Illinois. The Cardinal and Archbishop of Chicago was a leading figure in the Americanization of the Roman Catholic church in the United States. Mundelein was educated at seminaries in New York and Pennsylvania, he studied theology in Rome and was ordained there in June 1895. In 1909 he was named auxiliary bishop of Brooklyn, N.Y. and in 1915, without previous administrative experience, became archbishop of Chicago. As Archbishop, Mundelein refused to sanction national parishes for immigrant

Roman *Catholics*-a measure designed to encourage their integration into the mainstream of U.S. *culture*-and he made English the language of instruction in parochial schools. He was created a cardinal by Pope Pius XI in 1924. Mundelein was a prominent figure at the International Eucharistic Congress held in Chicago in 1926, attended by Roman Catholics from around the world. He founded St. Mary of the Lake Seminary at Mundelein, Il. A town near Chicago named in his honour.

> "Love so that you bear outwardly as well as inwardly the image of Christ crucified, the model of all gentleness and mercy."
> St. Paul of the Cross

God wants nothing of you but the gift of a peaceful heart.
Mister Eckhart

A MID-LENTEN REVERIE

Since the end of the Christmas season, many of the readings of the Sunday and weekly masses selected passages from the Old Testament. They introduced us to stories of great interest and how they related to the New Testament; "what is concealed in the Old Testament is revealed in the New Testament." Here are some very brief comments that hopefully will help us in our understanding of these biblical passages. These readings deal with three books of the Old Testament: Joshua, Judges and Samuel. Many find Judges the most interesting and exciting book of the Old Testament. The time of the Judges is a time of transformation for Israel. It can be adequately understood only when taken against the background provided by the book of Joshua and in consideration of the changes a people must undergo when passing from a nomadic to an agricultural life, from a loose confederation to a unified kingdom. The place of Judges in relation to the past and the future can be shown as follows:

Joshua	1250-1225	Period of conquest
Judges	1225-1025	Period of transformation
Samuel	1025-965	Period of consolidation and expansion

To understand the frequent wars narrated in Judges, the gentle reader must be reminded that the conquest of Palestine by Joshua was limited in scope, restricted for the most part to the hill country of Judah and Samaria. To understand the social transformation that took place during the period of the Judges, you must remember that the generation of Israelites who conquered the hill country around 1225 B.C. had spent almost forty years in the desert, and their conquest of CANAAN represented the invasion and conquest of a civilized land by people who were semi-nomadic and culturally barbarians. Settling down required a transformation from the semi-nomadic life of the desert to the sedentary agricultural life of Canaan. That these were as a result of barbaric times can be seen from some of the incidents related in Judges 1:7; 8:16; 9:5; 11:31; and 19. Beside the social transformation, there was also a political transformation. Before and during the conquest, the tribes had been led by Moses and Joshua. During the period of the Judges, there was no longer any central authority or centralized apparatus of government. Israel consisted of a loose confederation of tribes, whose only bond was the SINAI pact and its symbol-the Ark of the Covenant, located at Shiloh in the central hill country. The subjection and oppression of the tribes by neighboring nations during the period of the Judges was a result, therefore, not only of Israel's sins but of her political disunity. Under Samuel, the last of the Judges, the tribes realized the necessity of a central government if they were to survive. This in due time led to the institution of the monarchy in Israel under Samuel and Saul.

The book of Judges is named after its principal protagonists, the twelve Judges. These men are not primarily judicial magistrates. They are military leaders sent by God at critical moments in Israel's history to save the nation from destruction. As is true of most of the books of the Bible, the primary purpose of the author of Judges is to teach religion rather than to record history. What he proposes to teach his contemporaries and us that while GOD cannot brook sin and rebellion and that He invariably punishes the defections of His people. He also always saves them from extinction. Implicit in this teaching is the exalted conception of the sanctity and fidelity God demands from those whom He has chosen in a special way to be His representative people on earth-an idea as valid today as it was at the time Judges was written. Here is a quick summary. In the Book of Joshua, the chosen people had FIDELITY but had INFIDELITY. This INFIDELITY led to their cycle of (1.) sin, (2.) punishment, (3.) repentance, (4.) forgiveness and then this cycle would be repeated over and over again.

Chapters 10 and 11 of Judges are an excellent example of the infidelity of the chosen people, repeated and asked for forgiveness. God in His mercy then sent them a charismatic leader (a judge) who conquered their enemies. The Israelites then lived in peace and harmony with God but slowly evil crept in and the cycle would be repeated. Let us begin to finish this reverie with some significant passages on JEPHTHAH. Oppressed by the Ammonites (10:6), the people of Transjordan between Bashan on the north and Moab on the south (10:6-18), the Gileadites, a clan of Manesseh, located just south of Bashanm, called upon Jephthah to lead their forces against the oppressors. (Any map of the division of Canaan can be found in any Bible and will clearly indicate these cities and tribes.)

Jephthah was born of a harlot. His father had other sons who, upon growing up, found out about Jephthah's background and drove him out of town: "You shall inherit nothing in our family" (Judges 11:2). Jephthah turned into an outlaw, heading up a gang of raiders. His reputation as a skilled fighter and leader spread. When the Gileadites could find not leader, in desperation they turned to Jephthah, he accepted. "The stone rejected by the builders becomes the cornerstone." The spirit comes upon Jephthah, and he leads the Israelites to victory. Jephthah's vow (11:30) was probably fulfilled literally when he returned victorious over the Ammonites (11:34-39). This episode, along with many others in the book of Judges, shows the barbarous state of affairs during this period and also the strange things that can be done in good faith out of unenlightened theological motives. Jephthah never should have made a deal with God after God had promised him victory.

Well, my friends, we are now about halfway through Lent and just possibly our Lenten resolutions may need a "shot in the arm" (keep smiling). So why not add this resolution to your all ready made resolutions: To read Joshua, Judges, and Samuel during the last three weeks of Lent, one book a week. You'll never regret it and the Lord can never be outdone in generosity, your reward will be great.

HAVE A HAPPY AND HOLY EASTER, and I hope you will find your next Easter morning (certainly might bring back a long forgotten but happy memory)!

A YEAR FOR PRIESTS—
A REVERIE

The following article was written by the Very Reverend James Presta, S.T.D. '82.

On June 19, 2009, the Feast of the Sacred Heart of Jesus, Pope Benedict XVI proclaimed a year for priests. The special jubilee year of grace coincides with the 150th anniversary of the death of St. John Marie Vianney, the Cure D'Ars, the patron saint of parish priests, who died in 1859. The Pope called for a year to pray for the spiritual perfection of the priest, to pray that priests will grow in holiness so that they can teach and assist God's people in the ways of spiritual perfection. The Year for Priests will conclude in Rome on June 11, 2010, the Feast of the Sacred Heart, when Pope Benedict hopes that thousands of priests will gather with him in the Eternal City for the closing ceremonies of this special year for priests.

Here at the seminary, we have taken seriously this Year for Priests in a number of ways. Please allow me to share those ways with you:

1. Each morning at 7:00 a.m., as we begin our Meditation time, we offer a "Prayer for Priests" as a community.
2. On Thursdays, whenever the liturgical calendar permits it, we celebrate the Votive Mass of Jesus the Eternal High Priest, so that we can offer Mass for the priests of

the Archdiocese and around the world. Also, on some Fridays, we offer the Votive Mass of the Sacred Heart, asking Jesus to make holy our beloved priests who serve the Church so faithfully and generously each day.

3. We have purchased a beautiful icon of Jesus the Priest which is venerated in our seminary Chapel.
4. Once a month, we celebrate Evenings of Recollection and focus a talk on different aspects of the priestly ministry of St. John Vianney and how it relates to our seminarians as they discern their call to the priesthood. During the evening, the Blessed Sacrament is exposed on our altar and our men are asked to keep silence in the Seminary as we contemplate the Lord's love for priests and all God's people.
5. Each seminarian has been given three books this year to focus on our priesthood theme. One is a book by Fr. George Rutler on the life of St. John Vianney. Another is a book of meditations for seminarians called Radical Surrender: Letters to Seminarians by Fr. Michael Najim, published by the Institute on Priestly Formation for this special jubilee year of the preist. We also have a beautiful pamphlet published by Magnificat with reflections on the priesthood and prayers for priests.
6. On Wednesday, October 21, our seminary community traveled to Mundelein Seminary to see a one act play by Leonardo Di Fillipis called Vianney. The seminarians were inspired by the performance and it helped them to focus on the life of St. John Vianney and how his life and ministry touches their vocational journey to the priesthood.
7. In October, fourteen of our seminarians traveled with three seminary priests and myself on a Pilgrimage to Canada. We were able to see so many beautiful Catholic

Shrines. Most notable was St. Joseph's Oratory in Montreal, the world's largest shrine dedicated to the foster-father of Jesus Christ. During the pilgrimage, the seminarians reflected on various aspects of the call to priesthood and were able to pray for priests and priestly vocations throughout the four day sojourn through Catholic Canada.

Our 32 St. Joseph seminarians have taken seriously this Year for Priests as they look at various aspects of priesthood and how they feel inspired and challenged by the Lord's call to priestly service in His Church. Our seminarians have been reflecting on the lives of those priests who have become saints to draw inspiration for their priestly vocation. They also have so many priests in their lives that have inspired them to consider God's call to priesthood. The priest who baptized them; the priest who heard their first confession or gave them their first holy communion; the priest who comforted their family with the Anointing of the Sick when a relative was infirmed or near death; or the priest who visited school or trained them as an altar server. Indeed our college seminarians have been inspired by many priests, those in heaven and those here on earth, and they dare to courageously, generously and faithfully respond to God's call to service in the Church as future priests. I am confident that you also have stories of priests who have inspired you to be faithful in the practice of your Catholic faith. I am sure you have met priests who are inspirations to you and your loved ones. I am positive that you know so many priests who have given wonderful priestly zeal and enthusiasm to carrying out their sacred duties each day! Join me and join our St. Joseph seminarians in thanking God for priests who so selflessly and generously serve the Lord's Church.

In the winter issue of "The Carpenter's Workshop," you will read about the seminarians of St. Joseph College Seminary who tell their vocational stories about why God is calling them to the Holy Priesthood of Jesus Christ. You will see this in many reflections offered by our men. In particular, I call your attention to the summer apostolate reflections of our men who spent ten weeks in parishes around the archdiocese of Chicago, living in rectories with priests, shadowing parish priests in their duties and offering their service to the Lord's people in the parishes. These men will share how they have been touched by God's spirit to dream about the possibility of one day being ordained a priest of Jesus Christ! I found their stories so inspiring and full of hope for me as a priest of twenty-three years! I am sure they will inspire you as well!

> Enjoy our winter 2010 issue of "The Carpenter's Workshop."
> I wish you a most blessed New Year!
> In the Most Sacred Heart of Jesus,
> Very Reverend James Presta, S.T.D. '82

P.S. Please allow me one final note: After much reflection and with the blessing of Cardinal George, I will be leaving St. Joseph College Seminary after fourteen years of service as Rector. It has been a tremendous blessing to be the pastor of this college seminary over these many eyars and to have met some very fine young men who have taken seriously the mission of this place: to discern the call to priesthood! By the way, I will continue working with seminary formation after I leave here. As of July 1, 2010, I will be full-time member of the Mundelein Seminary faculty. More to come in the next issue! For now, please pray for me as I will pray for all of you!

Now, gentle readers, let us begin to end our Reverie by reading about St. John Vianney, the Cure of Ars (1786-1859) that our friend Robert Ellsberg has written about him in his book "All Saints".

The early life of John Vianney contained no foreshadowing of greatness in any field. He was born to a peasant family in a village near Lyons. Though he desired nothing else but to be a priest, his humble background and lack of education made it unlikely that he could ever realize such a vocation. Nevertheless with the help of private tutoring he secured a place in seminary. His studies were interrupted when he was conscripted to serve in the army. On his way to a posting in Spain he deserted and went into hiding for several years in a neighboring village. Only with an amnesty in 1810 was he able to resume his formation. For all his zeal, Vianney proved to be a miserable student. It was only with grave reservations that he was recommended for ordination. In the end, however, his evident piety and goodness won the day. As one of his sponsors noted, "The Church wants not only learned priests but even more holy ones." Thus he was finally ordained at the age of twenty-nine. He served for a brief time as curate in his home parish. And then in 1817 he was named the parish priest of Ars-en-Dombes, a village of 250 souls, as remote and insignificant a place as his Bishop could find. To Vianney there was nothing insignificant about his new home. The size of the village was unimportant. He regarded himself as answerable for the salvation of his flock. This was an awesome charge, which he accepted with all the determination of a soldier ordered to hold his position. Compensating for lack of learning, he girded himself for his responsibilities by ascetic zeal. This did not go unnoticed. It was said that the new cure lived on nothing but potatoes. He never seemed to sleep. When not visiting parishioners or performing the sacraments he could invariably be found in the church, fixed in silent adoration of the Eucharist.

The cure's sermons were simple and unsophisticated. His theology was rudimentary. His efforts to elevate the spiritual level of his community by combating the evils of profanity, public dances, and work on Sunday seemed, even at the time, to verge on the naïve. But what gradually dawned on his parishioners and began to work its gradual effect was the consciousness that their souls mattered to this holy priest and that he suffered for their sins. For all his simplicity, there was one area in which Vianney acquired a reputation for genius: his extraordinary gifts as a confessor. It was said that he had an ability to read souls. With disarming simplicity, the Cure' d'Ars was apparently able to discern the secrets of his penitents, and unlock the barriers that prevented them from knowing and loving God. This gift attracted a growing stream of penitents which gradually expanded so as to lay claim to nearly all of his waking hours. Fixed in his cramped confessional, shivering in the winter, stifling in the summer, he would sit ten, twelve, as many as eighteen hours a day.

Toward the end of his life the railroad provided special trains to accommodate the heavy traffic of pilgrims to the famous confessional in Ars. By the time of his death in 1859 Vianney was one of the most beloved figures in France. Various honors were bestowed on him. Napoleon III, in a curious gesture, sent him the medal of the Legion of Honor. Vianney refused to take it out of the box, remarking, "I don't know what I have done to deserve this except to be a deserter." Certainly Vianney never sought or anticipated such fame. It was literally one more cross that he shouldered. Vianney could not imagine any more important calling than to serve as the parish priest of the village of Ars. This was the post where he had been placed to care for the souls of his flock, ready, like the good shepherd, to lay down his life for them, if that were required. St. John Vianney was canonized in 1925 by

Pope Pius XI. At the same time he was named patron saint of all parish priests.

Let us now end this Reverie by reading a prayer for Priests composed by Cardinal Dougherty, Archbishop of Philadelphia:

A PRAYER FOR PRIESTS

Keep them, I pray Thee, dearest Lord,
Keep them, for they are Thine-
Thy priests whose lives burn out before
They consecrated shrine.
Keep them, for they are in the world,
Though from the world apart;
When earthly pleasures tempt, allure,
Shelter them in They heart.
Keep them, and comfort them in hours
Of loneliness and pain,
When all their life of sacrifice
For souls seems but in vain.
Keep them, and O remember, Lord,
They have no one but Thee,
Yet they have only human hearts,
With human frailty,
Keep them as spotless as the Host,
That daily they caress;
Their every thought and word and deed,
Deign, dearest Lord, to bless.

Mary, Queen of the Clergy, pray for them.

The priesthood is a masterpiece of Christ's divine love, wisdom and power.

"Jesus, Mary, I love you, save souls."

A RELIGIOUS REVERIE

Psalm one is a preface to the whole Book of Psalms; it outlines the lot of the good and of the wicked.

PSALM 1
True Happiness

I
1. Happy the man who follows not
     the counsel of the wicked
   Nor walks in the way of sinners,
        nor sits in the company of the insolent,
2. But delights in the law of the LORD
         and meditates on his law day and
         night.
3. He is like a tree
     planted near running water,
   That yields its fruit in due season,
      and whose leaves never fade.
      (Whatever he does, prospers.)
  II
4. Not so the wicked, not so;
      they are like chaff which the wind

drives away.
5. Therefore in judgment the wicked shall
not stand,
nor shall sinners, in the assembly of
the just.
6. For the LORD watches over the way of
the just,
but the way of the wicked vanishes.

What follows now are some articles that were printed in the Catholic New World, a newspaper for the Archdiocese of Chicago, IL. CNW, May 10-23, 2009 (Two Articles) Who Is Our Mother? And On Life Issue, Cardinal George says Obama on 'wrong side of history'.

Who is our Mother?
By Francis Cardinal George O.M.I.

On Mother's Day, each of us does something extra to tell our mother that we love her and are grateful for her love. If out mother has died, Catholics remember her at Mass in a particular manner. Mothers' Day began as a religious remembrance, although it was secularized fairly early, becoming, like most major civic holidays, a commercialized commemoration. One year when I was still in grade school, I went to my sister's high school to watch her perform in the students presentation of a play called, "I Remember Mama." It was the story of how a mother of a poor family gave her children confidence in the future by assuring them there was a bank account to cover their financial worries. Because there really was no bank account, Mama always convinced her family that they should not use the "savings" until they were absolutely sure they had to do so.

Because of her love and skill, the family weathered every crisis without turning to the non-existent bank account. Mothers give confidence to their children. Mothers want what is best for their children.

The Catholic devotion to the Blessed Virgin Mary as our mother comes from the fact that we are incorporated into Christ by baptism. As members of Christ's body, His mother is ours. We find a confirmation of this relation to Mary because of our relation to her son in the words spoken by Jesus from the cross to his mother and his beloved disciple (John 19: 26-27). Just before dying, Jesus tells Mary that John is her son, and then he tells John that Mary is his mother. Practically, this meant that Mary, left alone at Jesus' death, has a son to take care of her. "... the disciple took her to his home." Spiritually, it meant that Mary was mother to the disciples of Jesus, including ourselves. She gives us confidence in our life of faith, encouragement in cooperating with the grace won for us by her son. She wants us to become Saints.

Catholics also speak of the church as their mother, for she is the womb in which we receive grace through the sacraments. Her instruction sets out the way to the fullness of life, in this world and the next. Her worship, because it unites us to Christ, gives us confidence in God's love for us. The fathers of the Church explained that no one can call God "Father" without recognizing the church as "Mother."

Devotion to the Blessed Virgin Mary and love for the church go hand in hand. Both Mary and the church mediate our relationship to Jesus Christ. When someone makes his or her separate peace and decides that they have no need for mediation in the life of grace, the church disappears from their life, sometimes without their even realizing it.

Catholic social teaching calls for agencies of the state to take care of needy people when other means of helping the poor are not available. The state should help to provide the means for all to live with dignity. When the state's "mothering" becomes smothering, some people speak of a "nanny state." Dorothy Day, who was a peace activist and a person committed to living with the poor as one of them, used to speak, with a certain sarcasm, of "Holy Mother the State." The state helps to give citizens confidence and provides a "safety net" for those whose lives are most threatened; but our emotional ties to our country, while very deep, usually fall short of the kind of devotion that mothers inspire. One can change citizenship; immigrants do it regularly. One has only one mother. Mothers' Day provides an occasion, if necessary, to reconcile our relationships: with our proper mother, with the Blessed Mother, with the church. Alienation and estrangement are signs that life is disordered in some fashion. Mothers' Day is a moment for putting our fundamental relationships in right order, in loving order. Then the day will be happy, and our lives will be full. God bless you.

Sincerely yours in Christ,

Francis Cardinal George
Archbishop of Chicago

ON LIFE ISSUE, CARDINAL GEORGE SAYS OBAMA ON 'WRONG SIDE OF HISTORY'
by Peter Finney Jr., Catholic News Service

Kenner, La.—President Barack Obama is a "very gracious and obviously a very smart man" but he is on the 'wrong side of history" when it comes to his fervent support of abortion rights, Cardinal George told the 2009 Louisiana Priests convention April 21. Cardinal George, president of the U.S. Conference of

Catholic Bishops, told 200 priests from the seven dioceses of Louisiana that, while he wants Obama to succeed in his efforts to right the economy, enhance world peace and help the poor, the president needs to understand that the Catholic Church will not allow the life issue to be abandoned. In a question-and-answer session that followed his keynote speech to priests on offering compassionate ministry to people who are hurting, Cardinal George offered a candid assessment of his 30-minute meeting with the president at the White House March 19. "I think on the life issue he's on the wrong side of history," the cardinal said. "I think he has his political debts to pay, and so he's paying them." Cardinal George said his conversation with the president was polite but substantive. "It's hard to disagree with him because he'll always tell you he agrees with you," he said. "Maybe that's political. I think he sincerely wants to agree with you. You have to say, again and again, 'No, Mr. President, we don't agree (on abortion).' But we can agree on a lot, and we do, and that's why there is so much hope. I think we have to pray for him every day."

Cardinal George said he told the president he was concerned about his decision to rescind the Mexico City policy, which resulted in providing taxpayer money to fund abortion over seas. "He said we weren't exporting abortion," the cardinal said. "I said, 'Yes we are.' He would say, 'I know I have to do certain things here . . . . But be patient and you'll see the pattern will change.' I said, 'Mr. President, you've given us nothing but the wrong signals on this issue.' So, we'll see, but I'm not as hopeful now as I was when he was first elected." The church and the president find common ground on supporting social programs that lift up the poor, but Cardinal George said on the issue of abortion, "I think we're up against something a little bit like slavery. These are members of the human family, genetically indivuated, (with) a human father and a human mother," he said. "What their legal status is, of course, you can debate, and we have . . . . John Paul II says you cannot simply live comfortably with an immoral legal system, any more than you could live comfortably with slavery, and therefore you have to work to change the law. "It's a society-dividing issue, and on this issue, we're with Abraham Lincoln and he's with Stephen Douglas, and he doesn't like to hear that, but that's where he is." The cardinal was referring to the seven debates held in 1858 between Lincoln and his opponent for an Illinois seat in the U.S. Senate. Slavery was the main issue discussed in all of the debates. If even the incremental restrictions on abortion—such as the ban on partial-birth abortion or parental notification laws—are rolled back. Cardinal George said pro-life advocates could feel desperate because they fear "abortion will be a human right, and of course, if it's a human right, it can't be qualified." Cardinal George said Pope John Paul II, with the help of Muslim and Latin American countries, successfully fought the Clinton administration's efforts to declare abortion a fundamental "human right" at the 1994 U.N. population conference in Cairo, Egypt. "Whether or not the present pope will be able to do this a generation later, I don't know, because we're going to be faced with it again," the cardinal said. But you can't go on indefinitely. For 80 years we were a slave republic, and it took a terrible war to end that. And now for 40 years we're in an abortion regime, and I'm not sure how that's going to end."

CNW, June 7-20, 2009 "New Push For Conscience Clauses" by Catholic News Service. Washington, D.C. The President of the U.S. Bishops Conference Washington, D.C.—The president of the U.S. bishops' conference and two members of Congress have called on President Barack Obama to make good on something he said in his May 17 speech to University of Notre Dame graduates, namely that he wished to "honor the conscience of those who disagree with abortion." In a May 22 statement, Cardinal George said he was grateful for Obama's promise to support conscience clauses. At a May 19 press conference in Washington and in a letter sent that day to the president, Reps. James Sensenbrenner, R-Wis., and Chris Smith, R-N.J., urged Obama to forgo rescinding the Bush administration's conscience-protection regulation. They also asked Obama to "commit to defending conscience protections in future rule-making." In his statement, Cardinal George said health care professionals and institutions "should know that their deeply held religious or moral convictions will be respected as they exercise their right to serve patients in need." He noted that since 1973 federal laws have protected the conscience rights of health care providers.

Protecting conscience rights "will strengthen our health care system and enhance many patients' access to necessary life-affirming care," the cardinal said. He said he welcomed working with the administration and other policymakers to advance goals Obama has set out for reducing abortions. "A government that wants to reduce the tragic number of abortions in our society will also work to ensure that no one is forced to support or participate in abortion," Cardinal George's statement said, "whether through directly providing or referring for abortions or being forced to subsidize them with their tax dollars." Earlier this year, the U.S. Department of Health and Human Services proposed rescinding the conscience clause that gives federal protection to the conscience rights of health care providers. The rule, which took effect two days before Obama took office, codifies three longtime federal statutes prohibiting discrimination against health professionals who decline to participate in abortions or other medical procedures because of their religious or moral objections. The letter from Sensenbrenner and Smith to Obama stressed that the president should use all the tools at his disposal "to keep conscience protections in place and reduce the number of abortions in the United States." "The religious and moral views of health care workers should be respected," Sensenbrenner said during the press conference. "Workers should have the right to refuse to participate in an abortion procedure without the fear of losing their job or being discriminated against."

In his speech at the University of Notre Dame, Obama called on people with differing views on abortion to find common ground. "Let's work together to reduce the number of women seeking abortions by reducing unintended pregnancies, and making adoption more available, and providing care and support for women who do carry their child to term," he said. "Let's honor the conscience of those who disagree with abortion, and draft a sensible conscience clause, and make sure that all of our health care policies are grounded in clear ethics and sound science, as well as respect for the equality of women," he added. Smith noted that he and Sensenbrenner were simply asking the president to make sure "that his deeds match his words." He said the president could act on the words of his commencement speech by stopping the efforts of his administration to rescind current conscience regulations. "Protecting conscience is the truly pro-choice position and respects the diversity of opinion in our society as well as the sanctity of life," he added. Dr. David Stevens, president of the Christian Medical Association, said in a May 18 statement that if Obama is "truly concerned about finding common ground, he should meet with doctors and patients who would be affected" by the lack of conscience-protection clause. He said the regulation was needed to protect doctors, nurses and other health care professionals from discrimination based on their religious beliefs.

CNW, Aug. 16-29, 2009 THREE PATHS OF DISCIPLESHIP. Catholicism is first of all not a set of ideas of a collection of causes. It is a way of life, a way of following Jesus Christ. It teaches what Christ expects of us and gives us the sacraments to give us strength for the journey; and it also offers a whole range of ways to follow Christ with others, first of all in our families and parishes but then also in various movements and callings that offer distinctive paths of discipleship. During the first week of August I was with three different groups, each with its own path to holiness, its own way of following Christ.

THE SISTERS OF CHARITY

On August 1, the six Congregations of Religious women who look to Mother Elizabeth Ann Seton as founder joined the Daughters of Charity of St. Vincent de Paul at the basilica in Emmitsburg, Md., where Mother Seton is buried and now venerated as a saint of the church. She began her religious congregation 200 years ago, a moment in a life of constant conversion. She converted to the Catholic faith after the death of her husband, took care of her own and other children, began the Catholic school system in the United States and founded the Sisters of Charity in our country. Mother Seton took as a model for her way of life St. Louise de Marillac, who was responsible with St. Vincent de Paul for the beginnings of the Daughters of Charity in 17th century France. Elizabeth Seton found in the Vincentian way of life the confirmation of her own love for the poor, her hospitality towards all, her gift for friendship and her total dedication to doing the will of God just because it is the will of God. These values remained constant in her life, even as she changed often to meet the altered circumstances of her own life and of those whom God gave her to love and protect. She was introduced to Christ truly present in the Blessed Sacrament and to His mother Mary by Catholic friends in Italy; and these friendships with Jesus and Mary were the anchors of all she was and did, of her way of life and her ministry in the church. The Daughters of Charity and the various Congregations of the Sisters of Charity keep alive Mother Seton's way of following the Lord. Theirs is a path of discipleship well adapted to following with integrity the Catholic way of life as consecrated women in the United States.

THE KNIGHTS OF ST. PETER CLAVER

From Emmitsburg, I went to New Orleans, La., to join in the celebration of the 100th anniversary of the founding of the Knights of St. Peter Claver. Our own Bishop Joseph Perry is the national chaplain for the Knights and the Ladies Auxiliary of St. Peter Claver. He joined the national officers of the Knights in creating a major event that filled the New Orleans Convention Center with 5,000 Knights and their families. It was good to see so many I recognized from our parishes in Chicago. With them for their centennial celebration were representatives from most of the other Orders of Catholic knighthood. The Knights of St. Peter Claver are one of two African-American associations that have existed continuously for over a hundred years, the other being the NAACP. The Knights embody a distinctively Catholic way of life, a way of following the Lord in His church. Founded with the help of the Josephite Fathers a century ago in Mobile, Ala., they offered services to their members and their families that were part of membership in most fraternal organizations at the time: life insurance, death benefits, help for widows and children; but they did all this and continue to do it in the context of the Catholic faith. They have had a particular interest in educating African-American children, whom they sponsor and for whom they raise scholarship money. They are husbands and fathers particularly concerned, with the help of their wives, in being faithful to the teachings of the church and in assisting one another to live as Catholic men. I became a member when I began my service as Archbishop of Chicago, and I welcome their assistance at ceremonies as well as in the life of our parishes.

THE KNIGHTS OF COLUMBUS

After the convention of the Knights of St. Peter Claver, I went to Phoenix, Ariz., for the annual meeting of the Supreme Assembly of the Knights of Columbus, Founded in New Haven Conn., more than 100 years ago, the Knights have developed from a fraternal organization founded when Catholic men were not welcome in other such organizations into a strong example of Catholic action in the world. To the services given members, especially through their insurance program, the Knights have added support for priests and seminarians, work to advance a culture of life, devotion to the Blessed Virgin Mary and concern for the poor. They do the works of mercy, they care for the sick, they are involved in humanitarian efforts around the globe, they support Catholic education and work to preserve religious liberty. They call their members to conversion of life through service to others. The annual assembly is more and more international, with Knights from every State of the Union, from Mexico and Central America (including Cuba), from Canada, the Philippines and Poland. Bishops can count on their help in many difficulties today, and they stand always ready to help the Holy Father and the church. They model a way of holiness in the world and contribute strongly and uniquely to our Catholic way of life. I was grateful to be invited to give an address at the States Dinner in Phoenix this year, because it gave me the opportunity to express the bishops' thanks to the Knights and their leaders. Three gatherings, three ways of discipleship in one universal church: moving from meeting to meeting was like making a pilgrimage among people whose faith tells them they are not captured by nature or history or genetic determinations, as the world often tries to convince us we are. Rather, they know that they are free in Christ Jesus, whose disciples they are. May God bless them and all of us in and through this same Jesus Christ.

Sincerely yours in Christ,

Cardinal Francis George, OMI
Archbishop of Chicago

CNW, Nov. 22, Dec. 5, 2009, THE MEANING OF PRIESTLY, EPISCOPAL MINISTRY (in place of the Cardinal's regular column). The Year for Priests proclaimed by our Holy Father, Pope Benedict XVI, aims to renew among ordained priests a sense of the sacred vocation that is theirs in the Church, drawing ever more confidently on the grace that was given them with the laying on of hands (1 Tim 4:14). It is also an opportunity for the whole Church to thank God for this grace, which is given to those called to Holy Orders for the sake of others' salvation. It has already moved some of the faithful to thank their priests for their lives of self-sacrifice for Christ's people. In this gratitude, we bishops, who shepherd our Churches with and through our priests, join wholeheartedly. Pope Benedict XVI, in a recent homily, spoke about the Church's "sacerdotal form," explaining that the category of priesthood is an 'interpretative key of the mystery of Christ and, in consequence, the Church . . . Jesus Christ's priesthood is no longer primarily a ritual one but an existential one," the pope preached; the ordained priesthood affects every dimension of the Church's life. Ordained so that

Christ's headship of his Church might be visible and so that the baptized will know where they must gather if they want to be visibly one in Christ, priests are called to every-greater depths of pastoral charity by the demands of their ministry. To appreciate the many dimensions of priestly ministry, it helps to consider what the Catholic Church would be without the sacrament of Holy Orders.

The priest teaches the people in Christ's name and with his authority. Without ordained priests, the teaching ministry would fall primarily on professors, whose obligation is first to seek the truth in the framework of their own academic discipline and whose authority to teach derives from their professional expertise. The priest governs the people in Christ's name, exercising Christ's authority in collaboration with the bishops. Without ordained priests, the only instance of real governance in any society would be that of civil and political leaders. Their authority comes from God through the people they have sworn to serve; but, in Catholicism, secular kingship confers no religious authority and a civil government has no right to deprive the Church of freedom to govern herself by her own laws and under her own leaders. The priest counsels people to see the hand of God directing human affairs, using the discernment of spirits to govern souls and to free people from what oppresses them. Without ordained priests, counseling passes into the hands of therapists, dedicated to their clients and skilled in examining the dynamics of human personality, but without consideration of the influence of God's grace. The priest leads his people in prayer making possible the real presence of Christ, the head of His Church, under the sacramental forms of bread and wine. Without ordained priests, the Church would be deprived of the Eucharist, and her worship would be centered only on the praise and thanksgiving, the petition and expiation open to all by reason of baptism. Without ordained priests who love and govern their people in the name of Christ and with His authority, the Church would not be connected to Jesus Christ, the great High priest, as Christ Himself wants us to be joined to Him. Without ordained priests, the Church would be a spiritual association, a faith community, but not fully the Body of Christ.

During this year for Priests, we bishops are called to reflect on our relationship to our priests, to help them grow in holiness, to deepen our fraternity with them, to unite them with us around Jesus Christ. We are called as well to examine the ministry that is properly ours by reason of the fullness of the priesthood given us at Episcopal ordination. To us bishops, gathered into this conference established by the Holy See in order to strengthen our unity with the Holy Father and among ourselves the words of St. Ignatius of Antioch speak across nineteen hundred years of the relationships that constitute our own participation in the sacrament of Holy Orders and in the governance of the Church. On his way to martyrdom in Rome, Ignatius wrote to the Philadelphians: "For all who belong to God and Jesus Christ are with the bishop; all who repent and return to the unity of the Church will also belong to God, that they may live according to Jesus Christ." And again, in his letter to the Trallians: "Your submission to your bishop, who is in the place of Jesus Christ, shows me that you are not living as men usually do but in the manner of Jesus Himself, who died for us that you might escape death by belief in his death. Thus one thing is necessary . . . that you do nothing without your bishop . . ."

If such is not the universally accepted sense of Catholic communion, we bishops must look to ways to strengthen Church unity. Relations do not speak first of control but of love. If there is a loosening of relationship between ourselves and those whom Christ has given us to govern in love, it is for us to reach out and re-establish connections necessary for all to remain in communion. As you know, we have recently begun discussions on how we might strengthen our relationship to Catholic universities, to media claiming the right to be a voice in the Church, and to organizations that direct various works under Catholic auspices. Since everything and everyone in Catholic communion is truly inter-related, and the visible nexus of these relations is the bishop, an insistence on complete independence from the bishop renders a person or institution sectarian, less than fully Catholic. The purpose of our reflections, therefore, is to clarify questions of truth or faith and of accountability or community among all those who claim to be part of Catholic communion. Our pastoral concern for ecclesial unity does not diminish our awareness of our own mistakes and sins. There are some who would like to trap the Church in historical events of ages long past and there are others who would keep the bishops permanently imprisoned in the clerical sexual abuse scandal of recent years. The proper response to a crisis of governance, however, is not governance but effective governance. Loss of trust, we know, weakens relationships and will continue to affect our ministry, even though clerical ranks have been purged of priests and bishops known to have abused children and the entire Church has taken unprecedented means to protect children and to reach out to victims. In any case, the sinfulness of churchmen can not be allowed to discredit the truth of Catholic teaching or to destroy the relationships that create ecclesial communion. Relations in the Church and among priests and people are mutual. The faithful need the bishops in order to be Catholic, and the bishops need the faithful in order to be Catholic pastors. Pastors are given authority by Christ to govern the Church not according to their own whims or desires but according to the will of Christ and to keep the faithful united around him. Every pastor has councils for this purpose: to listen to those to whom he has been sent to guide and govern. I believe I speak for all of us here when I say that the bishops look forward to the dialogues that will clarify and strengthen the conditions necessary for all of us to be Catholic.

The Church, as St. Paul reminds us, has the mind of Christ (Phil 2:5). If we are not of his mind, not of one mind, we cannot preach who Christ is to a divided world. The Second Vatican Council reminded the entire Church that we are to be a leaven for the world's transformation. Catholic communion is to be the counterpart of human solidarity. Recently, we have tried to be such a leaven in the debate about health care. It is not for us to speak to particular means of delivering health care; it is our responsibility, however, to insist, as a moral voice concerned with human solidarity, that everyone should be cared for and that no one should be deliberately killed. This voice and these concerns are not novel. My predecessor as Archbishop of Chicago, Cardinal Bernardin, speaking to the National Press Club in 1994, said that concern for health care "requires us to stand up for both the unserved and the unborn, to insist on the inclusion of real universal coverage and the exclusion of abortion coverage, to support efforts to restrain rising health costs, and to oppose the denial of needed care to the poor and vulnerable." Participating in the same debate fifteen years later, we are grateful for those in either political party who share these common moral concerns and govern our country in accordance with them. The challenge to governing effectively and pastorally as bishops and priests is to be public without being co-opted and to be who we are without being isolated. We approach every issue from the perspective of the natural moral law and the Gospel of Jesus Christ, for issues that are moral questions before they become political remain moral questions when they become political. To limit our teaching or governing to what the state is not interested in would be to betray both the Constitution of our county and, much more importantly, the Lord Himself. Jesus Christ is the Savior of the whole world, of our public lives as well as our private lives, of our business concerns and of our recreational outlets, of our families and of our institutions, of the living and of the dead. In His name and as bishops of His Church, we gather now to seek His will for His people, and with His authority we govern. May Christ bless and guide, with the power of His Spirit, our deliberations and this meeting of our conference.

Thank you,

Francis Cardinal George, OMI
President

CNW, Feb. 14-27, 2010. Conversion from peace lovers to peace makers, stories of violence in warfare in Afghanistan. Stories of violence in warfare in Afghanistan, Iraq and Pakistan continue to impact political life but, listening to our neighbors and many parishioners, stories of violence closer to home are also heard. In choosing themes for discussion this year, the members of the Archdiocesan Pastoral Council several months ago honed in on violence in our homes, on our streets and in our public conversation. Domestic violence is more widespread than many would like to believe, and it affects all social classes. Talking with the Archdiocesan Women's Committee about violence in the schools and gang violence on the streets, one woman pointed out that children learn violence at home before they become violent elsewhere. A number of initiatives for addressing domestic violence are being put in place and should begin to influence ministry in the parishes soon. Everyone prays for peace; the challenge is then to work effectively to reduce violence and create peaceful homes and neighborhoods, to move from peace loving to peace making at home. Pope Benedict, speaking of peace as the world entered a new calendar year last month, treated peace making as a cosmic endeavor. "If you want to cultivate peace," the pope said, "Protect Creation." Peace is a state of harmony between God, His human creatures and all the rest of creation. The Holy Father explains: " . . . environmental degradation is an expression not only of a break in the harmony between humankind and the creation, but of profound deterioration in the unity between humankind and God."

Because God is intimately involved with all of creation as maker of heaven and earth, making peace anywhere is not something we can do without God's help. Peace is a sign of God's presence, and violence is a sign of sinfulness. In this perspective, conversion is part of peace making. It's good to spend a few moments reflecting about conversion as the church prepares to enter into the season of Lent, a time when we recognize our sinfulness and pray for the grace of conversion.

Conversion requires effort on our part. Jesus called His first disciples to repent because the kingdom of God, in the form of Jesus himself, was among them. But Jesus also knew that no one can reform his or her life alone. "It is easier for a camel to go through the eye of a needle than for a rich man to enter the kingdom of God." The Lord then explained where to go for help: "What is impossible with man is possible with God" (Lk 18:25-27). The help from God that we can count on as we pray and work for peace gives us a power otherwise beyond our efforts. With the grace of conversion, our faith deepens and our heart expands. Our impulse to generosity is pushed toward self-sacrifice. From giving money and things we move to giving ourselves. Real peace is not the fruit of negotiation but of forgiveness, on God's part and ours. Making a good sacramental confession is to make peace at the most profound level. In giving absolution from sin, the priest prays that the Lord may transform our lives through His "pardon and peace." In the celebration of the Eucharist, having found the courage to call God our Father, we pray for peace as we prepare to receive the body and blood of Jesus, God's Son and our Brother: Lord Jesus Christ, you said to your apostles:

> I leave you peace, my peace I give you.
> Look not on our sins, but on the faith of your church,
> And grant us the peace and unity of your kingdom . . .

The peace of soul found in converting to God's way makes possible peace in the home and the neighborhood; it opens up ways to bring peace to nations and harmony in creation. I hope that the discussions on peace making will continue this year and that our prayers and efforts will bring an end to violence at home and peace among peoples abroad. God bless you and give you His peace.

Sincerely yours in Christ,

Cardinal Francis George, OMI

Let us end this Reverie with Psalm 53, a lament over widespread corruption.

> I
> The fool says in his heart,
> > "There is no God."
> Such are corrupt; they do abominable
> > Deeds;
> > > there is not one who does good.
> God looks down from heaven upon the
> > children of men
> > > to see if there be one who is wise

and seeks God.
All alike have gone astray; they have
Become perverse;
there is not one who does good, not
even one.
II
Will all these evildoers never learn,
they who eat up my people just as
they eat bread,
who call not upon God?
There they were in great fear,
where no fear was,

For God has scattered the bones of
your besiegers;
they are put to shame, because God
has rejected them.
III
Oh, that out of Zion would come the
salvation of Israel!
When God restores the well-being of
His people,
then shall Jacob exult and Israel be
glad.

"Let us rejoice and give thanks, not only that we have become Christians, but that we have become Christ! Do you grasp this? Do you
understand the enormous grace God has given us? Stand in awe and rejoice—we have become Christ!"

FINIS